Natasha Lands Down Under

Katherine McCaughan

ISBN: 978-1-934666-36-4

Printed in the United States of America

Cover Design by Summer Morris

Published and distributed by:
High-Pitched Hum Publishing
321 15th Street North
Jacksonville Beach, Florida 32250

Contact High-Pitched Hum Publishing at
www.highpitchedhum.net

Contact author at www.katherinemccaughan.com

This is a work of fiction. The literary perceptions and insights are based on the author's experience. All names and places not historical, characters and incidents are either products of the author's imagination or are used fictitiously.

Natasha Lands Down Under

Chapter 1

Natasha dreaded lunch time most.

Shrieks of laughter and fake retching greeted the smell of the liverwurst sausage in her sandwich. She wanted to throw it at her new classmates, to scream at them, but most of all, she wanted to hide. Instead, she smothered the sandwich in wrapping paper and, her classmates trailing her like a swishing dragon's tail, deposited her lunch in the garbage can. A boy with thick glasses bumped against her, probably accidentally, but she glared at him, and he turned away, laughing.

Natasha perched on a bench, frowning. *How would they like to be in a foreign country, in a new school and not understand a word anyone said?* As she tugged at the folds of her too-short skirt, two girls sat down beside her, copying her movements.

"*Duraki*," she said, looking straight at them. They glanced at each other.

Natasha gave a quick smile. *Good, she could call them 'stupid' in Russian and they didn't even know.* She yearned to fight back, but yesterday, when she had complained after her first day of school in Australia, Mama had said it was the worst thing she could do.

Yesterday they had called her "bloody-new-Australian," whatever that meant. They could not understand why she was Russian but came from Shanghai in China. Many Russians lived in China as the two countries shared a border, but this was obviously something these young Australians did not know.

Yesterday some boys reeled off Russkie, Bolshie and Commie, as well as Ching Chong Chinaman, until a teacher stopped them. Natasha knew she was not Communist, nor

Chinese. At dinner, Papa explained in World War II, Russia had fought on the same side as America, England and Australia. Aunt Vera, her father's cousin, noted that even though Australia was on the winning side, it was now hard to get refrigerators or cars.

At school, though, everyone thought Australia was perfect. They did not know how much better things could be in other places, like in Shanghai.

In Australia people did not have *amahs* and had to clean their own houses. There were no rickshaws or pedicabs. Most streets were spotless and very quiet. There were no hawkers selling their goods, no coolies balancing bundles on bamboo poles and crying out to warn people in their way. Natasha had to figure out what was normal here, as *normal* differed, apparently, from one part of the world to another.

Wanting to fit in better, she decided she needed to change her hair. Also, she would ask Babushka, her grandmother who had traveled to Australia with the family, to make her a longer skirt and some plain, not embroidered, clothes. Plaid blouses, the same as the other girls wore.

When the bell rang, she lined up at the white line. Yesterday she had become lost, wandering the halls, checking the classrooms for the only people she knew, Aunt Vera's two sons. At least today she knew where to go.

Indoors it was cool, the light dim. At the front of the class, Natasha slid into her desk, waiting until the whispering and giggling settled down. When only the teacher was speaking, she could follow the words better.

Miss Robinson turned to her and repeated a word, pointing with a ruler and smiling. "Paper, Natasha, paper." The ruler smacked against the upheld sheet. Nodding, Natasha retrieved a sheet from her desk.

"And pencil, see? And your workbook." Miss Robinson leaned down and pulled out the correct book. "This one. Can you say it? Workbook." Natasha repeated the word carefully.

A boy in the back row snickered, but when the teacher raised her eyebrows at him, he stopped immediately.

Miss Robinson seemed so tall and angular, but her face softened and was almost pretty when she smiled. Babushka would say her green dress with its white collar was fresh looking and fitted her well. Her grandmother would check the seams and could tell if it were *khorosho sdelano*, well made, or just thrown together.

The teacher and many of the students had pale hair and eyebrows the color of sand. Freckles, like squashed insects, covered their arms, legs and even their faces, giving them a cover to hide behind. Natasha pulled at her black braid and could almost feel how dark her eyes were. Mama said she had inherited her Armenian grandfather's swarthy coloring and black eyebrows that wiggled like centipedes when she talked. But these Australians made her feel dark on the inside, too. While she could not speak English, she felt like a shadow slipping between them.

As she concentrated so hard, the afternoon sped by. When the bell sounded, the others hurried to leave. She watched, exhausted, a headache throbbing behind her eyes. Two girls she had not noticed before paused as the others jostled out. They smiled, and when she quickly cleared her frown and smiled back, they waved goodbye. For a fleeting moment she felt released from the prison of her silence. Maybe she would eat lunch with them tomorrow. Maybe they would be her first Australian friends.

After Miss Robinson reviewed the new words, Natasha replaced her workbook, up-ended her chair on the desk, and slipped silently down the stone steps. Finally, she could return to her temporary home where Babushka and her two sisters were waiting.

The eucalyptus trees shading her path down the hill filtered the warmth of the November sun. Natasha wandered along, touching the strange plants like bottle washers, fascinated by the tough grass that looked like green fingers protruding from the earth. Everyone had disappeared and she could pretend she was alone in the whole world.

Red brick houses lined up like soldiers down the slope, similar, yet with different color trim or bushes. Stillness enveloped her in a way that never occurred in Shanghai. She missed the throngs of people and the musky smell of perspiration, the clang of the Chinese language and the women patting her hair and smiling, smiling at her.

Repeating her new words, she murmured, "pencil, pencil," and then "vork—" She stopped. "*Nyet.*" The Russian word for *no* slipped out. "W—w—," she blew through her lips, "workbook." *Tomorrow will be a week*, she thought. *A whole week that we've been in Australia.*

The park in the valley, her halfway point to Aunt Vera's house, was empty, so she meandered in and flopped onto the sweet-smelling grass. Lying flat, she stretched out and gazed up at the vast endless sky. This same sky had covered her in Shanghai, but now her world had turned upside down.

She missed her old school, her neighborhood friends and Shura, the parrot who lived in the apartment above. And what about the old beggar who was always on the street corner? He could die and she would never know. A tiny cry escaped her throat. It was all so different! People and places had disappeared as if she had only dreamed them.

Their first days in Sydney had been warm and clear and the nights crisp and cool. Her parents marveled to be in a free country and encouraged Natasha to understand the customs and learn the language. But beneath their smiles, problems loomed. She heard her parents whispering at night. She saw them adding up numbers on paper and anxiously checking prices.

Papa could not speak English and worried about getting a job. Today he had an interview at three o'clock. Would he return happy, or upset like the last time? Mama, too, had replied to an advertisement in the newspaper. What if they could not find work? They could not go back to China, not now with the Chinese Communists in control.

She willed herself to think of something else. A dog. Mama and Papa had promised her a puppy when they were settled in their own home. When things seemed too hard, she would think about having her own dog.

The ground underneath her felt hard and the grass tickled her bare legs. She stared at that great sky that covered everyone she loved, and then in her own language, but with her address in English, she recited, "I am Natasha Sergeevna Kiranovsky. I live at Aunt Vera's house at 77 Waratah Street, Lindhurst, New South Wales, Australia, the Earth, the Universe. It is November, 1950, and I am ten years old." She let out a long sigh.

The fresh air with its perfume of gum trees felt clean and sparkling new, not dusty like the smell of Shanghai. Getting up, she smoothed her skirt and started up another hill. Aunt Vera and her two sons would still be at the house. Yesterday Vladimir, who was just her age, and Peter, two years older, had shown her the way, but today they had hurried home to dress to go out for dinner.

As she mounted the hill, she could see their house near the top. Beside the gate, yellow flowers bloomed on a fat frangipani bush, the fallen petals resembling tiny discarded banana skins. Aunt Vera stood chatting over the fence to a lady dressed in a blue hat and white gloves. They turned as she approached.

* * *

A few minutes later, turmoil erupted at Aunt Vera's house.

"Ahyaa! *Kakoy uzhus*! What a disgrace!" Aunt Vera shrieked. "How could you, Natasha? You're a—, you're—" Her arms flailed while she struggled to find words strong enough. "*Disgrace* is too nice a word. You can't imagine how disgusted I am."

Natasha's heart pumped furiously as her aunt's words struck her like a barrage of bullets. What had she done that had been so wrong?

"What came over you, child?" Her aunt's eyes had turned a darker blue while a spider's web of red veins draped the yellowed whites. They blazed in a reddened blotched face. "Terrible, just terrible behavior!" Aunt Vera's body vibrated with emotion, intensifying the scent of her flowery perfume. Even the hairs in her nostrils quivered. Her two sons came running to the living room as their mother's raised voice echoed through the house, and now stood watching from the door.

"*Ya izvinyayus!* I'm sorry," Natasha apologized. Maybe she had not said *sdravstvuiti* properly to the lady at the fence? Maybe her smile and saying hello were not enough? The lady had said goodbye rather quickly. Natasha sidled to Babushka as a fresh barrage of angry words assailed her. "I'm sorry, I'm sorry," she repeated.

Aunt Vera turned on Babushka. "*Kakuyu devochku ti vospitivaesh?* What kind of girl are you raising? She doesn't know how to behave. How to be a lady." The bun on top of her head shook each time she jerked her chin. "Can you believe it? Natasha spat. Actually spat! And there was Mrs. Sedgwick. Oh, I could have died on the spot."

So that was it. But Papa and the men in China did it all the time.

Her aunt continued. "The whole neighborhood will be laughing at the uncouth Russians. Natasha, they don't DO that here. *Oy, yoy yoy*! Finally, I thought they had begun to accept us and now this!" Her puffy face looked like bread dough to Natasha, who wanted to poke it and see how long the dent would stay.

Natasha started to explain but was met by another volley of words. "I've sponsored your family, let you stay in my home," her hand swept the small space, "guaranteed you won't need government assistance, and this is how you repay me." A thin gleam of sweat glistened on her upper lip.

Babushka's face had flushed a deep pink. "She's never done anything like this before, and she's sorry. We both apologize."

Elena, Natasha's four year old sister, stared, her eyes wide. Natasha clenched her jaw and repeated, "*Ya izvinyayus.* I'm sorry."

Natasha saw a smirk spread across Vladimir's face. Her fear flipped to anger that seethed inside her. Babushka was still trying to placate Aunt Vera. "It won't happen again. She knows now it's not done here."

Elena whimpered and ran to her parents' temporary bedroom, slamming the door. Natasha felt Babushka's body stiffen and they both listened for baby Sonia's cry, but for the moment the baby remained silent.

"Can we speak more quietly?" asked Babushka. "You have every right to be upset, Vera. Natasha was copying the men in Shanghai. She now knows it's wrong and has apologized."

Aunt Vera's snort of disgust seemed to Natasha to be as ugly as the spit she had rid herself of in the front garden. Unfortunately, Mrs. Sedgwick was the doctor's wife and the richest person Aunt Vera knew.

"I don't know how I'll face Mrs. Sedgwick again. Come, Vladimir, Peter. The taxi is waiting. At least I know my boys know how to behave."

Vladimir smiled behind his raised hand. His body was all angles, elbows, knees, even his nose. Peter, ignoring Natasha, quickly swallowed the remains of a cream tart.

With a final sniff, Aunt Vera straightened her gold dress, and swept like a tornado to the door. Natasha stared at her aunt's puffy ankles and fat feet stuffed into high-heeled shoes and compared them to Mama's slim ankles, which tapered so finely they looked like they might snap from supporting a whole person.

Vera swung around and threw out a final insult. "You're just like Katya. Watch out or you'll end up like her, too." To Babushka she added, "And don't use too much salt in your cooking. It's hard to get these days."

The door slammed and Babushka gave a start. "Oh dear. Well, at least the baby's still asleep." She patted Natasha's shoulder. "While we're in her house, be careful. *Khorosho, maya golubka?* All right my little dove? You must never, ever spit here in Australia."

"Papa does it."

"I know the men in China do it. But in Australia it's not done."

From the bedroom a small voice asked, "Have they gone?"

"It's over, Elena dear. You can come out." Babushka smoothed wisps of gray hair back into her bun as Elena, clutching Irina, her favorite doll, joined them. "We have to be grateful to Vera, girls. Our family owes her a great deal."

Natasha pouted. "She yelled so hard I couldn't think. Can she really tell me what to do? I hate her giving me orders."

Babushka laughed. "You hate anyone giving you orders."

"When we have our own home, she won't be able to yell at me." Natasha flopped onto the sofa. "All she had to do was talk to me. I wouldn't have done it again."

"It's her way. She's very emotional. Come on. I need help with the table." Babushka started for the kitchen. "Mama and Papa will soon be home. *Gospodi, pomogi im naitee rabotu sevodnya.* Dear God, help them find work today." She crossed herself, having spoken the name of the Lord.

Natasha followed Babushka, trailing a hand along the silk brocade sofa that ran the length of the small room. "Will you tell them?" she asked. "Will you tell Mama and Papa what I did?"

"I'd like not to, with all their problems. But they need to know, just in case Vera says anything. Don't worry, I'll tell them you've been punished.

Chapter 2

In the tiny kitchen, Babushka reached for a choko, a green pear-shaped vegetable that looked to Natasha like it had a bad case of acne.

"Who's Katya? How did she end up?"

Babushka's thick fingers slithered along the shaft of the choko as the knife sliced easily through the skin. "Never mind about Katya. Vera was upset and saying anything that came to mind." She dropped lard into a frying pan on the stove, which dissolved with a soft hiss. A fly buzzed loudly outside the screened window.

On a table in the corner, a large pot covered with layers of bleached and floured cloth sat atop a bowl of warm water. It contained a mound of rising dough that Vera would use to make *piroshki*, to sell at the Russian Orthodox Church in Strathfield.

Elena screwed up her nose. "I don't like chokos."

"They're free. That's why they're good." Babushka threw the peel into the newspaper-lined garbage pail. "We'll plant a vine when we get a house too."

"What did Katya do that was so wrong?" Natasha asked again.

"She didn't do anything actually wrong. Ask your mother. She'll tell you. Now come on, you two. You know what you have to do." Babushka added the choko to the frying pan and the fat spat and sizzled, making it impossible to continue talking.

Natasha set the table, which only seated four people, so the families ate in shifts. She hissed at her sister, "Do you like it here?" The heavy green brocade at the windows oppressed her, and she hated the black metal swans that flew across one wall. She would have liked to inspect the porcelain ballerinas on the mahogany side table, each figure on its own bed of crocheted lace, but she and her sister had been warned never to touch them.

Elena shrugged as she set her doll, Irina, on the sofa and arranged her dress.

"We'll leave as soon as Mama and Papa get work. Then we won't have to listen to her yelling anymore."

Elena carefully smoothed Irina's hair.

"Why don't you answer me? You never speak to Aunt Vera and hardly to Vladimir or Peter."

Elena's voice was a whisper. "If I don't say anything, then they can't see me, so they can't get angry with me."

Natasha banged down a fork. "Invisible. That's how I feel at school. Invisible. But it doesn't work. You don't become invisible. You just become a big fat lump of a person who doesn't count." She swatted a napkin against the table.

Elena shielded her ears with her hands and squeezed her eyes shut. After a few seconds she checked to see if Natasha had stopped.

"Look, I'm sorry, but they can see you. I wish I could become invisible to Aunt Vera just by not saying anything. Her yelling jumbles me up inside. All she ever talks about is her tasty cooking, her great sons, her wonderful sewing, yak-yak-yak! The boys are awful. Fatty and Skinny. Don't you think they're just like the picture of Laurel and Hardy that Vladimir showed us yesterday?"

Babushka's voice called, "Come here, Natasha." In the kitchen, Babushka said, "Leave Elena alone, and don't talk about people like that. It's not nice, especially after everything Vera has done for us." She tasted the soup simmering on the stove, and added salt. "Elena is not even five years old. You're a lot older and understand far more."

Natasha leaned against a kitchen chair, frowning. They all felt Elena was so fragile, treating her as though she were special. Mama had said her sister resembled a flower, gentle, easily bruised, bending with the grasses in the wind, whereas she, Natasha, behaved like a solid oak tree. She stood firm in her convictions and made everyone else sidestep around her ideas. But since coming to Australia, she sometimes wanted to just curl up in Mama's lap and cry.

"Anyway," Babushka continued, "you haven't told me how school was today."

Natasha took a deep breath. "They laughed at my lunch. I'll never take sausage again. I hate them."

"All of them?" Babushka asked.

"Yes." But a small memory of the last minutes of school returned. "Well, maybe except for two girls. They waved to me. I'll look for them tomorrow."

"It's getting better already. We know how well you'll do."

Natasha glared at her grandmother. Everyone always thought she would do well, whatever she did. They thought that everything was easy for her, whereas it was her determination that helped her succeed. Nobody ever praised her. They only said, "Well, of course Natasha did well." It made her as angry as she now felt at Aunt Vera. "What happened to Aunt Vera's husband, Uncle Viktor?"

"Remember we told you. *Rak*. Cancer. Happened very quickly. He died a year after they came to Australia, God bless his soul." Quickly Babushka crossed herself. "His photo's beside the sofa. Luckily he left enough for her to keep the house and take care of the boys for a while. He'd been quite well off in Shanghai. Owned a furniture store."

"He probably couldn't stand living with *her*," Natasha mumbled. "And I don't like the boys much, either. Peter's too fat and Vladimir wants everything his way."

"So do you. And don't call Peter fat. He's just a little chubby."

Natasha moved to a safer topic. "I've been watching for kangaroos—"

"My friend Agnes told me they are only in zoos in Sydney. She's lived here two years and—"

The sound of the front door opening was followed by Elena's joyful shriek. Natasha rushed to her parents as they trudged wearily into the house. Babushka wiped her hands on a tea towel as she joined them to hear their news.

Chapter 3

Natasha hugged Papa as he came in, burying her face in his neck and inhaling his aroma of perspiration and tobacco smoke.

"How did it go?" Babushka flipped the tea towel over her shoulder.

Mama's lipstick had faded and her perfume smelled musty. "Well," she slid a glance at her husband. Natasha had understood years ago her father was a quiet man who only became talkative when discussing history or books, but not ordinary things like clothes, or food or even what had happened that day. Realizing his wife was waiting for him, Papa raised his fedora and nodded for her to continue.

"I have a job," Mama unpinned her hat and shook free her dark curls, "but Sergei has not as yet." She hung her hat next to Papa's jacket on the coat tree beside the door.

"*Slava Bogu!* Thank the Lord!" Babushka crossed herself. "It's a beginning. But we'd better move those," she took down the jacket and hat, "into my room. Vera says they make the place untidy."

"What's it for, then?" Papa asked.

Babushka rolled her eyes. "To look nice, that's what it's for. Tania, my dear, congratulations." She hugged her daughter-in-law against her armful of clothes, and then turned to her son. "You'll get a job soon. Anyone would be lucky to employ a hard worker like you."

"Can we buy our own home now?" Natasha asked.

Papa was loosening his tie. He scratched his ear and turned away, his body looking as if the bones had melted.

"In good time, dear," Mama said. "After all, we've only been here a week. People say there's lots of work. It's just that I can speak English," she put her hand on Papa's arm.

"Learning a new language at my age is not easy." Papa shrugged off her hand and bent to scoop up Elena. "Thank heavens the children will pick it up easily." He straightened and added, "What time is that teenager coming to tutor me. Seven?"

"There's time for dinner," Babushka answered. "You'll feel better after you've eaten."

Elena leaned towards her mother. "You didn't work in Shanghai, Mama."

"She's only working here until we get settled." Papa kissed Elena as he set her down and eyed the liquor display on top of the buffet. Several bottles and a crystal decanter stood on a white crocheted mat. Mama frowned as he poured a shot glass of vodka. "Sergei," she said quietly.

"*Na zdorovie.*" Raising his hand in a half wave, he threw his head back to swallow. "No caviar to chase it down. I wonder if we'll ever live like that again." As he placed the glass down, he said, "I'd better replace that bottle tomorrow. We don't want her to complain."

"She likes it enough herself," Mama began, but then glanced at the children and stopped.

Papa patted the pocket where he kept his pipe and Russian/English dictionary. "I'll get changed."

Mama's eyes followed him out. "Is Sonia asleep?" she asked.

Natasha nodded. "Babushka says she's better at sleeping through noises than me."

Merriment returned to Mama's eyes. "You always wanted to know everything going on when you were little. Still do, don't you?" Babushka's voice called them to dinner. "I'll get the baby," she added.

At the table, Mama fed mashed carrots to Sonia, who was seated on her lap. "I will type and file for Mr. O'Brien," she told them. "He's the Administrative Manager of Freemont Products. His secretary, Edna Bruce, said I hardly seemed like a New Australian at all. She's a *Pom*, what they call someone from England, and said I seemed like a 'good sport.' "

Mama laughed. "They speak a different kind of English here. Sonia, open up. Good girl." Sonia's large solemn eyes followed her mother's movements. "Edna arrived here two years ago, but it only cost her three pounds! Can you believe it? She has to stay three years but doesn't get assigned a job like a refugee."

"We pay our own way," Papa said, helping himself to potatoes. "I don't take charity from anyone, even the government."

Mama added, "Well, she married an Australian and is expecting a baby in a few months. I am to take over when she goes into hospital."

Papa was toying with his potatoes, his fork making scratching noises on the plate. To Natasha, his wonderful blue-gray eyes which, in Shanghai, had always reminded her of a merry sea, now resembled a cloudy day.

"Maybe your company has a job for Papa?" Natasha suggested.

A muscle twitched in her father's temple. "Thank you, dear. I have more interviews set up. And there's always the Snowy River Scheme."

"Sergei," Mama frowned as she massaged Sonia's back, "we need you here. At least we are not assisted migrants who have to live in hostels and get separated for work. Vera told me about that dentist, Molotoff from Bubbling Well Road, who has to work as a janitor for two years. Lost all his money to the Communists and came here as a refugee. All that education and now he's a janitor!"

"You can't leave us, son," Babushka passed a plate of chokos. "We couldn't manage without you in this strange land."

"The Snowy River's not that far. I'd get back often and it wouldn't be forever." Papa's voice deepened. "I *have* to work. How else are we going to make it here in Australia? I'll work at anything — day or night. Nick Orloffsky has three jobs, and I'd do that if I could." His glare swept his family. "We have to make this work. The children must be educated. That's the one thing no one can take from them."

The family ate in silence. Natasha stared at her plate, praying that Papa would not leave to find work. Things were too different. She needed him and knew Mama did, too.

After dinner, Mama wiped Sonia's hands and face as the baby struggled and whimpered. Natasha watched. Sonia's hair, eyes and eyebrows were dark, just like their Armenian grandfather, too. Would it be hard for Sonia at school to be so dark, or would it be easier as she would speak English? She felt a momentary stab of empathy for her young sister for whom life was still a perfect warm cocoon in the nest of her family. It would be so nice to stay at home and not have to face the kids at school.

After clearing the table, Natasha left to prepare for bed. She wanted to be out of the way when Babushka told her parents of her problem with Aunt Vera.

First, however, she set off for the lavatory which, as in most Australian homes she had seen, was housed in a tin shed at the end of her aunt's back garden. Elena refused to go alone, even in the daytime, because of the overpowering smell and the spiders' webs that crisscrossed the corners of the outhouse. Natasha hated going, too, but gritted her teeth and forced herself. The evening had darkened to night, so she took a flashlight to shine her way down the path, and then, as there was no light in the shed, she rotated the flashlight to light up all sections of the shed in turn, in case of a spider or mouse.

The smell in the shed worsened each day until Thursday, the day the "dunny man" came to collect the full barrel. First he would bring a fresh barrel to the shed and would fit the seat onto it. Then he would hoist the full barrel onto his left shoulder. Excrement often sloshed over his torn, filthy singlet that was already streaked with a mix of urine and feces. It mingled with the sweat on grease-covered arms that were bronzed from the sun and heavily muscled from his work. With his right arm extended for balance, he would lug the heavy load down the driveway and heave it onto the waiting truck.

Sitting on the wooden seat, Natasha held her breath for as long as she could and then took shallow breaths with a hand covering her nose. A wad of newspaper squares, for cleaning up afterwards, hung on the wall beside her. She wrinkled her nose in disgust. Homes in Shanghai had much cleaner, inside toilets made of cool, white porcelain. Sometimes in Shanghai, she had enjoyed just sitting and thinking. But not in Australia.

Back outside, in the white glow of the moon, she negotiated her way with the flashlight through menacing shadows. She cringed when a leaf grazed her skin and stifled screams when she walked into spider webs. Her feet steered clear of the silvery trails left by snails, and away from lizards that darted out. She could not knock over any potted plants or rocks, as she had been told venomous red-back spiders lived under them. Arriving back at the house, she felt as exhausted as if she had undertaken a great adventure.

Natasha washed in the sink of the pink bathroom they all shared, and changed into pajamas. Before going to bed, she returned to the empty living room and examined the photo on the table beside the sofa. A middle-aged man with large ears was staring into the camera. Uncle Viktor. She barely remembered him. The features on his narrow, long face all dipped down at the edges, as though gravity had reached up and pulled at them. There was something of Peter's bored expression on his face, but for some reason he looked incredibly sad, like a clown after his last performance.

Natasha felt sorry for him and for a few moments felt sorry for Vladimir and Peter. She remembered years ago in Shanghai when Uncle Viktor had lifted her into the air and then thrown her even higher, scoffing at her terror. Yes, and this brought back the memory of him boxing with the boys and telling them to "put up their dukes."

Looking back at the photo, she realized he was a lot older than his widow. Had they been a happy family? Mama had told her cancer was a growth inside a person. Could he feel something expanding inside him, pressing against his ribs and squashing the other parts together until he couldn't breathe?

She shivered at the thought. Quietly she slipped back to her temporary bedroom and climbed into the twin-sized bed she shared with Babushka, whose voice she could hear from the kitchen. Sometimes, while she slept, Babushka would release gas and Natasha would hold her nose until the air cleared. In the morning she would pretend it had not happened. Now, lifting the blanket to climb into bed, the medicinal scent of Babushka's ointment permeated their thin cream blanket with the lettering, *U.S. Army.* Papa bought it at the Army Surplus shop, which had the best bargains.

Natasha settled against the pillows to reread the book that she had brought from China. With her eyes half closed, she gazed at the alphabet letters, which were so different from the new ones she was learning. The Russian letters looked furry, like friendly insects scurrying over the page, whereas English letters looked so stick straight, without any interesting curlicues or character. They resembled soldiers all lined up.

The English language was harder than Russian. Take the word *climb.* Miss Robinson had told her not to worry about the *b* on the end. She said you pronounced the word *clime,* not *clim*. Strange. And Mama had tried to explain about *through* and *thorough* and *rough* as they were all pronounced differently. For the hundredth time she wished that she didn't have to learn English at all.

From the third bedroom she heard the sound of laughter as her sisters were readied for bed. Natasha tucked her brown bear, Ivan, securely in beside her.

Usually she loved to read but tonight her eyes wandered off the page to examine what was really Vladimir's bedroom. He and Peter were, at present, sleeping in their mother's room. Painted white, Vladimir's room had dark green curtains and a grey linoleum floor. A metal table and chair that Vladimir used as a desk stood in the corner. A wooden low-boy, a small wardrobe with a few drawers, backed against one wall, while a shelf holding three books, a cricket bat and ball, was screwed into another wall.

Natasha wondered where the rest of his books might be. She had so many books because Papa kept bringing new ones home. Would he do that in Sydney too? He had not so far. And stamps. She loved him talking about the different countries as they stuck stamps into her album. But that had not happened since they had arrived either.

How else was her life going to change?

Chapter 4

Gazing at the paint on the bedroom ceiling, Natasha blinked to keep the tears away. Only six months ago Papa had told them they were moving. They had just finished dinner and she knew he was going to tell them something important.

Every day she would hear about visas and exit permits, and about her parents' friends leaving Shanghai, moving to Russia, England, North or South America. The population of her school had halved and when her teacher left for England, her class had been combined with the grade above.

That evening back in Shanghai, Papa had waited while Chang Ma, their amah, served tea and cake. Natasha was impatient. "Where? Where are we going?"

"Hush," Mama said. "Wait." Chang Ma glanced up but continued her work, her blue tunic with its frog fasteners glowing in the soft light.

As Chang Ma bowed out of the room, Papa rested his elbows on the table. He looked worried, the way he did when Natasha had done something terribly wrong. Like the time she had let the old beggar with the mole on his chin come inside and sit in Papa's chair. She wanted to watch the three mole hairs bobbing up and down. The beggar had propped his ragged boots on Babushka's white silk footstool and was rolling a cigarette from the tobacco in Papa's silver cigarette box when Chang Ma had rushed in. Later, with this same concerned look, Papa had explained it was dangerous to let strangers inside, so she had never let him in again, but from then on they had been friends.

Finally, Papa had spoken. "*U nas yest razreshenie poyekhat v Avstraliyu.* We have permission to emigrate to Australia. My cousin Vera will sponsor us."

"*Avstraliya? Pochemu v Avstraliyu*?" Natasha groped to understand. "Why Australia? I don't want to move to Australia."

Elena, sitting on Babushka's knee, stopped eating and gazed at her sister. Papa unrolled his tobacco pouch and tapped his pipe against the ashtray. Natasha kicked at the table leg and Mama placed a calming hand on her knee. "It doesn't make sense. Only Mama can speak English."

Papa filled his pipe then raised his eyes. "You know how many of our friends have left. Even the U.S. consul has been ordered to leave. Now, we have our chance." He placed his pipe in the ashtray and drew forward his glass of tea. "It's too dangerous for foreigners here now. You've heard the gunfire. You are nine years old—"

"Nine and a half," Natasha corrected him.

"Right. Old enough to understand." Papa toyed with his glass.

Mama added, "The Communists are in power now and we can't stay."

"You mean Mao Tse-tung?" Natasha asked.

"Exactly. Foreigners have to close their businesses and leave."

Papa took a sip of tea. "Soon I won't have any way to make a living. The garage is gone. We don't have much left to trade. What I do now is 'black market' which means it is illegal." He wiped the back of his hand across his mouth. "I'm a law-abiding person. But how are people to live? I have a family to feed!"

Natasha's lips quivered. "*Eto moi dom*. This is my home!"

Everything around her, familiar and ordinary, suddenly seemed so precious: the old brown wallpaper with pink flowers, the deeply carved Chinese furniture and the silver samovar tea service. Above it, a watercolor painting of a Chinese peasant, balancing a load on a bamboo pole, hung from a picture rail. A standing lamp, its pink lampshade sporting a tasseled fringe that trembled with any movement, stood at the side of the painting.

All the family's important discussions occurred around the oval table in the dining room. Outside, rain pattered gently against the window, while indoors the occasional fizz of the fire punctuated their conversation.

"We have no choice," Papa said. "We have to leave."

Babushka crossed herself with three fingers the Russian way, bowing in the direction of the lampada, a small red vase with a wick whose flame flickered under the silver icon with its picture of Jesus. "God has his reasons for my life changing as it has. Australia will be the fourth country I have lived in."

Natasha had thought she knew everything about her grandmother. "Where else have you lived?" Babushka's wispy gray hair and soft pink skin were like a safe haven into which she would burrow when the world would not give in to her.

"*V Kitaye, kanyeshno*. There's China, of course. But I grew up in Russia, in Vladivostock, where your father was born, and I also lived in Japan. You are young and in no time Australia will be home. I've lost many things, but while I have my family," she gave Elena a squeeze, "material things are not important."

Papa lifted his unlit pipe. "We've had the Japanese occupation, then the war and now the Communist takeover. The French concession has lost its privileges, so our safeguards are gone. It's too dangerous to stay." Flickers of yellow firelight reflected on his broad forehead.

"Mrs. Popov and Shura are still upstairs." Natasha had a special relationship with their upstairs neighbor.

"She and her parrot will probably leave soon, too."

"What about Uncle Andrusha?" Natasha asked about her father's brother.

"We're lucky to get out before him, that's all."

Natasha peered sideways at her father. “If we stayed, would we die like those people on the street? I’d hate to be a dead body with people walking right past me.” For a time she had not been allowed out in the morning until the truck that collected dead bodies had passed. People dragged the corpses to street corners and covered them with straw mats, but sometimes a shoe stuck out, or hair or a hand was visible.

Papa took off his glasses and rubbed his eyes. “People have no money and starve, or freeze to death. Or they’ve been killed fighting or even committed suicide. Children should grow up without seeing such things.” Pushing himself from the table, he moved to the window. He stood motionless, his fingers toying with the sheer curtain as the rain splattered against the glass. The last of the evening light had faded and the terraced houses were slipping into darkness. Somewhere a dog barked three times, then stopped.

“No,” Papa’s voice sounded stronger, “no. We wouldn’t die. But life would be difficult. For instance, there would be no more piano lessons."

“Good,” Natasha interrupted.

Papa turned and clicked his tongue. “And no more *piroshki*. None of the good foods you like. No more pretty dresses, or new books. But it’s not just *things*. It’s dangerous. Dangerous just to go out. We don’t know what might happen next or whom we can trust. What new laws we might break. And look at the weight of money I carry around,” he pulled a large wad of 10,000 *yuan* notes from his pocket, “just to buy normal things. They’ve printed so much money that it’s worthless, totally worthless.”

“Sergei,” Mama frowned as she leaned forward. “She’s still a child.”

“*Ya znayu*. I know, I know.” Papa sank back into his chair. “The government makes life so hard. You can never get a straight 'yes' or 'no' answer to anything." Silence sat like a presence at the table as Papa reached for his tea.

Natasha swallowed hard. It had seemed so exciting to *think* about moving, but now, being wrenched from her home felt like jumping into a tornado. She felt Mama patting her arm and she reached for her mother's hand. At once her eyes widened.

"Mama, where's your ring?" The familiar bump of the gold and emerald ring that Mama usually wore was missing.

"We sold it two days ago to buy the tickets to leave."

"Will you get it back?"

"*Nyet, dorogaya.* No, darling. It's only a ring."

Babushka crossed her arms and said, "Your mother didn't feel that way about her ring."

"That was different." Mama gave a dismissive wave. "This ring didn't have the significance of my mother's. Now you see, Natasha, that we have to leave?"

Natasha nodded. "Will we wait until the baby comes?"

Her mother caressed her stomach. "Yes. It's only six weeks."

"But how can I go to school if I can't speak English? Why can't we go to Russia like Gran and Grandpa?"

Mama spread out her hands. "I didn't tell you about their letter, did I?"

"Will they visit us in Australia?"

Mama's face froze for a second. "No. That won't be possible."

Natasha wondered if she was about to cry. Did this mean they wouldn't see her grandparents ever again?

Babushka sighed. "Poor Aleksei and Lilla should have waited."

Mama drew herself upright. "My parents were to write to tell us if we should join them in Russia. We waited and waited, but with the blockade, little mail was getting through. We had heard that life was hard there, but after the war, life is not easy anywhere. Finally, we received a letter which said that we should definitely join them."

Natasha looked at Mama. "Well, then, why aren't we?"

"They wrote that we should leave immediately after you finish your university studies."

"But…they know how old I am."

"Exactly. They know, but anyone from the government reading the letter would not know. They used a code to warn us not to come."

"But what could the government do to them?"

"You don't understand. They could lose their jobs, not get ration coupons or, God forbid, be sent to a labor camp."

Babushka shook her head. "All these problems. I hope it doesn't affect the baby. You've already been sick once this pregnancy. And this could be Sergei's son!"

The door to the kitchen creaked and Chang Ma entered. She poked quickly at the fire and then began placing the used dishes onto a black lacquer tray. She asked in her part-English, part-Russian, part-Chinese, "You want I take Elena?" The amah had been with the family since the day Mama returned from hospital with Natasha.

"*Nyet, nyet,*" Babushka answered, giving Elena's hand a kiss. Chang Ma bowed and left the room.

When the sound of running water could be heard from the kitchen, Papa spoke softly to Mama. "You know, Chang Ma asked to come with us."

Mama nodded. "It's impossible. She's worried and who can blame her, with a brother who fought against Mao and, now in Formosa— ah, I mean Taiwan."

"She is no relation to us and with the White Australia policy—" his mouth tightened. "Yet I feel terrible leaving her."

Babushka suggested, "Maybe we can help her get to Hong Kong?"

"That's a good idea." Papa's shoulders relaxed.

Natasha asked, "How did you choose Australia for us?"

Mama answered. "Australia accepted us first. We're lucky Vera can sponsor us. Australia has opportunity and freedom. And the weather is wonderful, too."

Natasha sat back in her chair trying to remember this Aunt Vera. If only they could have moved to Russia instead of Australia. But her grandparents' coded message was rather scary. "Mama, why did Gran and Grandpa go back to Russia if it's so hard there?"

"Russia had lost so many people in the war, the government made promises to lure people back, but the promises have not been kept. So we are moving to Australia for your future. You, your sister and the new baby."

Outside a gust of wind rattled the window and sent a heavier burst of rain running down the pane. Natasha huddled closer to the warmth of the fire. Wherever they went, it was important to all be together. The father of a boy in her class had been taken away by soldiers and he and his mother had left Shanghai without him. She shivered at the thought of being without Papa. She realized Mama was smiling at her with a glow of expectation as if she was ready, almost anxious to start again.

"It will be an adventure. A new beginning with a new baby in a new land." Mama gave her a quick hug.

"Will you teach me some English words before we get there?"

"Of course."

Papa added, "She's teaching me, too. First, how to sign my name in English."

Chapter 5

By the time they arrived in Australia and Natasha started school, she knew quite a few words, but they were hardly enough to hold a conversation, let alone learn school subjects. And Aunt Vera had turned out to be so awful.

Vladimir's bedside lamp shone harshly, too close to her eyes. She wished she could shade it, but she was told that it did not belong to them and to "make do" for the moment. Everything in Australia seemed a bit wrong, and she always had to "make do."

Mama came into the room and leaned over to kiss her goodnight. "What a day you had today," she began softly as she nudged in beside Natasha on the bed. Natasha nodded and suddenly tears filled her eyes.

Her mother's arm encircled her. "You learned not to spit." Natasha nodded again. "And some people yell when they are upset."

"Why couldn't she just talk to me?'

"Vera lost her husband and the boys lost their father. She is our sponsor. It's thanks to her that we are here."

"Then I hate her even more."

"You are so fierce, Natasha." Her mother spoke in her smooth voice. "You need to let life carry you along, not butt your head against it. You also learned that when you are dependent on someone, you have to put up with things you don't always like."

Natasha rolled her eyes. "I know, make do, make do."

"That's right. You can see how badly Papa feels because he hasn't found work. We won't depend on Aunt Vera for a second longer than we have to."

"Aunt Vera said I was just like Katya. Who's Katya and what did she do?"

"So you want to know about Katya," Mama smiled and looked over Natasha's shoulder. "She was a cousin of my mother's. A few years older than Gran and very beautiful, *but* she had a strong mind and a terrible temper. Everything always had to be the way she wanted it."

"Sounds to me like Aunt Vera."

"Be careful, dear," Mama sighed. "Now, to Katya. Katya's strong character and temper became well known throughout our neighborhood, then throughout the school and whole countryside. That meant all the men, well, boys at first and then men, also knew. As she was so beautiful, a few tried to find out if everything said about her was true."

Mama went on, "But if Katya showed the slightest sign of disagreeing with anything these men said, they left immediately, convinced she was bad tempered after all. Well, time passed. All the other girls were getting married, but not Katya. As she got older, her beauty began to fade. Her father became disgusted he had this strong healthy woman to whom he had given so many advantages but who couldn't find a man to marry. He complained all the time, even though Katya worked hard helping her mother."

Natasha began to feel a little sorry for Katya.

Mama continued. "Katya grew angry with her father and left home. Nobody heard from her or about her for a long time, and then one day, another cousin, Misha, was travelling in the country and stopped to stay with an army friend for a night. And there, in this middle-class house in a small country town, he found Katya. She was working as a maid."

"A maid?"

"Like Chang Ma used to be for us. She cooked and cleaned for this young family. Poor Katya had given up hope of marrying and looked for a way to support herself. At first she had tried to be a governess and private teacher, but she lost her temper and that was that. So this was all she could do," said Mama.

"Misha was so embarrassed and ashamed. In front of his friend, he pretended he didn't know her, but they had a long chat before he left. She asked him not to tell anyone even though she would never return home. Misha, however, couldn't keep it to himself. Everyone in town found out. It was such a disgrace for our family. So there it is, the story of Katya."

"I like Katya. I don't care if I'm like her. There's nothing wrong with being a maid." Natasha moved her legs to a cooler place beneath the sheets.

"It was a different time then. Today there are many ways a woman can support herself. She could be a secretary, a nurse or a teacher."

"I don't want to be a secretary, a nurse or a teacher. I want to be an architect or a doctor."

Mama smiled. "You don't need to worry about it yet. Anyway, how was school today?"

"Awful." Natasha stifled a yawn. "Just horrible." She gave her bear, Ivan a hug.

"It will get better. What new words did you learn?"

"Workbook. Recess…um," Natasha thought for a moment, "Pencil. Cricket. Atlas. Orange juice."

"Good." Mama patted her shoulder. "But Babushka tells me you've had nightmares again."

Natasha did not want to tell anyone about the huge military boots that grew and grew until they reached up to her head and crowded out her lungs so she could not breathe. She would wake in a sweat and be so grateful that it was just a dream.

"Tell me if your dreams bother you, all right?"

Natasha nodded. "Mama, they laughed at my lunch again." She smoothed down the blanket on her knees. "I nearly cried. But I did what you told me. I pretended they were laughing at someone else. It didn't help. They kept it up and I wanted to *hit* them—"

Mama interrupted. "You must never give in to how you feel. They'll give up if you ignore them. Be proud of your Russian heritage. Soon you will be able to speak two languages and I'll bet they can only speak one."

"One boy called me Chinese again today."

Mama laughed.

"I want to change my hair. And what are we going to do about my lunch? They all have these thin sandwiches with black stuff. Vegi-something."

Mama kissed her forehead. "Let's make you a sandwich with jam."

"And white bread, not black Russian bread."

"That's easy. Now, say your prayers."

Natasha's head nodded back against her mother. She whispered her prayers and then snuggled into bed with Ivan. She was aware of Mama pausing at the door before leaving the room.

"Tomorrow," she murmured to Ivan, "tomorrow I'll see if those two girls will have lunch with me."

Chapter 6

"Come here, sweetheart." Natasha's mother spoke to her in English one rainy Saturday morning as they sat at a small wooden table in the kitchen.

On the other side of the wall in the living room, the rest of Natasha's family squashed in with Aunt Vera and her sons. Over the four months of their stay with Aunt Vera, everyone contrived to keep Natasha and her aunt apart. As she sat with her in the kitchen, Mama was knitting a red sweater for Elena.

Natasha worked on a drawing of their old home in Shanghai. She ignored her mother's request and peeked into the living room to see Papa puffing on his pipe, his head immersed in a three-week-old Russian newspaper.

"You deserve a quiet weekend," Babushka was saying to him. "Trying to understand English all week must tire you out."

Papa had finally found work as a motor mechanic at a service station and car repair garage in the next suburb, and the familiar grease smell had returned to his hands and overalls. He studied English every Monday and Friday evening, but his progress was much slower than Natasha's or even Elena's.

Papa glanced over the top of the paper. "You're trying to learn English, too."

"I've given up. I practice and practice and think I've learned a new word and the next day, pouf!" Babushka's hand spun out, "it's gone. I'm too old. 'No spik English' will have to do."

Aunt Vera laughed. "We'll send you when door-to-door salesmen come around."

Natasha turned back to her drawing. Again Mama spoke to her in English. "I want to show you something." Her cup of tea waited while she turned her knitting around to begin a new row.

Natasha pretended not to understand, and thought, *That will show her. If I never learn English, maybe we'll go back to Shanghai and have a place of our own.* Hunched over her paper, she carefully outlined the high sloped roof of the three-story terraced house.

Her mother put down her knitting, took a sip of her tea and said, "You can understand me. I know you can."

"*Nyet, ya ne mogu.* No, I can't," Natasha answered loudly. She sat up and considered her picture. Something was wrong but she could not tell what it was.

Mama readjusted the sweater and the needles clicked soothingly as she began another row. "I want you to speak to me in English, please, Natasha."

"I don't know any English and I don't want to." Suddenly Natasha slashed a hard black line through her picture. She was forgetting what the house had looked like, where exactly the windows had been. How awful! She felt like a traitor to everything important to her.

Her mother's voice came to her as if from a distance. "Babushka said she heard you speaking in English with Vladimir."

"She's lying. I can't speak English to anyone, especially to Vladimir. He doesn't make sense in any language." Natasha scrunched up her picture into a ball and squeezed hard. "*Glupi malchik.* Stupid boy."

"Ssh. He'll hear you." Mama glanced quickly into the living room. "And Babushka doesn't lie. She would be very upset to hear you say that." Mama continued in English. "You are making it hard for us. Even Elena helps Aunt Vera to dust while you're at school. How do you think you might be able to help?"

Natasha didn't speak, just glared at the wooden grain of the table. How did her mother make her feel she was in the wrong without making any fuss at all? Not like Aunt Vera who made a fuss if all she said was "good morning."

"When you've mastered English," her mother continued, "you'll be a part of Australia in a way your father and I never will. We will always be immigrants, but you and your sisters have a chance to succeed on equal terms with everyone else."

"*Ya izvinyayus*. I'm sorry." Apology followed apology in her aunt's house.

"If you come here, close to me," her mother leaned towards her and spoke softly, still in English, "I'll show you a photo of the house we just bought."

Natasha stifled a scream and raced to her mother who laughed, put down her knitting and reached into her pocket. "You understood everything I said, didn't you?"

"Show me! Show me, please!"

"As soon as you tell me in English that you'd like to see the photo."

Natasha complied quickly. She desperately wanted to see this new home. Her aunt's house seemed like a prison from which she was ready to explode. She wanted a place for just the six of them, her own family, in peace.

"Here it is." Mama held out a smudgy black and white photo of a small brick bungalow. Three steps led to a tiny porch that sheltered the centrally placed front door. Windows on either side signaled two rooms facing the street. A brick fence bordered the bare front yard, while wire netting enclosed the sides.

"It's so beautiful," Natasha whispered.

Her mother laughed. "Well, it's the best we could do right now."

"I love it. I just love it. Can I bring my new friend to visit?"

"You have a new friend? That's wonderful! What's her name?"

"Lorraine Baker. She's in my class and she's really special. Yesterday she asked me to be her friend, so when we move I'll ask her to come after school. I don't want her at Aunt Vera's."

Natasha had been thrilled when she returned to school after the Christmas summer break and such a popular girl had asked to be friends. Lorraine was always one of the first chosen for teams even though she was not a good athlete. She always acted as though she excelled at everything and everyone seemed to believe her. They would be standing around in a group and Lorraine would toss her long golden hair and stalk off, expecting the other girls to follow. And they did.

Now, Natasha would stalk off with her. With Lorraine as her friend, she was sure that she, too, would be popular. But deep in her heart, she was frightened that when she returned to school on Monday, Lorraine might have forgotten what she had said on Friday afternoon.

Wow. A new home and a new friend. Natasha watched her mother closely as she asked, "Will there be anyone else living in our house?'

"Just us. Maybe you'll be lonely?"

Natasha scowled. "Don't joke, Mama. When do we move in?"

"In three weeks."

"Three more weeks here?"

"Yes. And promise you will behave."

"I always behave."

"You always try. But sometimes your temper gets the better of you."

Natasha leaned forward and peered into the living room again. Vladimir squatted on the floor, twisting the volume knob of a wireless radio up and down as a little girl's voice sang, "I love Aeroplane Jelly, Aeroplane Jelly for me." He glanced up, and, catching her eye, poked out his tongue. Peter sprawled on the sofa, sucking a licorice stick and reading a comic book. Elena huddled close to Papa, combing her doll's hair.

Aunt Vera commented on the harsh sounding noises Sonia was making and burst into laughter, her gold fillings glinting in the glow of the lamp. Natasha turned back to her mother. "If you tell *her* to leave us alone, then we'll get on better."

"You know what we owe her."

Natasha breathed, "I know, I know," and picked up the photo again. She studied it closely, then straightened out the picture of the house she had drawn. "My homes," she whispered, comparing them.

The drawing with the hard black line through it now looked sinister, and the tear in the paper made a window look as though it were crying. The tall Shanghai house had three stories divided into two apartments. The first and second floors had been Natasha's family's apartment, while old Mrs. Popov and Shura, her parrot, had lived upstairs. Shura squawked and squawked whenever Mrs. Popov went out. They would hear the tap of the old lady's walking stick alternating with her heavy tread on the stairs and Shura's raucous accompaniment all the way down the hall as she left for another game of mahjong.

* * *

Of the different apartments Natasha's family had lived in, mostly in the French Concession area of Shanghai, the last was the best because it was almost like a house. Her father's business, a car sales and service garage he owned with his brothers, occupied a small building just around the corner on Avenue Joffre.

Papa was born in the city of Vladivostock in Russia and moved to China with his parents at nine years of age. Motor vehicles fascinated him and his brothers and the garage was a dream-come-true for them. Once, during the time China was occupied by the Japanese, Natasha had been visiting the garage with Mama and Babushka and had created quite a scene. As she was four years old, she insisted that she could walk home alone. Finally, she was allowed to stay at the garage an extra half an hour after Mama and Babushka left.

It had been a cool, breezy October day with a bright sun that threw long, dark shadows. Natasha felt very grown-up, staring out from the window as dust rose in swirls from the road. Uncle Andrusha patted her on the head and told her what a big girl she was, and Maurice, a red-haired young man in striped overalls, gave her a toffee when no one was looking.

Finally, Papa kissed her goodbye and waved as she set out proudly on the short walk home. Just when she reached the corner shots rang out and she broke into a run. More shots. People fled in all directions. Ladies screamed and cried out.

Natasha didn't cry or scream. She ran and ran. A wailing pedicab runner thundered past, his passengers swaying dangerously and clutching at their hats. Hawkers on the sidewalk hid behind their barrels, heads cradled in their arms. The usually dignified letter writer crouched in a doorway, his pots of ink and brushes scattered on the ground.

Natasha concentrated her eyes on the pavement's cracks that disappeared under her feet, while the boom of the shots reverberated in her ears. She knew she must not, under any circumstances, fall down. She had to keep going until she reached home.

Her coat unbuttoned and flapped madly and then the ribbons to her prettiest red hat unraveled under her chin. At first she clung to them but then gave up and let the hat fall away. She prayed for Mama's forgiveness, but knew better than to run after it. At last, she sped past the park where she played and ran into Mama running to meet her.

Babushka was huddled at the front door, waiting to let them into their house. Natasha was red faced, and her chest heaved. She felt hot and sweaty and sticky. Now, safely at home in Mama's arms, she cried. Her body shook with fright and for quite a while she could not speak.

"I shouldn't have allowed her to return alone." Mama enveloped her in her arms. "My baby, my poor baby." She pressed Natasha's body hard against her own. "I will never, ever, give in to tantrums again."

"It had been quiet for so long. How were we to know they'd start up again?" Babushka crossed herself. "*Blagodayru Boga* that she is all right. Thank God, thank God." Chang Ma flittered around them, trying to be helpful.

"My darling." Mama's face rubbed her daughter's forehead.

Natasha felt she had to confess. "I lost my hat, Mama. My good one."

Mama's eyebrows shot up in bewilderment. "Your hat?"

"While I was running. It flew off."

"My darling, a hat is nothing. Nothing. We'll get a new one."

"If I had stopped running to pick it up—"

"Don't say another word." Babushka shivered "If you hadn't kept running…oh, my goodness."

Natasha sat away from Mama. "How long will the shooting last?" As she shrugged off her coat, the boom of shots was heard again. She froze, wide eyed.

"It's getting less frequent," Babushka answered. "But God only knows when it will stop."

Babushka prepared Natasha's favorite food, *pelmeni* dumplings for dinner, and for the afternoon, Mama indulged her every whim. Outside, an occasional shot reminded them of what had happened, but they only glanced at each other and did not speak of it again.

They waited for Papa but he was late and Babushka kept adding more water to the pot of chicken broth simmering on the stove, waiting until the last minute to add the dumplings. Her cheeks glowed with a damp shine whenever she emerged from the kitchen. Finally, Mama called the garage from the phone on the wall at the foot of the stairs. Natasha and Babushka waited nearby.

"Andrusha, is Sergei there?" As she listened, Mama's body stiffened. "He left *then*?" Her voice rose too high. Natasha saw how scared she looked.

After a slight hesitation, Mama spoke again. "No, Natasha's fine. But Sergei? He's not here. Oh my Lord, what's happened? It's so long!" Her knuckles had turned white where she clutched the phone.

Babushka crossed herself and prayed aloud to the Lord, "*Gospodi, Gospodi*!"

Mama listened to the voice on the line, her dark eyes darting around the room as her panic mounted.

Babushka took her arm. "*Shto on govorit*? What's he saying?"

"Andrusha's going out to see what's happening." Mama hung the phone up slowly. "Sergei ran out with the first shots to make sure Natasha was safe. They haven't seen him since."

She leaned against the wall. "They thought he was here with us." Even though it was not cold, she wrapped her cardigan tightly around herself. "He says we should stay here. Oh my goodness. What could have happened?" She paced the floor, her hands fluttering like lost birds. Chang Ma watched gravely from the kitchen doorway.

Natasha crept up to her room. It was all her fault. If she had only returned home with her mother, Papa would be safe at home, too. From downstairs she could hear her mother and grandmother comforting each other, Babushka breaking into prayer, asking God to bring Papa home.

Natasha buried her face in the pillow. Her throat tightened as her father's image filled her mind, his kind gray eyes, his slow smile and the way his laughter always started with a giggle. And what if something terrible happened to Uncle Andrusha? It would be her fault, too. Now, Uncle Andrusha's face, older and a little livelier came into her mind. She loved them both so much she felt she would burst from loving. Fear spread through her, seeping into her bones, her heart, her stomach. She was far more frightened now than when she was running home from the shooting.

The minutes dragged. Mama's footsteps echoed loudly in the silence. Chang Ma tried to coax the women to drink tea. Sporadically, Babushka's voice rose to a wail as she prayed for Papa's safe return. "*Gospodi*, I pray that he does not come home in a coffin like the men the Japanese tortured."

"Shush," Mama whispered. "She might hear."

Babushka lowered her voice. "What if he's been taken to the Bridge House?" she hissed. "Oh dear. No, no. We can't think like that."

Even Natasha had heard of the Bridge House. People taken there by the Japanese did not always come out to tell what happened. The one time she had walked past it, Mama had kept her head averted and rushed past as if the building were on fire.

"He'll be back soon, I'm sure of it." Mama's voice did not sound sure, but anxious and afraid.

Natasha wanted to join them but felt it was all her fault. Outside, the world grew dark as evening approached. The tree close to her window swayed with the wind and occasionally its branches brushed the glass. She huddled on her bed, watching the edges of her furniture blur as shadows crawled over the room.

The boom of shots replayed in her mind and she cringed in fear for her father. She reached for Ivan and huddled into her pillow. *Please God, save my Papa. I'll be good forever and do whatever Mama and Babushka tell me. I promise, I promise.*

When the phone finally rang, she raced to the door of her room. She could see Mama listening intently with a hard stony face. After a few seconds she closed her eyes and whispered, "But Sergei? Is he there?' She listened with all her being, nodding her head in reply.

"*On tam?*" Babushka asked. "Is he there?"

Mama shook her head. "No sign of him yet." Her attention was suddenly seized by the voice on the phone. "Oh, no. Konstantin? Oh, dear God." Even from the landing, Natasha could see the way her mother had started to tremble.

Babushka pulled at Mama's sleeve. "What?"

Mama slumped against the wall. "There are a number of bodies in the grounds of the Pavilion. Oh, dear God. Konstantin Levitsky was shot."

"May God have mercy upon his soul," Babushka crossed herself again. "The poor man. And dear Maria. But Sergei? He's not there? That must be a good sign."

"Sh, sh!" The receiver was pressed hard against Mama's ear. "I see, I see."

"What? What?" Babushka's hand was at her throat.

"He says there are men leaving the Pavilion grounds. If Sergei was there, he should be on his way."

"*Gospodi Bozhe moi.* Pray God he is not lying somewhere on the street. Poor Konstantin. I saw him at church last Sunday. What will Maria do?"

A key rattled in the lock. "Sergei?' Mama's voice was high pitched.

"It's Papa!" Natasha raced headlong down the stairs. Mama dropped the phone and ran to her husband with Babushka close behind. The receiver dangled on the end of its black cord.

Papa looked terribly tired, but very relieved, his eyes red-rimmed and his hair disheveled. Mama hugged him so hard, he laughed, saying he could not breathe.

"What happened? Where have you been all this time?" Babushka demanded.

"One minute. Let me catch my breath." A shiver passed over Papa's body. "A drink, Chang Ma, please." He slumped into a chair, his head down, while Mama and Babushka hugged with relief. Chang Ma quickly returned with a glass of vodka and another of water.

"My God, it's wonderful to be here with you all." Papa shook his head in disbelief. "It's so good to be alive." He took a quick sip of his drink. "And the taste of vodka—like heaven." He downed the rest of the small glass.

"Tell us, Papa."

"After Natasha left the garage," he straightened in his seat, "I heard shots and ran out to bring her back. She had disappeared, but soldiers were coming down the street from the other direction. They were shouting and firing their guns into the air. They rounded us up. All the men who happened to be in the street. Rounded us up like cattle."

He reached for Mama's hand and went on, "They took us to the Pavilion and then we had to wait. No one knew what was going on. We stood around, waiting, terrified and worried. It was cold in the Pavilion but most of us were too scared to walk about or even stamp our feet, what with the guns a few feet from our faces. I didn't know if Natasha was safe, I was *so* worried. Come here and let me kiss you," he extended an arm to her.

Natasha ran to him and snuggled into the familiar curve of his body, breathing in his aroma of perspiration that was tinged with something new. "What's that smell, Papa?" She pulled away and knelt on the floor beside him.

Mama answered. "I can smell the gunpowder, too. Oh my goodness. What happened next?"

Papa sat up. "After what seemed like an age the Japanese ordered us into lines. Five men in each. Again we waited, still not knowing what was going on. Next they marched one line of men at a time out into the grounds, beyond the birch trees, you know where I mean?" Papa's eyes swept over their solemn faces. "And then, every so often we heard a shot, and we knew—oh, God, we knew what that meant." He shuddered, and his voice drifted to a stop.

"Maybe Natasha should go upstairs?" Mama suggested.

"No, Mama, please."

Babushka patted Papa's shoulder. "She'll hear about it from her friends. She should know the truth from her father. Go on."

Papa drew a deep breath. "Yes, the shots. But still we didn't know *why*. Why one man and not another!" Again he fell quiet, and no one wanted to break the silence.

Papa sipped some water. "Then, finally, when I felt I couldn't stand the suspense another minute, my line was marched out. We passed bodies on the ground and I tried not to look. But the blood—so red, so bright. Someone had vomited and the smell. I can still smell it."

His hand tightened around his glass. "They stood us so that they could see us clearly. I was so aware of the soldiers and how close they were, their guns. 'Take out your wallets,' they commanded. I obeyed. 'Anyone with U.S. dollars will be shot. No black market activities will be tolerated.'"

"Oh, dear Heaven," Mama dropped to the floor by Papa's feet. "You have them. You always have them."

"I know. I stood there with my wallet in my hands, knowing U.S. dollars were inside. I cursed that washing machine I sold yesterday. There was no way to get the money out—they were watching too closely." A muscle in his temple was throbbing.

"The Lord heard my prayers," Babushka cried softly. "*Blagodayru tebya Gospodi*!"

Natasha couldn't wait. "What happened?"

"They worked down the line, taking the wallets, opening them and checking the money inside. I said my last prayers. I saw all of you in my mind and all I wanted was to hug you and be sure you would be safe." Papa's voice broke and again he stopped.

"When the soldier took my wallet, my hand was shaking so badly. I was sure…so sure that this was 'it.' Forty U.S. dollars were in there. I'd put them in just this morning."

"God, Sergei. What happened?"

"The soldier flicked the wallet open. I glanced at his face. It's imprinted on my mind. His thin moustache, the waxy shine to his skin. I gritted my teeth and waited for the shot, but he shoved the wallet back at me and moved on. They herded us back past the Pavilion with the others who had only Nationalist money. I was too scared to look. My Lord, I didn't know I could be so scared. All I wanted to do was get out of there," he said.

"The thought that they might recheck kept passing through my mind…now that I knew what they wanted. We waited in another part of the grounds until they had worked through all the lines. No one in my line was shot, but there were several shot after us."

"Yes. Konstantin Levistsky."

"Konstantin? Oh, no." Papa banged his fist on the arm of his chair. "What did he ever do to hurt them? How do they expect people to live with a crazy currency that's out of control?"

He lowered his face into his hands. "Konstantin, Konstantin. Yes," his voice was muffled, "I saw him but I was so worried about myself. How terrible! The poor man looked so frightened, and all I could think of was myself." Papa sat up and ran his fingers through his hair. "How do you know?"

Mama stroked Papa's arm. "Andrusha called," she said softly. "He went to look for you. We must call and tell him you're safe. Just tell me. Why didn't they see the dollars?"

"When they let us go, I got away as fast as possible. I hid in an alley and checked my wallet." Papa reached into his pocket. They all crowded around as he opened his wallet. Only Nationalist money was visible. Then Papa lifted a flap of leather behind the Nationalist money to show the American dollars.

"I couldn't believe it! The way the money was placed in my wallet made the U.S. dollar bills invisible unless you lifted this flap. And that soldier, bless him, didn't bother to check."

"Praise our good Lord." Babushka hugged him, tears streaming down her cheeks.

"The phone," Mama said. It still dangled where she had dropped it. "I had better call Andrusha. And Chang Ma, please pack some food for Maria."

Papa took money from his wallet. "She'll need some ready cash," he said. "But give it to her amah." He raised the wallet and kissed the leather. "I'll keep this wallet for as long as I live."

Natasha stood, watching her family. She felt as though she was on the outside looking in at them. In her mind she embraced them in arms that stretched out into protective encircling wings. She felt such a huge and overwhelming love, she wondered how it could all fit into her body. The ghastly prospect of losing her father was so terrifying; she felt she would never be able to get beyond such a horror. As she watched him, Papa turned and she ran to him to be engulfed by his solid arms.

* * *

Now, from the kitchen of her aunt's house, Natasha could smell the aroma of her father's pipe. The family had left

China together, Papa had not had to go to the Snowy Mountains to get work, and soon they would have their own home.

Slowly she scrunched up her drawing of their Shanghai home, and again examined the photo of the house her parents had bought.

Chapter 7

On the day of Elena's fifth birthday, a pink linen cloth covered the dining table in their new home on William Street. Crimson napkins rested at each place setting and five pink balloons decorated the ceiling light fixture.

As preparations for the birthday party continued, Natasha lay sprawled across her bed, her head over the side and her toes tracing patterns on the wall. Absently she listened to Elena's excited voice chattering with Babushka. Aunt Vera was coming with her sons and bringing Babushka's friend, Agnes.

Natasha's parents had warned her to behave, so she rehearsed answers to imaginary questions Aunt Vera might ask. If prepared, maybe she would stay out of trouble.

Why did no one else have problems with Aunt Vera? Natasha frowned at the ceiling. Surely her parents could see how she twisted things to her own benefit. Yet they never let on that she had stretched the truth or lied.

The door to her parents' room opened and Mama's footsteps clicked into the hall and proceeded to the dining room. She could hear Sonia making baby noises so she must be with Mama. Then Natasha heard Papa's deep voice as he entered the house from the back.

So, she thought, they are all there except me.

What would it have been like if she had never been born? The family would have been the five people in the dining room. Would Elena and Sonia have been born? Maybe Papa would have had a son. Would he prefer a son? Why? Vladimir, who was just her age, was not more clever or nicer or…anything. She would not want to be him and she was glad there were no boys in her family.

Natasha flexed and pointed her toes. She stared hard at them. They were part of her body, the outside part that people saw and that proved she existed. The "real" her was in her head, she decided. What was it that made her "Natasha?" Could someone else have been born with her body but a different spirit inside?

Was it just luck that she had been born, like Papa thought, or part of God's grand design, like Babushka said? This "Natasha" inside her reacted badly to Aunt Vera and had the problem with Lorraine. Another person in her body could be indifferent to Aunt Vera, the way Elena was, and might still be friends with Lorraine.

Maybe she could be another person inside her body. Natasha wondered if she could teach herself to have different reactions to things. She would try and see.

Swinging her legs to the floor, she could already feel the new person seeping into her bones. This new person would be *so* good and *so* easy to get on with. Everybody would love her.

She jumped up to change her clothes and brush her hair before the guests arrived. Would her family notice the new Natasha? She could already imagine Mama praising this new person. Maybe this new person should have a different name. She tried out various names—Lara, Irena, Valia. They felt so different, not like her at all.

But she wasn't giving her ordinary self a new name. That would remain Natasha. No, she was giving a new name to her new inner self.

Then she thought of the fairytale about beautiful Vassilisa, who, with the help of her magic doll, outwitted the witch Baba Yaga, as well as her terrible stepsisters and stepmother. Vassilisa spun such beautiful cloth that the Prince asked to see her and wanted to marry her on the spot. That was the right name. Vassilisa.

From the wardrobe she removed the dress Mama had suggested she wear. Pale blue gabardine with a white lace collar, it made her feel pretty without being fussy. When she was dressed, she stood in front of the mirror attached to the dressing table and stared hard. Still staring, she settled onto the small stool in front of the dresser.

As she smoothed down her hair, she decided there must be something strange about the old Natasha that made her difficult. Elena never fought with anyone, but she never stood up to anyone, either. How would Elena have handled Lorraine? She would just have accepted that Lorraine didn't want to be her friend anymore.

A week ago Lorraine had asked Natasha who in her family helped her with her homework, since her father could not speak English and her mother worked. Natasha had answered she did it herself and her mother checked it when she got home. Lorraine had laughed and said Australian parents helped their children do *all* their homework.

Natasha had probably made a mistake by asking if Australian parents needed the practice to do school work. Lorraine had not been the same after that, so it wasn't a complete surprise when she ended their friendship.

But then Natasha had done it. She had lost her temper again. At that point, Elena would probably have run away. What Natasha should have done was left with her nose held high. Well, it was too late, now.

As she brushed her hair, she heard a car pull up and then Aunt Vera's loud laugh. She rose and, from the window, watched her aunt paying the taxi fare. A tall older woman emerged from the taxi and stood, staring at the house. Hidden by the curtains, Natasha witnessed the parade coming up the driveway.

Aunt Vera wore a fur coat over a green satin suit with a matching hat and veil. In her arms she cradled a huge bouquet of lilies. Peter, looking hot, fat and uncomfortable, and Vladimir, trailed behind her. Both boys wore dark suits, white shirts and ties, like miniature businessmen. The older woman came up last.

Natasha bit her lip. *Aunt Vera looks like she's going to visit the Queen and her sons are the pageboys. Brother, she must be so hot in that fur. I'm hot in this light dress.*

Suddenly she realized how critical she had been. "That's what's wrong with me," she said aloud. "I criticize her. Today, I'm changing. Today, I'm Vassilisa who is too clever to be in trouble." Eager to show off her new self, Natasha joined her family. When the front doorbell rang, Elena raced to the door, squealing with joy.

"Hello, hello, hello, my darlings!" Aunt Vera's voice echoed through the house. Her large breasts led the rest of her body into the hallway. She handed Babushka the lilies and they hugged, mashing the flowers between them. The scent of the flowers and the musk smell of mothballs from the fur coat mixed with Vera's heavy perfume.

Next she turned to Sonia in Mama's arms and pinched her cheek, causing Sonia to whimper. "This is how I like them. Before they can talk and walk." The folds of her chin wobbled in time with her laughter. "Though this poor child is rather late, isn't she? Probably her sisters never let her get a word in. That's a family of girls for you."

She hugged Mama and Papa briefly, while Babushka cried out and embraced the older woman who laughed and hugged her back.

"Agnes, Agnes," she repeated as the two rocked together while the family watched. Then the new lady reached out her hand to Papa. "Sergei!" she exclaimed. Mama was next to be hugged. "Tania, my dear!"

Natasha felt in awe of Babushka's friend, Agnes. She wore a loose black silk coat over a simple beige dress. The materials looked expensive but old. She held her head high and her silvery-blue hair was curled in ringlets and held by a jeweled hair net. Her fingers sported several rings and her hands fluttered elegantly, jangling many bracelets. Agnes' large brown eyes laughed even when her mouth didn't.

"My goodness, look at these young ladies," Agnes said as she was introduced to Natasha, Elena and Sonia. When Natasha called her Agnessa Vyacheslavna, her name and patronymic (her father's first name), which was the polite Russian way, Agnes laughed again and suggested "Aunt Agnes," the Australian way.

Aunt Vera reached into her shiny black handbag and, with a great flourish, produced a large envelope. "For the birthday girl," she said and added immediately, "Don't I get a kiss and a thank you?"

You didn't give her a chance, Natasha thought, but then reminded herself that she was Vassilisa today and would no longer criticize.

"Thank you, Aunt Vera." Elena reached up to kiss her cheek. "And thank you, Peter and Vladimir." Glancing at her mother, she asked, "Can I open it now?"

"Let our guests come in first."

Aunt Vera nodded quickly to Natasha while Mama and Papa greeted the boys. Agnes patted Elena's head and slipped a small, wrapped package into her hand.

As Babushka hung up Vera's coat, she said, "*Ooh, kak krasivo*! It's so lovely." Her fingers stroked the thick fur. "Muskrat, is it?"

"It's just an old standby coat I have," Vera said, waving a hand. She adjusted her skirt and straightened the cream silk blouse she wore under her suit as she checked herself in the hall mirror. With a squeal of surprise, she grabbed for her purse and took out a lipstick. Reddening her lips, she exposed semi-circles of sweat under her arms.

The boys hung back, hands in pockets, casting glances at their mother and then at their hosts. They both looked embarrassed. Vladimir giggled and looked away.

Mama led the way into the living room and seated the guests. In contrast to Aunt Vera, she looked prim with her simple gray skirt and cardigan and crisp embroidered white blouse. Pearl buttons on the cardigan complemented her earrings. Natasha knew she would probably wash the blouse this evening and wear the same clothes to work on Monday.

"Drink, Vera?" Papa asked.

Vera seated herself in Papa's chair. "Maybe a little sherry." Agnes nodded her agreement to sherry also. When he handed them their drinks, he asked, "And the boys?"

"Lemonade, please," they answered almost in unison. Peter glanced at his mother and asked, "Is there any food?" His lips always looked shiny, as though he had just eaten something lathered in butter.

"You'll wait, Peter. Remember your manners." Aunt Vera laughed as she spoke. "You can see why my boys have such good manners. I never let them get away with anything. And Tania, my dear, I believe congratulations are in order?"

"You mean my job?"

"Galia told me you are moving up to take Edna's place."

"It's just while she has her baby. But it's nice to have the extra pay. Elena, why don't you unwrap your gifts now?"

Elena tore the wrapping from Aunt Vera's gift, and then gazed at the two pieces of paper blankly.

Aunt Vera leaned forward to take the papers. "These are stock certificates," she explained, revealing the cleavage of her breasts inside the v-shape of her neckline. Once, when they were living at her home, Natasha had glimpsed her aunt's massive brassiere through the half open door of her bedroom. Propped on a chair, it looked like a Viking breastplate, set to battle the world.

Aunt Vera's voice continued, "These stock certificates are for a new company and although inexpensive now, they could be quite valuable in time. When you marry, you'll appreciate them."

"Thank you so much, Aunt Vera." Elena looked quite baffled by her gift.

Aunt Vera picked up her sherry. "Better than a silly toy that gets broken in a day."

Mama took the certificates. "I'll take care of them for you, dear."

"This one now." Elena picked up Aunt Agnes' gift.

Mama turned to their guest. "Agnes, you didn't have to bring anything."

"Of course I did." Agnes winked at Elena. "We have a birthday to celebrate."

Elena ripped the paper from the gift. "A book."

Mama read the cover, "*What Katy Did* by Susan Coolidge. It's in English and will help you learn."

"I like it, Aunt Agnes. Thank you." Elena smiled and then asked. "Can we go outside to play?"

"Good idea," Mama answered. "It's a wonderful day to be out in the sunshine."

The children jumped up and Elena was skipping towards the door, when Aunt Vera's booming voice stopped them. "They can't go outside in their good clothes."

She looked exasperated. The children stared back at the adults. "Do you know how much those suits cost? They're not like girls' clothing that you can sew yourself and just wash. These are real suits."

Mama stood quietly and took Natasha's hand. "It would be better if you played in the girls' room. There are puzzles and books and soon it will be time for birthday cake."

Natasha and Elena exchanged glances as they obediently filed out towards their room. Natasha knew her mother was warning her, but now that she was Vassilisa, she would not have commented anyway. When they were safely in the bedroom, the girls started to giggle.

Vladimir scowled. “What are you laughing at?” His dark hair, which had been brushed into a wave off his face, now fell forward.

Remembering her vow, Natasha stopped laughing and answered in a serious tone. “Nothing really. We just laugh when we get away from the grown-ups, that’s all.”

“You girls are stupid and your little sister makes funny noises.” Vladimir sniffed as he gazed around the room.

Peter, his hands in his pockets, also examined the room critically. His nose was wrinkled as though there was a bad smell. “I bet all you have are stupid dolls.”

On their matching chenille bedspreads Elena had arranged her dolls and on Natasha’s, Ivan reclined. Under the window an open shelf was crammed with books.

“Look,” Vladimir said, “there are no cricket bats or any footballs. There’s not a decent thing in the room.” He picked up Ivan. “You’re the same age as me and you have a bear.” He threw the bear to Peter.

“Give him back,” Natasha demanded. The boys played catch with Ivan over her head while Natasha grabbed for him as he flew past. “I want my bear.”

“You want him, you get him.” Peter threw the bear up to the top of the wardrobe.

Natasha was about to yell at him, but then decided Ivan was safer up there until they left and tried to divert their attention. “Look, we have books. In English and in Russian.” Elena, slumped on her bed, gazed fixedly at her black lacquer party shoes.

“How do you play with books?’ Vladimir laughed. “You don’t even have any comics.” From inside his suit jacket, he pulled two rolled-up comic books, their covers wrinkled and torn. “See. Superman. But you can’t have these. They’re mine.”

"I don't want them," Natasha answered. "We have good puzzles and games." She opened a drawer and reached for a pile of board games and puzzles.

"Look. Snakes and Ladders and Checkers. Papa will let us play with his chess set if we ask. Here," she placed the games on the floor between the beds, "you boys can choose."

Peter stared at her with a petulant, bored expression. "I'm too old for these." His foot swung out, kicking the pile. The boxes crashed against the bed frame and pieces of puzzle slithered across the floor and under the bed.

"Stop it!" Natasha yelled, and then forced herself to ask calmly, "Why did you do that?"

"Stupid games." Peter turned his face away. "Made for babies." Vladimir snickered. Elena dropped to her knees, reaching for the pieces under the bed.

Natasha glared. "Look at all the pieces. You'd better help pick them up."

"You must be kidding." The sides of Peter's mouth arched down as he spoke. "That's what girls are for."

"What's that supposed to mean?"

"Girls do housework, not boys."

"Boys do housework, too. I saw you cleaning up your garden when I came that day with Mama."

"That's different. The yard is a man's place." Peter turned and stared out the window.

"*And* you ironed shirts, too. I remember when I stayed at your house." Natasha moved closer to him.

Peter, being two years older, was a good six inches taller than Natasha, and looked down his nose at her. "Get away from me, *girlie.* This room's too small for all of us. I don't like girls so close to me."

"Look, it's your fault that we can't go outside." She mimicked Aunt Vera's voice, "The boys' suits are too good to be worn outside."

Peter spun around. His hand seemed to come out of nowhere and connected hard with Natasha's face. She grabbed at her cheek, feeling the rush of blood to her face. Her eyes watered, but she was determined not to cry. The stinging sensation in her cheek bewildered her. No one had ever hit her before.

Elena's head jerked up at the smack of Peter's hand and she let out a piercing scream.

Almost immediately, the door flew open and adults crowded around the doorway. Vladimir pointed to Natasha. "She started it," he insisted, while Peter, his hands in his pockets, gazed at the floor. Elena rushed to her mother and sobbed into her skirt.

Vladimir's voice rose higher. "She was nasty about you, Mama. She copied your voice and blamed us because we couldn't go outside to play."

"I should have known." Aunt Vera gave an exaggerated sigh. "Life's a trial when that child is around."

"Oy, oy," Babushka shook her head, her hand to her mouth.

Papa seemed embarrassed and clicked his tongue, looking as though he wanted very much to be somewhere else. Agnes stood back, her large eyes watching them all.

"I'm sorry," Natasha began, her hand still covering her cheek, "but Peter—"

"Don't try to blame someone else," Aunt Vera scolded. From the dining room, Sonia's cries added to the commotion.

Mama, satisfied that Elena was not hurt, intervened quickly. "Come on, everyone. It's time for cake. Let's go to the table." She took Elena's hand and brushed a tear from her cheek. "It's all right, darling."

"But Mama," Natasha tried again, "Peter hit—" Sonia's cry reached a crescendo in the dining room.

"No complaining. Come along, please." Mama's voice was stern as she hurried to Sonia and lifted her from her high chair. Natasha followed, her hand still covering her left cheek. Elena glanced at her but Natasha frowned back.

Anger grew inside her. The adults had refused to listen to her side, but as Vassilisa, she was not going to cause problems. She quite liked this new feeling of martyrdom. If she should die now, eat a poisoned piece of cake or be bitten by a spider, Elena would tell the truth and they would finally see her great self-control.

Vladimir slipped her a quick look and smirked. Peter, however, completely ignored her. As if nothing had happened. *He's just like his mother*, she thought. *He pretends things and then acts as if they are true.*

But her conscience pricked her. Was what she had said so bad? She had only repeated what Aunt Vera had said, although she probably should not have mimicked her voice. Maybe Peter didn't like being the reason for them staying indoors. But that was not *her* fault.

Natasha held back as Mama seated everyone around the table, and then took the seat between Papa and Babushka. At least she would be safe there.

Now, everyone's attention was focused on Elena and the cake Mama carried in. As the candles flickered, they sang "Happy Birthday" in English the way Elena wanted. Elena watched, a shy smile playing around her mouth, her eyes glistening with recent tears. She blew out the candles and laughed aloud when everyone clapped. Mama cut the cake carefully to avoid getting cream on her clothes.

The whole party acted as though the confrontation had been forgotten, and Natasha began to relax. Reaching for her cake, she removed her hand from her cheek.

"What's that?" Mama stopped what she was doing. "That mark on your face?"

"She hurt herself," Peter answered quickly.

Babushka clasped her hands to her chest when she saw the mark. "*Bozhe moi.*" She reached out to Natasha.

Elena spoke up. "Peter hit her."

"She ran into my hand." Peter's cheeks reddened.

"That Natasha is always causing problems." Aunt Vera waved a hand in disgust. "Can't even let her sister enjoy her birthday."

Mama ignored her. "Tell me what happened, Natasha."

Before she had a chance to reply, her aunt cut in. "Do you think she'll tell you the truth?"

"I always tell the truth." Natasha glared at Aunt Vera. "You just don't like to hear it."

"Natasha, go to your room," Mama commanded.

Natasha pushed Babushka away and ran to her room, slamming the door behind her. Oh no, she had done it again! And she had been trying so hard.

She grabbed her pillow and burrowed her head into its softness. She wanted Ivan but he was on top of the wardrobe. Why was she always in trouble? From the dining room she heard raised voices, but she did not care what they were saying. Her mind replayed her final words to Aunt Vera. She should have stopped after declaring that she always spoke the truth. It was the next part that got her into trouble.

She was angry with herself. She had figured out how to act before the guests had arrived, but had not been able to keep her thoughts to herself. The "new" Natasha should not have been critical of Aunt Vera, but the "old" Natasha had sprung up inside her and taken over.

Her door creaked open and she glanced up to see Papa standing just inside her room and shaking his head. "Oh dear. We have trouble again."

She nodded and closed her eyes.

"Let me see your cheek." She sat up and turned the left side of her face towards him. "It's only superficial," Papa decided. "The welts will be gone soon. Does it hurt?"

Natasha shook her head. "Not any more. But it did. When he hit me."

"I believe you, and you've been very brave and not made a big fuss."

She smiled. At least some of her new behavior was being recognized.

"Peter was wrong to hit you. I've told him that. Now, if you can apologize to Aunt Vera, we'll see if we can salvage the rest of the visit, for Elena's sake."

"Will Aunt Vera apologize to me for saying I'm always trouble and I lie?"

"To her it seems that there always *is* trouble when you're around."

"But it's not fair. Peter hit me and he should be the one in trouble."

"We've told him he was wrong and he must never touch you girls again. I think he knows we mean it. He'll have a tough life if he resorts to fists over small disputes. But it's not up to us to make him apologize. I'm sure Aunt Vera will take care of him when they go home."

Natasha stood. At least Papa talked to Peter about the way he had hit her. She would apologize to Aunt Vera and try to save the "new" Natasha.

When she returned to the dining room, everyone fell silent and even Sonia stared at her with wide eyes. Peter turned away and folded his arms. Natasha took a deep breath. "I'm sorry, Aunt Vera."

Aunt Vera nodded her large head. "You have to learn to control your tongue, young lady, or you'll end up just like Katya."

Natasha was about to say she liked Katya, but Mama's pained expression stopped her. She gritted her teeth. Inside, she could feel the bristles of anger scratching again. Her tongue was itching to tell Aunt Vera that Peter better learn to control his temper, too, but Mama's alarmed look reminded the new Natasha to take over. With a straight back she strode to her seat.

"Have another cup of tea, Vera." Mama's face now looked taut, like she, too, might explode from the words she wasn't saying. "Or some more wine?"

"We'll have to leave soon. My boys have so many activities they are involved in."

"I'm sure they have."

Aunt Vera cleared her throat. "By the way," she said, "did I tell you that Vladimir has been called one of the best tennis players his age in the state of New South Wales?"

Natasha's eyes widened. Vladimir had come second in their school. That was all. He had not even won. Who would have called him one of the best young players? Vladimir was smirking and basking in his mother's praise.

"I think I'll get a private coach for him." Aunt Vera bristled with pride. "He might even play for Australia when he's older. He's a young Ken Rosewall."

Natasha put on her sweetest voice. "Aunt Vera, last week you told us that Vladimir was going to be a doctor."

"Oh that," her aunt waved a dismissive hand, "That was just conjecture. Besides, doctors don't travel the world the way tennis players do. No, Vladimir has proven how good he is at tennis." She smiled at Vladimir's proud look, but Peter was scowling.

"And Peter will probably be chosen for selective high school." Now, it was Peter's turn to look proud. "Yes. His teachers have said how well he does. And everyone knows a child from a selective high school can go on to university. Won't it be wonderful? The first child in our family to go to university will be my own son. It's such a bonus that the government pays just about all the costs with scholarships. Yes, I can see it now."

Natasha gazed around the room at everyone. No one disputed anything Aunt Vera said, although Agnes seemed to be smiling down at her hands. Both boys sat there, exalting in their mother's praise. A powerful urge to stamp on their feet and bring them back to reality swept through her. She had never heard about Peter's great scholastic abilities before. He was just fat Peter, a sullen, unpopular boy two years ahead of her.

Vladimir threw her a sideways glance and suddenly Natasha realized he knew how much his mother exaggerated and, in a way, he was embarrassed. How awful to have a mother like that!

Now, Natasha examined her aunt more carefully. Ugh! She would hate to have her body and personality. For the first time she felt a little sorry for Aunt Vera, being stuck with who she was. It must be hard for her, like Mama said, being alone with the two boys. Luckily, Natasha had Mama, Papa *and* Babushka.

Mama smiled and said, "How wonderful that your boys are doing so well. I'm sure we'll hear all about their successes."

"I wish Viktor, may he rest in peace, had lived to see. He would be so proud. He always said I was the best thing that ever happened to him. And to give him two sons, well, nothing was too good for me after that. He always said he liked a woman with some meat, not a scrawny skeleton. That fur coat was his last gift to me." A small cry escaped her throat, and Babushka leaned over to give her niece's arm a quick squeeze.

"God bless his soul," Babushka whispered. "We all miss him." Her voice rose as she added, "But you've managed very well by yourself."

"Yes, yes, I have. But it's hard, being alone."

"Of course," Babushka agreed. "He spoiled you all."

Agnes nodded. "He tried to make a good life here. He just didn't have time."

Aunt Vera's eyes took on a dreamy look. "He worshipped his sons, his heirs. Ah, Viktor. Now *there* was a man! Big and strong and when he spoke, everyone paid attention. He tried so hard to build up his business, and now here we are, without him. Funny, you know. Sometimes I think if I had died instead of him, he would already be married to some woman half his age." She stopped and her glance flittered nervously around the room, as though she had said more than she had intended.

With a laugh, she rushed to say, "But he would have been so proud of Peter's cleverness and Vladimir's athletic ability. His boys!" Pride glowed in her eyes. "Did you know the tennis scores will be in the newspaper?"

"We'll look for them," Mama said as Papa stood and walked behind her, his hands resting on her shoulders so that his wedding band glinted in the light. Today his stubby fingers were clear of the grease that usually outlined his fingernails. Mama's hand reached up and covered his left hand. "You have every right to be proud of your sons. We are all lucky to have such wonderful children. Natasha has—"

Aunt Vera's chair scraped on the floor as she pushed back from the table. "We really must go. Boys, come on." When Aunt Agnes placed her napkin on the table and stood, the rest of the family also rose. Vera asked, "Sergei, can you call a cab?"

The farewells took another fifteen minutes. Vladimir found a moment when Natasha was alone to sidle up and whisper, "You're just jealous. You know that you'll grow up to be just someone's wife and you'll have to do whatever your husband tells you." He giggled as he waited for her response, but Natasha turned away.

Relief flooded her when the cab's horn sounded and everyone crowded towards the front door. As Agnes said goodbye, she leaned down so her powdery cheek touched Natasha's. "You're a strong girl," she whispered. "You'll grow into a strong woman. Don't let anyone," she glanced towards Aunt Vera, "stop you from being who you are." She winked and Natasha returned a wide smile. She really liked Aunt Agnes.

The family followed the guests as Aunt Vera laughed and waved her way down the driveway, her large coat swinging out and warding off anyone who came too close. Natasha hung back as the family saluted the departing cab. Finally, they returned to the dining room.

"A fresh cup of tea, please, Tania," Papa said with a sigh as he sank into his chair. "In peace," he added, taking out his pipe. It seemed as though every member of the family breathed a sigh of relief.

"We can just be 'us' now, can't we?" Elena picked up her new book.

"I like Aunt Agnes," Natasha said.

"She's not really your aunt," Babushka said as she gathered used cups, "but I think she likes being called that."

Elena examined her book. "Why is there writing inside the book?"

Papa unrolled his pouch of tobacco. "It's a second-hand book. Someone else enjoyed it before you."

Moving towards the kitchen, Mama said, "Natasha, come with me. Let's have a look at you while I get Papa his tea."

At the sink, Natasha stood beside her mother. "It feels all right, now."

Mama held her by the shoulders as she examined her cheek. "The mark is fading. It will be gone soon." She leaned forward and kissed her daughter's forehead.

Natasha hugged Mama, but as she let go, said, "Sometimes I want to prick Aunt Vera to see if she knows what's real. What kind of business did Uncle Viktor have?"

"He was a carpenter and worked for himself."

"But he had a business?"

"In Shanghai he had a furniture store. In Sydney he worked alone. He planned to grow a business but he became ill after only a year here."

"I see." Another of her aunt's exaggerations. "What were you going to tell Aunt Vera about me?"

"How quickly you are picking up English." Mama smoothed back her hair. "We are very proud of you."

Natasha smiled. "Did you know that Vladimir came second in tennis at school?"

Her mother filled the kettle, lit the burner and placed the kettle on the flame. "Yes," she finally said, "you told me when it happened."

"Vladimir is called 'John' at school."

"John?" An amused smile flickered around Mama's mouth.

"Peter told me he changed his name because the kids laughed at 'Vladimir.'"

"I don't think his mother knows."

"Probably not. Did you notice how she changes her story when things don't work out. Next week she'll say he's about to become a world-famous scientist or something."

Papa entered the kitchen. "Natasha, tell me," he took her hand, "will anything Vera says about her sons make a difference to how you live your life?"

"No. But it seems unfair."

"Then forget it," Papa gave her fingers a squeeze. "I hope Vera talks to Peter. Those boys could do with some direction. They need a man in the house."

"Don't you volunteer," Mama interrupted quickly. As she switched off the flame under the whistling kettle, she leaned her head against Papa's shoulder. "I was just shaking inside," she whispered, "just seething, when she was going on and on. We have children, too!"

Natasha was straining to hear the words, but the telephone interrupted and Mama left to answer it. "It's for you, Natasha," she called.

Lorraine's voice answered her "hello." "I wanted to tell you that although we're not best friends anymore, you can still talk to me and be on my teams, even if you have old fashioned hair. But if you talk back to me again, that'll be the end." She hung up.

She replaced the receiver slowly. How strange! She and Lorraine had been best friends for two months until Lorraine decided she preferred Beverly, a girl who constantly ate mints while she scratched at the pimples on her legs. Lorraine had told Natasha they were no longer to speak to each other and she could not be on her teams. Natasha had been devastated at the news and had yelled at Lorraine, calling her a bird-brain who couldn't tell a true-blue friend from a…a…mouse trap—so there! Furthermore, she told her that she didn't deserve a true friend because she didn't know how to *be* one. Inside she felt heartbroken, and was sure no one at school would ever be her friend again.

Later, when everyone had left the circle that had formed with all the shouting, another girl, Jan Hunt, had come up to her. A large blonde girl with short curly hair and a shy smile, Jan confided she had been Lorraine's best friend before Natasha. Jan told her that when Lorraine had ended their friendship and chosen Natasha as her next best friend, she, Jan, had hated Natasha. However, she had not been brave enough to say anything and she was still not allowed to speak to Lorraine or be on her teams.

Well, Natasha thought as she wandered back to her bedroom, at least Lorraine knows I fight back. There are some good things about being me just the way I am. Probably Lorraine will replace Beverly with someone else soon anyway. But the comment Lorraine had made about her hair! That hurt. Was it really so old fashioned?

On the floor of her room lay one of Vladimir's comic books. She picked it up and flicked through. Just rubbish, she decided. Then, very carefully, she tore it straight down the center and hid it under her mattress. Tomorrow she would throw it in the outside garbage. Feeling guilty, but somehow vindicated, she lay down on her bed, propped her feet on the wall and traced the shape of a butterfly with her toes.

Maybe on Monday she would ask Jan if she wanted to eat lunch together. Jan was sensible, even if she did not fight back and was not as pretty or popular as Lorraine. She would make a good friend. Somehow she knew Jan would tell her the truth about her hair.

Chapter 8

Soon after Elena's birthday, Natasha caught the flu and stayed home from school for several days. With two beds and a crib, her bedroom felt crowded, so she rested in Babushka's room instead. Although smaller, the single bed faced the sunny back garden and through the white lace curtains, she could gaze at the eucalyptus trees and the shrubs that now edged the square yard. Buffalo grass formed a patch of green in the center. The garage sat at the end of the driveway, and behind it, hidden from view, five brown hens and a rooster inhabited a chicken coop.

Natasha spent her last day at home wrapped in Babushka's soft down comforter, reading or staring at the flickering motion of the sun-dappled garden. When Sonia settled down for her nap, the world slid into total peace. In the silence she could hear her grandmother's slippers shuffling in the kitchen and the occasional clang of a pot or pan. At lunchtime, Babushka carried in a cup of lemon tea and a bowl of sugared rice with raisins. Her padded hand tested Natasha's forehead and she pronounced her recovered.

In the late afternoon, Natasha set her book onto Babushka's dressing table which angled across the corner of the room. A profile photo of Uncle Sasha sat propped against the mirror. With her finger, she traced the sepia head-and-shoulders shot. Her uncle had a strong chin, broad nostrils flaring, and deep-set eyes gazing eternally towards the window. His glossy hair, slicked straight back, ran in ridges away from his face.

Babushka's gold embossed icon of the Mother and Child hung above the dressing table. At dusk, Babushka entered to perform an evening ritual. Climbing up on a stool, she struck a match and lit the wick in the *lampada*, the red vase of lamp oil attached to the base of the icon. The pink flare quivered and danced around the walls, leaking a hint of paraffin odor, and then steadied into a soft glow in the twilight.

Down from the stool, Babushka bowed three times towards the icon, crossing herself each time. Natasha watched the flesh on her grandmother's upper arms swaying gently as her fingers, three together in the Russian way, reached back and forth to each shoulder. After the third bow, she picked up the photograph, kissed Uncle Sasha's face and replaced it carefully.

Finally, she turned to Natasha, her smooth shiny skin stretched tight over wide cheekbones, her smiling gray-blue eyes twinkling in their crinkled recesses. Wisps of hair had escaped from the bun at the nape of her neck, and fluttered around her face. Opening her arms, she enfolded Natasha against the cooking smells in her apron.

"Babushka, why don't you have a photo of me on your dresser?"

"Sasha's the one I'm worried about. *You* I have right here." She squeezed Natasha tightly. "Dear Sasha, God be merciful. I haven't heard from my precious son since…well, the last time was from Singapore before it fell to the Japanese in 1942."

"1942? But that's nearly nine years ago. When will you know what happened to him?"

"In the Lord's good time, I guess." She swayed slowly, holding Natasha against her, the shadows etching deeply the lines in her face. "I worry so much about him."

"What about Uncle Andrusha?" Disentangling herself from Babushka's arms, Natasha asked about her father's older brother.

"Andrusha is on his way here right now. But Sasha, dear Sasha," Babushka picked up a pillow and held it close to her chest, "it's been so long." With determined effort, she stripped the pillowcase from the pillow. "Hop up now so I can change the sheets."

Natasha slipped off the bed, thrust her arms into her dressing gown and feet into slippers as Babushka dislodged the sheets and continued. "Before we left Shanghai, Papa wrote to everyone asking for help to locate Sasha. Of course he'd been to the Red Cross many times, but he went again to tell them we were leaving. He went everywhere we could think of. And when we moved here, your parents wrote to give our new address and to ask again about Sasha."

"Didn't you write, too?"

"You know it's too hard for me. I can manage a little reading. But writing? No, I wasn't as lucky as you with school every day."

"Hasn't anyone heard anything about Uncle Sasha?"

"No one seems to know what happened to him." For a few seconds she stood in silence, then sighed and completed stripping the bed. Next, she opened a cupboard door, removing a fresh cream-colored sheet and duvet cover.

Outside, the sun had slipped below the horizon. The glow of the lampada trembled in one corner, the rest of the room in soft shadow. A kookaburra cackled harshly and was joined in chorus by more, the laughter rising to a high pitch and then decreasing. Babushka screwed up her nose. "I can't get used to that racket."

"I don't notice it any more. You know, I don't really remember Uncle Sasha. Except…didn't he swing me around in the air?"

"You remember that? You were only two years old when he left for Singapore. He loved you so much. He would play with you for hours and you loved it."

"He chased me around the kitchen. Oh, and he used to steal biscuits for me." Natasha laughed at the memory she had nearly forgotten.

"You two were great friends." Babushka flipped out the sheet and began smoothing the edges under the mattress. "He's my youngest, you know. A mother worries about her youngest. Somehow they never seem old enough to…" The old woman shook her head sadly, and then crossed herself before stuffing the feather quilt into the duvet cover. "I pray he is alive and well somewhere in this world. May God be watching over him."

Fitting the fresh pillowcase onto the pillow, Natasha asked, "Did he write to you?"

"He wrote that he started his new job and got himself an apartment. We know from his landlady that he left hurriedly just as the Japanese were invading. And that's it. Silence. All these years. It's the uncertainty that's so difficult. And will he be able to find us?" Her lips twitched as she said, "But God brought us to Australia without dear Sasha, and I shouldn't question the ways of the Lord." She flung the quilt onto the bed.

"The bed will be all nice and fresh for you," Natasha said brightly. Then she confessed in a more somber tone, "You know, I didn't like the trip here, except maybe the last bit."

"You're right. It was not an easy journey."

As many people were fleeing China, it had been difficult to get transportation for their family of six. The port of Shanghai was closed, and the only way they could get out was in the cargo hold of a ship traveling from the northern city of Tianjin to Hong Kong. That is why the family began the trip south to Australia with a 1,100 kilometer train journey north to Tianjin.

Elena was ill but they could not delay their departure, even though her condition deteriorated. Their furniture had been packed and crated, they had given up the lease on their apartment and their exit permits were expiring. They had to leave. Natasha remembered how Mama nursed a feverish Elena on the shadowy vibrating train. With so many people and suitcases stuffed with their most valued possessions, the small compartment felt claustrophobic. Babushka cradled the new baby and when she could, leaned over to cool Elena from the heat with a wet handkerchief. She smoothed back the hair sticking to her face and fanned her small body with folded newspapers. Natasha grappled with the fear she felt around her, not only for this trip into the unknown, but also for Elena.

The train rattled on and on and for hours they were jolted and bounced unceasingly. Papa opened the windows to capture any breeze, but soot gathered in their hair and on their bodies, and even invaded their mouths. Occasionally, the train stopped at a station and hawkers slithered between the moving throng of passengers to tap at the train windows, calling out the prices of their goods.

Towards evening, the train lurched heavily, throwing them all forward and then abruptly stopped. The conductor hurried down the corridor, shouting instructions in Chinese. Papa translated. Passengers were to get off with their luggage. Commotion erupted as people jostled each other and their belongings to obey.

Finally, Natasha's family stood huddled together with their suitcases on the overcrowded platform, Mama cradling Elena and Babushka shushing a whimpering Sonia. A hush descended on the entire assembly and a few people whispered and twittered nervously. Natasha clung to her parents, holding on to the back of her mother's blouse.

A platoon of soldiers marched onto the platform and at the sound of a whistle, fanned out among the passengers. Flashes of uniforms, shiny boots, pistols and swinging flashlights swept back and forth in front of her. The soldiers volleyed shouts and barked orders in Chinese at their captives on the platform, poking and prodding to enforce their demands.

Suddenly, Natasha's family became the focus of their attention and uniformed men surrounded them. The crowd of passengers shrank from them, as if distancing themselves from contamination. Abruptly, the soldiers wrestled the family's suitcases away and splayed them in a circle on the ground.

"*Yao-shi*!" they demanded.

"Keys," Papa mumbled, reaching into his pockets. He spoke quietly to the soldiers, trying to buy time, to find out what they wanted. Finally, he had no choice but to hand over the keys. Her parents obeyed the soldiers' waving arms and stepped back, exchanging desperate glances as two soldiers squatted down to open their suitcases. Mama rocked Elena while Babushka, her eyes closed, prayed and clutched the baby close to her chest.

Natasha's heart raced. She gritted her teeth and prayed, too, to be somewhere else, anywhere as long as it was safe and peaceful. Why were people always fighting? First there was the Japanese occupation of Shanghai and everyone was terrified of the Japanese, then after World War II ended, fighting broke out between the Nationalists and the Communist Chinese, and you didn't know who was in charge from one day to the next. Now, although the Communists had won, there were still soldiers to be obeyed.

Papa kept talking to them, trying to find out what they were after, shielding his family with his body and outstretched arms. But the soldiers snapped at him and shoved him aside, as if he were no more than a fly in their way.

Natasha's all-powerful Papa was totally helpless, and she felt her own defenses crumbling. Guns and power were what counted and they had none of either.

Mama, fingering the bracelets on her wrists, sidled closer to her husband. She and Babushka had decided to wear all the jewelry they still possessed, even though they knew solid gold was not allowed out of the country. The soldiers prattled to each other as they flung the family's suitcases wide open. They shuffled through carefully packed embroidered linens, threw aside valued books and government sealed photographs, and jumbled important papers and manuscripts. Laughing, one man held up Mama's silk underwear while others delved into the pockets of Papa's suits and jackets. They exposed the family's lives to all the watching eyes on the silent platform.

Exasperated, one soldier turned to Papa. "*Jin*!" He raised his baton. "Gold. Where is the gold bullion?"

"What bullion?" Papa's face showed his astonishment. "The only money we have is in our wallets."

The baton whacked the side of Papa's head, forcing him sideways onto Mama. As she grabbed for him, he tripped and splattered to the ground, a bloody gash on his temple. Elena let out a shriek of protest as Mama dropped to her knees, cradling Papa's head. The soldiers ignored them, looking for secret compartments in the suitcases. Babushka, whimpering, took Elena's hand and led her aside, while Mama tended to Papa's cut.

Too scared to cry, Natasha felt the anger inside her boiling up. She wanted to pummel the soldier who had hurt her father, but he was yelling at Papa and gesticulating wildly. The family crowded around Papa as he shook his head and brushed at his clothes. He waved Mama aside and staggered to his feet.

After another few minutes of fruitless search, the soldiers gave up, abandoning the suitcases and their contents all over the platform. The family was left to gather their belongings from the dust, to somehow jam their goods back into suitcases in time to re-board the train for the rest of the trip. Two men from their carriage helped Papa load their luggage.

Back in their compartment, Mama fashioned a makeshift bandage, and Papa kept his hand to his head to keep it in place. All the while, Natasha kept watching the soldiers. She was still afraid, but also angry, wanting to strike back, yet hoping desperately they wouldn't notice her family again.

For some time after the train set off, no one spoke. Although many Chinese people rode the train, Natasha's carriage consisted mainly of Europeans of various nationalities. Once Mama and Papa's fright had subsided and they were sure the other passengers were sympathetic, they began to whisper and talked well into the night. They speculated on possible reasons for being singled out, but could come up with no plausible explanation.

With the danger over, other passengers sent offerings of food and drink. Men trickled in to commiserate with Papa, the women helped Mama and Babushka with the children. Another Russian family was in the carriage, and they exchanged seats with some Belgian people to be nearer to discuss what had happened and help in any way they could.

In Tianjin, a doctor treated Elena and Papa. Elena's health improved quickly and Papa's wound was healing well. Now, the family boarded the ship for the four-day trip to Hong Kong. The passenger liner was luxurious, but they were to travel in the cargo hold with many other people fleeing China. Space was limited, so each family was restricted to the floor space they occupied when lying on their fold-up beds to sleep. Privacy was nonexistent. There were toilets but no bathrooms below decks, so the odor of perspiring bodies mixed with the smell of seasick passengers and oily lubricants from the ship.

The suffocating lack of fresh air most disturbed Natasha, the heat, the stuffiness and smells she could not escape. It was July, the time of typhoons in the South China Sea, and for several days, storm clouds blanketed the sky and fierce winds whipped up the ocean. As the liner rolled and lurched, most passengers were seasick. Inside the hold, bodies lay prostrate, moaning in time with the ship's upheavals. The trapped sick-smelling air was like a pungent shroud enveloping them all.

Each evening Papa took Natasha on a short walk up on the deck. She reveled in the sharp gusts of fresh wind that cleansed her lungs and revitalized her mind. The cold sprays of salt water seemed like a benediction, but too soon her father insisted it was time to return below. The time on deck for the refugees was strictly limited and they had been warned to keep out of the way of the "proper" passengers.

For the first half of the trip, Mama was seasick, so Babushka had charge of the children and Natasha had to help clean up any mess with toilet paper, but no disinfectant.

Next to the family in the hold sat a thin hawkish woman in her fifties who wore long caftan-like garments of black silk. Her nose was large and hooked and her voice rasped when she spoke. To Natasha, she embodied all the witches of every fairy tale she knew. Mama reported to the family that the woman was traveling to Australia as a mail-order bride. She had sent a twenty-year-old photograph to a suitor who was paying her expenses and she was not at all concerned the man might be astonished at her current appearance. "If he doesn't like what he sees when I get there, too bad," she had told Mama. "I'll be in Australia and I don't care if I live there married or single."

At last, the liner cruised into Hong Kong harbor in brilliant sunshine. The island looked immense, rising up, up out of the water to its huge tree-covered crest. And the air smelled so sweet and clean. The name, Hong Kong, meant Fragrant Harbor, Papa told her. She stood looking up, breathing deeply, finally out of the hold.

The family checked into a small hotel on Hong Kong Island. Their next ship, which had not as yet arrived, was to leave for Sydney in a few days. Natasha relaxed a little as she felt her parents' anxiety lift, but she remained anxious about the next leg of their trip. Still, for a few days, she enjoyed a holiday feeling. The family rode the Star Ferry to Kowloon and Natasha leaned over the railing to stare deeply into the water that had so buffeted her ship. Here the waves looked small and friendly, lapping happily at the sides as though asking her to come in and play. But she knew better. She knew how treacherous they could be and the effect they could have on a ship and its passengers.

Natasha enjoyed the days, but at night, dreams interrupted her sleep. Her body twitched and she caught her breath as soldiers' boots marched through her head, trampling everything in sight. On some nights the boots expanded like inflatable balloons, while on others the noise of crunching on gravel grew louder and louder. In the morning, she was embarrassed by the dreams, but as dusk fell, she was reluctant to go to bed.

Their scheduled departure date came and went and still their ship had not docked. Every morning Papa visited the shipping company and each time was told the ship was due any day. Although their hotel was not expensive, the costs were adding up, and once again Natasha felt shadows creeping over her family. Papa had to keep asking for extensions to their visas to stay in Hong Kong at the police station. Nearly a month passed before Papa learned that their ship had been damaged in a typhoon, was limping back to port and would need extensive repairs before it could sail again.

Mama was furious they had not been told earlier so they could find another way to travel and save hotel costs. Papa unhappily speculated that the ship had probably been commissioned for the Korean War. So once again, Papa had to find a way to get his family on to Australia. Fruitless calls followed fruitless calls. All means of travel were fully booked.

Another month dragged by. Finally, Papa found a cargo boat whose captain was willing to take on a small contingent of passengers. Papa happened to be at the shipping office at the right time so, even though they had to wait another month, Natasha's family would form the second half of the passenger list of twelve.

Natasha readied herself to face another ordeal at sea, but this trip turned out to be magical, full of fun and freedom. As she and her sisters were the only children on board, they were treated with exceptional kindness by the other passengers and crew. Her parents began to taste the end of their journey. Traces of hope peppered their talk, swelling slowly until they were full of anticipation for their new life. The tinkle of carefree laughter and the confiding of hopes and dreams replaced the tension that had clouded their lives for so long.

In the evenings, a sailor played the accordion and the passengers began dancing sedate waltzes and ended with abandoned peasant dances. Natasha's parents seemed so beautiful as they danced, Mama, slim and elegant, her dark eyes flashing again and her body finally relaxing; and Papa, a dashing if somewhat short figure, his kindness all-embracing and his intelligence shining through his eyes. Suddenly, anything seemed possible in this wild adventure, and at night her nightmares became less frequent.

On some mornings, Natasha and Elena sat with Papa on the tiny deck in the sunshine that danced and dazzled on the waves. The fresh smell of the sea, mixed with the odor of fuel and tar, whipped around their nostrils by breezes that tousled their hair. Usually the girls played chasing games or climbed on Papa's knees. Elena loved to comb her father's hair. He would sit still and laugh as she styled it, while Natasha read aloud to them.

Sometimes, Papa told them stories of his boyhood. He and his brothers once owned a bear, which had lived in their backyard in Vladivostock. The bear was tethered by a long chain and the boys erected a tent for him to live in. Papa told them of bandits who lived in the hills above his home and stole fruit from their trees and clothes from the clothesline.

"They needed these things to live," Papa explained, "so we were never concerned about them. They were just *things*, after all. And that is why they never hurt our family, although they kidnapped a boy who lived a few houses away. His parents had complained to the police about what had been stolen."

"Was the boy all right?" Natasha asked. A spray of cold ocean water sprang up toward them, then died mid-air, and fell with a splatter, dribbling water onto the deck.

"They returned him after a few days. He was very dirty and hungry, but not harmed. Your uncle Sasha and I wanted to go into the hills to visit the bandits, but Babushka wouldn't hear of it. Sasha was such a brave kid, always wanting to do dangerous things. He was the one who got the bear for us. He bought it from a gypsy. When he'd get an idea into his head, you couldn't talk him out of it. Finally, I'd end up going along to make sure everything turned out safely. But we never did get to see those bandits."

"Why were they up in the hills?" Elena asked, holding onto her jacket against the wind.

"They were soldiers who had deserted when there was a change of government and they had backed the losing side." Papa turned his face into the sweet-smelling wind. "Politics," he added, "always winners and always losers."

The closer their boat sailed to Australia, the more impatient Natasha became, but a little scared, too. She could not imagine how this new country would look or what it would hold for her family. As they sailed through the heads, the much-touted beauty of the famous Sydney Harbor did not interest her. She had seen far too much water and only wanted to see land and the relatives she could not remember.

On the taxi ride from the wharf to their new temporary home, she drank in each unusual sight as an omen of their new life. After Shanghai and Hong Kong, the streets and buildings all looked squeaky clean, new and neat and somehow on a smaller, more earth hugging scale. Her aunt's house was near the top of a hill and it seemed to Natasha that the upper corner of each of the bungalows had been snipped off at exactly the same point as they climbed up the street. From the crest of the hill, the view was a sea of red-tiled roofs, with the blazing sun glaring hard, interrupted by only a few tall trees.

She hated the suspense of not knowing how or where they were to finally settle. But first, they needed to get through the months in their shared home.

Chapter 9

Natasha's family's new home on William Street was situated on flat land with no view, but on one side sat vacant land belonging to the local council. Overgrown with shrubs and trees, it was termed "the bush," by the kids whose squeals and shouts prodded Natasha to sit up and listen. Now, in her grandmother's room with the flame from the gold lampada glowing in the corner, she felt well enough to want to join them.

"*Lucsche?* Feeling better? Listen, there's the paperboy's whistle. Your friends will be going home for dinner soon."

For the next two weeks after Natasha returned to school, it rained. In Australia it seemed when there had been sunshine for too long, it would suddenly rain and rain and rain until the earth, parched for too long, turned into sodden slushy mud.

On the next Saturday, Mama raced out to the mailbox which was attached to the front fence. As she returned, she pulled the galoshes from her feet and shrugged off her coat, shaking it behind her in the small back porch. Puddles of water edged the grass, causing endless rings to expand and disappear on the surface with each rain drop. Across the garden a frog croaked rhythmically.

As she entered the dining room, Mama slipped an overseas envelope into Papa's hand. Papa checked the letter and, glancing at Babushka, disappeared into the living room. Mama followed, closing the door behind her.

The overhead light in the dining room lit up the gloomy day. Babushka was replacing missing buttons on Papa's shirts. Thread, needles and a large red tin, containing a myriad of buttons, littered the table. Babushka held a long cotton thread and needle up to the light. After a couple of attempts to stab the thread through the needle's eye, she said, "Here, Natasha, I need young eyes. Thread several, would you?" Casting a glance at the living room door, she added, "Must have been bills. Those two worry too much."

"Papa's overtime this week will help." As Natasha threaded the needles, Babushka matched up buttons from the tin with the ones on the shirts. "Two holes, four holes," she muttered, sorting and making a noise like mahjong tiles, while rain drummed a steady patter on the roof.

Natasha heard her parents' voices in the living room and Papa clearing his throat several times. When the door finally opened, she knew there was a problem. "I'll tell the children," Mama said as she wiped at her eyes. Papa took out his handkerchief and blew his nose.

Babushka looked up from the tin. "What's wrong?"

Papa bit his lower lip, then said, "Mother, come with me to your room."

Babushka arose, a splotchy blush creeping up her neck to her face, and followed him. Papa closed the door gently behind them.

Natasha spun round to her mother. "What's the matter?"

Mama frowned. "I'll get Elena and the baby."

"Tell me what's happened."

"Just a minute." Mama disappeared into the girls' bedroom.

Natasha started to follow when loud wails erupted from Babushka's room. She stopped, frozen. It didn't sound like her grandmother at all. Quickly she chased after her mother.

"What's wrong with Babushka?" A high-pitched cry rose shrilly from her grandmother's room, sending goose bumps racing up her spine. "What was in that letter, Mama?"

Both the young girls had been playing happily. Now, Elena's eyes filled with tears and the baby whimpered. Mama picked up Sonia and took Elena's hand. From Babushka's room, keening cries followed sobs and sharp intakes of breath. Natasha ran back to Babushka's door. It was still shut fast. What had happened? Had someone died? Who?

Outside a sudden gust of wind hammered the rain against the windows, and in the distance thunder grumbled and growled. Babushka's wails continued, soothed by Papa's murmuring voice. Natasha leaned her forehead against the cool wood of the door. Slowly the wails became less piercing and Babushka, her voice quivering, insisted between sobs, "No. No. I will never believe it." Silence followed by deep breaths. "No. I will wait. I will wait for him to return." Then a sob erupted and led to a fresh outburst of grief.

Natasha felt like she was choking. She clamped her teeth together to keep from crying out.

"Come away from the door." Her mother, with the baby in her arms, came up near her. "Come with me."

Natasha spun around. "Please. What's happened?"

"It's news of Uncle Sasha." Mama led the way back to the dining room. She wet her lips before speaking. "The letter is from an acquaintance, Mosia Petrov. He has written that he and Sasha fled Singapore together on a ship when the Japanese invaded. But the ship…the ship was torpedoed and it sank." Again she moistened her lips.

"Some people survived. Mosia was one. There were lifeboats and life vests. It was early morning but still dark and cold, he says. Mosia was able to get into a lifeboat. A passing ship picked him up a few hours later. He made his way to Argentina. That's where he lives now. He heard from mutual friends that Papa was trying to find Sasha."

"But Uncle Sasha? What happened to Uncle Sasha?"

Mama sighed and shook her head. "Sasha and Mosia had sat together at dinner the previous evening. It was the first night out of port. But in the morning, when the ship was hit, Mosia didn't see him. There was confusion, as you can imagine. People were pushing and shoving, trying to get into lifeboats. He never saw Sasha again, so he doesn't know what happened to him."

"Didn't he try to find him? Go to his cabin?"

"Natasha, the man was trying to save his own life."

"But, maybe Uncle Sasha got on another lifeboat? Maybe he's in South America somewhere? Maybe he was saved, too."

"I suppose there's a chance. A very small chance."

Elena clung to Mama, and Sonia began to wriggle in her mother's arms. Natasha stared at Babushka's door as muffled moans escaped from inside. The rain outside had settled into a soft patter. She moved towards Babushka's room and stood silently, listening. Once more she leaned her head against the door and waited for what seemed like an age. Mama sighed, but let her alone.

Hot tears filled Natasha's eyes whenever her grandmother's sobs grew louder. Through chattering teeth, Babushka began to question the Lord's reasons for this tragedy. Then she would refuse to believe Sasha had perished and insisted he would find them. Had it not taken so long for Mosia to hear about their search?

Natasha knew Babushka loved her, but there was no one, no one in the world except Uncle Sasha, who could comfort her right now. She leaned against the door as the wind increased and the windows rattled with the rain lashing at the side of the house.

Chapter 10

Natasha stood on the front porch with her mother and Babushka, watching their neighbors on William Street, Mr. and Mrs. Jenkins, walk down the driveway. Their two driveways ran parallel, and the Jenkins waved as they turned into their own. Babushka returned the wave. "Shame they're selling. At least they never complained about anything."

Elena was inside and pressed her nose to the screen door, flattening its whitened tip. Her pink hair ribbon hung loose. "Who will buy their house?" she asked.

"That's the problem," Babushka answered, "nobody knows."

Back in the kitchen, Mama picked up the tea towel she had abandoned when their neighbors had arrived. "It was nice they came to tell us they were moving. But they were not very friendly. They never invited us to their home even though we had them to dinner."

Natasha said, "Mrs. Parker across the street says they don't like," she switched to English, "bloody-New-Australians."

"Natasha!" Her mother twisted towards her. "Do you know what that word means?"

"What word?'

"You must never use the word *bloody.* It's a swear word. Do you understand?" Natasha nodded. "And secondly, you are not to listen to Mrs. Parker. She has too much to say about everyone." Mama flicked the tea towel, indicating the end of the conversation, and picked up a plate to wipe.

Babushka tied her apron strings and rolled up her sleeves to finish washing the dishes from their Sunday lunch. The steam from the hot water filled the small room and cocooned them in damp food smells. In the ensuing quiet, only the clank of metal pots interrupted their separate thoughts.

Natasha picked up another tea towel and rubbed at a warm teacup. She felt embarrassed, but also angry, because she had heard so many people say "bloody-New-Australians' all in one breath, as though the words had been invented together. Now, she realized, every time she heard those words, she and her family were being insulted.

Reaching up, she placed the cup in the kitchen cabinet and glanced at her mother, who was engrossed in her own thoughts. How could anyone say anything nasty about her? Mama was so beautiful and always so neat and tidy with her lacy-collared white blouse tucked into her pleated gray skirt. As always, her dark curly hair sat like a shiny cap on her head.

Babushka, her thick fingers busy in the sudsy water, turned to Natasha. "Why are you pouting? Your bottom lip will grow so big we'll be able to use it for a table."

The edges of Mama's eyes creased into a smile and the tension evaporated. "We've been lucky in our neighbors," Mama said. "Even the Jenkins. We had good people most of the time in Shanghai, too. Except maybe for that Chernoff woman who complained whenever one of the children cried."

Elena, who had left as soon as Mama raised her voice, now danced on pointed toes back into the kitchen. "Maybe our old neighbor, Mrs. Popov and Shura the parrot, will buy the house next door and we can be neighbors again," she said.

"That's not likely, dear." Mama handed Elena a pot she had just wiped. "Can you put this away?"

"She *might* come," Elena insisted. "Then Shura will be my friend again."

"Mrs. Popov hasn't enough money to leave Shanghai," Babushka said.

"No, you're wrong." Natasha picked up a plate. "She's rich. Remember, she owns the grocery store."

“Well, she doesn’t really own it,” Mama replied.

“The shop on Avenue Joffre. Remember?” Natasha’s eyebrows grew closer together. “She told me herself she owned it.”

Mama and Babushka exchanged a glance.

“It’s true.” Natasha’s voice rose. “Mrs. Popov took me inside the shop and got some toffee without paying. She wouldn’t steal it, would she?” Somehow, she felt as if she were justifying a lie.

Elena backed away and returned to the living room.

Mama said quietly, “Of course she didn’t steal it.” Her chin jutted upward as she made her decision. “I’m going to tell you a story. I’m afraid some of the things Mrs. Popov told you were not quite true.”

“Are you going to tell her?” Babushka angled a look at Mama. “And Elena?”

“Natasha is mature for her years,” Mama said, “and Elena,” she glanced around, “and Elena has disappeared.”

“She doesn’t like trouble,” Babushka said.

Mama sighed. “Just like her father.”

Babushka straightened her back. “He stands up for himself when he needs to. He’s a good man, your husband.”

“Of course he is. But I wish he would let me have more of a say in how we spend our money. I earn half of it, after all.”

“He’s a man, and men have to feel like they’re in charge. If you gave up work, he would still have to support you and the girls.”

“Times are different now, and since I…oh, never mind. Arguing with you isn’t going to help. Anyway, he’s always faithful. I can forgive a lot when I know I can trust him.”

“He’s given me a place to live,” said Babushka. “Of my three children, he’s the one who’s taken care of me.”

“Maybe Andrusha should help more.”

“Are you fighting?’ Natasha asked.

"Of course not," Mama answered quickly. "Where shall we go to tell you the story?"

Using her towel, Babushka pointed to the dining room. "I'll finish up here."

"Just wait a second." Mama retrieved her manicure set, nail polish remover and varnish from the linen closet and spread them on the table. Natasha sat beside her. On the other side of the sliding glass doors that formed one wall of the dining room, the garden glowed quiet and serene in the afternoon sunlight. Fruit trees and eucalyptus flourished along the fence and hydrangea shrubs filled in bare spaces.

Her mother leaned forward and placed a hand on Natasha's hair, smoothing it where it had escaped from her thick plait. "Think back to the time you went to the grocery shop with Mrs. Popov." She sprinkled nail polish remover on a cotton wool pad and began to rub the nails of her left hand.

"Okay."

"Did you see a man in the grocery shop when you went in?"

"Yes."

"And a young woman?"

"Yes."

"Now, do you remember how Mrs. Popov liked to play mahjong?"

"Yes. She went nearly every day."

"You have a good memory. You see, Mr. Popov, the man you saw in the shop, and Mrs. Popov used to own the grocery shop and lived in an apartment above it. The shop became a popular place to pick up whatever people needed. Vasa, Mr. Popov, worked very hard in the shop and occasionally his wife would help." Mama sprinkled more remover on the pad and began on her other hand.

"But Mrs. Popov liked mahjong, She liked to play so much that she went nearly every day. Meanwhile, her husband complained he was stuck in the shop and his wife would not help. They fought about this, so she brought a niece from the country, from outside Arsenyev, just across the border, to help in the shop." Mama's eyes rested on a cross-stitched bouquet of flowers on the tablecloth. Natasha waited for her to continue.

Mama picked up the red nail varnish bottle and shook it. In Shanghai a lady had come to their home every Friday to do Mama's and Babushka's nails, but in Sydney, Mama did her own and Babushka didn't bother any more. Mama kept shaking the bottle as she continued.

"In time the niece arrived. She was a pretty young girl, just sixteen years old. Her name was Olga and she was rosy cheeked and full of smiles. For a while after she started working in the shop, for several months, everything seemed to be working out very well. Mrs. Popov went to play mahjong whenever she wanted. Olga worked hard and seemed very happy, and Mr. Popov was pleased, too. But one day, Mrs. Popov's game was canceled and she came home when she wasn't expected." Mama stopped, put down the varnish and took Natasha's hand. "What she found was that her husband and her niece were in love."

Natasha's eyes sprang to her mother's. "But he was married to Mrs. Popov!" This was not how stories were supposed to end. Married people, like her parents, were supposed to love each other for the rest of their lives.

"That's true." Mama nodded solemnly, let go of Natasha's hand and unscrewed the bottle of varnish. "He was indeed. Mr. Popov was very wrong in what he did. What happened was that Mrs. Popov moved out and came to live in the apartment above us while her niece stayed with her husband. He owned the grocery shop, men usually own things, and so he continued to work there and to give his wife a little money." She began to apply the polish carefully to her left hand.

"Also, Mrs. Popov could go and get whatever groceries she needed without paying. Just before we left Shanghai, Olga had a baby girl whom they named Marina."

Natasha frowned. "Does Mrs. Popov still love him? She must have been so sad." Natasha could see poor Mrs. Popov, living alone, knowing the person most important to her, did not care for her any more.

Mama bent to apply polish to her right hand. "I'm sure it was very hard for her. I don't know if she still loves her husband. She never spoke of him or Olga or the baby. We heard the story from other people."

"What will happen to her now?"

"I don't know. I wrote to her a while ago, but she hasn't replied. Life will not be easy there, with the political situation."

"She still has her parrot. Shura loves her. I wish I had a pet. You promised me a dog when we got our own home."

"I know. But animals cost money. I don't know if we can afford one yet."

"A puppy wouldn't eat much. He could have some of my food."

"I'll talk to Papa. If a dog gets sick, it could get quite expensive. We'll have to discuss it."

"Please, please." Natasha could tell her mother was weakening. "You said you always keep your promises."

"I'll talk to Papa but even if he agrees, these things take time. We have to find out where to get a puppy, what breed. There are lots of questions. And Babushka has to be willing."

"I'll look after him. She won't have to, I promise."

"Darling, you are in school all day. Of course Babushka has to be involved. Don't go telling Elena yet. It's not settled."

Natasha leaned towards her mother. "Please, Mama," she whispered.

"We'll see. We'll see."

Elena ran in and climbed onto her chair. "What happened to Mrs. Popov?"

"She came to live above us in Shanghai." Mama had finished applying the polish and shook her hands with the fingers extended.

"I know that," Elena answered with exasperation.

Natasha asked, "Do many married people, you know, stop living together?'

"It happens sometimes. But you needn't worry. It won't happen here," Mama smiled, reached over and kissed her, holding her hands like huge elephant ears at the sides of her head. "Your father and I will always be together."

Natasha bit her lip. So Mama and Papa were just two people who decided to get married one day. "But how do you *know* we'll always be together?"

"I know because Papa is married in his heart. We, his family, are his whole life."

Elena leaned onto the table. "Do you think a family with children will come to live next door?"

"I hope so," Mama answered. "We'll have to wait and see."

The next day a 'For Sale' sign appeared next door. Small groups of people made pilgrimages to the house, disappearing inside for a while and then emerging and standing, chatting in the driveway.

"Who do you want to buy it?" Natasha asked her sister one day when the house had been on the market about a week. They watched as two older people and a young man got out of a car and walked up the driveway.

"I want nice people to buy it." Elena stared until the group went inside.

Natasha leaned against the window. "It's a big house, bigger than ours. It will probably be a family. I hope they have three girls, like us. And maybe a dog. But no boys like

Vladimir to ruin everything. We could put on plays, go to the pool. Wouldn't that be great, Elena?" When she turned, she found Elena had left the window and was totally engrossed in her dolls.

"That's all you ever do!" Natasha's hand flapped at the curtains. "Play with those silly dolls!"

"All *you* ever do is complain."

"No, I don't!"

"You like to complain better than you like to be happy."

Natasha pulled a face at her sister, who continued her game. Was it true? It did seem that she was unhappy a lot more than Elena. Sometimes, Natasha felt she had to dig too hard to get into Elena's consciousness, to where her mind was clearly focused on the outside world and not fogged in by her own imagination.

As there was nothing interesting to do, she wandered outside but today there was no one about. Well, she might as well get her quota of weeding done. Weed pulling was a task she and Elena had to do three times a week, until, Papa said, the lawn had established itself.

Natasha retrieved the weed tray from the garage and made her way to the front lawn. She squatted near a newly planted fir tree beside the porch steps, her body crouched over. She rubbed her nose against her knee, smelling the scent of her skin and the sweet smell of the grass. The sun warmed her back as her fingers tugged and prodded at the shoots growing from the earth. Beside her, a dandelion swayed its fragile prongs delicately in the breeze. Against her father's instructions, she blew at it and watched the scattering seeds waft away across the lawn. Little by little, a pile of weeds grew in her tray. She hated to begin weeding, would put it off on any pretext, but once she started, it seemed hard to stop, as though one more weed always needed her attention.

As she worked, she thought about poor Mrs. Popov and the twist in her life. Then she began to make up a story in which she heroically rescued a child, Sonia maybe, from a burning house. No, maybe not Sonia, because she couldn't risk Sonia or Babushka being hurt in a fire. It would have to be a stranger's baby, left alone by a terrible mother, and then maybe her family would adopt the baby. Or maybe she saved a dog and then the dog became hers and…

Voices drifted over from the driveway of the house next door and floated into Natasha's consciousness.

"You'd be very comfortable here," the young man was saying. "Shame the owners are out or they would tell you what a nice area this is. Not too many families with children to make a lot of noise. In fact, next door are just girls, and very quiet."

"Hmph," the old man responded. "Girls can make a lot of noise, just like boys." A throaty smoker's cough forced him to stop speaking. Hidden behind the fir tree, Natasha wondered whether she should get up from her crouching position so they would see she could hear them. She already disliked this man who didn't like children.

Abruptly the man's voice started up again. "The house itself isn't bad. Maybe a bit big for Ethel and me. But mate, I've another question for you. Are there any bloody-New-Australians on the street?"

Natasha's blood raced to her head and her cheeks ignited. Before she knew it, she had jumped up and yelled, "You bloody old Australians should watch what you say. We're just as good as you are and you could learn a thing or two from us. So there!" Then she raced up the driveway.

The tableau she saw stayed etched in her mind for years: the real estate agent in his dark suit standing open-mouthed, the old man frozen in the act of lighting a cigarette, the woman standing straight-backed in gloves and hat, her mouth a tight line bisecting her face.

Natasha raced around to the back door, through the house to her empty room and huddled on her bed with Ivan. Her cheeks burned and her mind was a jumble of emotions. She did not want that old man living next door. But what if he bought the house even after she had yelled at him? She couldn't imagine being polite to him.

Would the real estate agent complain? Maybe Aunt Vera was right and she was trouble to everyone. Sometimes she just could not control her temper and words were out of her mouth before she even realized she had thought them.

And maybe she would not get a dog because of this. Oh, no!

The sound of a car engine outside drew her to the window. The car with the prospective buyers made a U-turn and she could clearly see them in the back seat, but nobody looked out of the car window either at the house next door or at her house.

For the next few days, Natasha lived in fear. If someone said her name, she jumped in alarm, certain there had been a complaint. Whenever she thought of the incident, she blushed with embarrassment. Why couldn't she control her temper? No wonder she could never be Vassilisa.

Three days later, she was fed up with the suspense. After dinner, she spoke seriously to her parents. "I need to talk to you about something important. In my room would be best, I think."

Mama and Papa looked surprised. Papa got up, stretched and waited for Mama. She rose and wiped her mouth on her napkin. Elena and Babushka watched as Natasha led her parents down the hall to her bedroom.

Inside, Papa sat on Elena's bed while Mama perched on the small dressing table chair. Natasha's eyes scanned her parents. She wanted their good opinion more than anything. Outside, darkness shrouded the neighborhood and the street lamp lit up a circular patch of the footpath near the letterbox. Closing the curtains against the street, she sat on her own bed.

Intertwining her fingers, she took a deep breath and haltingly told her parents about the prospective buyers and the old man's "bloody-New-Australian" comment. Gritting her teeth, she finished the rest of the story.

When she had finished, they sat in complete silence. Then Papa took off his glasses and seemed intent on polishing them with his handkerchief. Mama stared at her clasped hands. Natasha waited for raised voices but Mama's tone was calm and mild. She told her she had indeed done something wrong. Young ladies did not yell at people and never used that word, 'bloody'. Had not Natasha promised not to use it?

But even as her mother spoke, she could tell her parents were not upset. The twinkle in Papa's eyes was working overtime, and after he put his glasses back on, he covered his face as if to conceal a smile. Suddenly, Papa giggled and then burst out laughing, his shoulders shaking and his hands on his knees.

Then Mama laughed. "Natasha, Natasha. You'll be the death of us." She shook her head, laughing as she added, "You and your tongue! How are you going to get through life if you can't control it."

Although her words said one thing, her laughter said something else. Natasha now felt proud she had stood up for her family. Maybe the old man would think twice before using that phrase again. Maybe he would get to know some new Australians and find out they were just ordinary people. He might even like them.

Mama told her again to watch her tongue, that yelling didn't solve anything, but no punishment was mentioned.

Natasha bit her lip. "Can I still have a dog?"

Papa glanced at Mama and asked, "Shall we tell her?"

Mama gave a little laugh. "Anyone with a quick temper wouldn't have the patience to look after a dog."

Natasha squealed with joy. “Where is she? Where is my puppy?” She hugged her mother so hard she nearly fell off her chair.

“Just wait, darling.” Mama laughed and playfully wrestled with her. “We’ve chosen a boy puppy and he’s only eight weeks old and still with his mother. We’ll get him in a week or two. Babushka thought a dog would be good for you, so you better thank her. She’ll help look after him.” Mama hugged her. “You’ll have to think of a name for him.”

“Happy. Oh, he makes me so happy, I’ll call him Happy. What is he like? What color? What kind?”

“He’s a mongrel. Labrador with a bit of spaniel. He’s white and brown and gentle. You’ll have to look after him very carefully.”

“I love him already. I just can’t wait.”

Papa chuckled. “Just don’t treat him the way old Mrs. Grinkoff looked after that Pomeranian of hers. Haven’t been able to stand Pomeranians since.”

“What did she do?”

Mama began, “Well, she fed the dog bits of the toast she was eating—”

Papa folded his arms. “That’s not what I meant.”

“I know,” Mama said. “Well, Natasha, Mrs. Grinkoff insisted on wiping the poor dog’s bottom after he went to the toilet.”

“Oooh. How awful! I’ve never heard of anything like that.’

“Neither had we, before we met her.”

“I won’t ever do that. Can I tell Elena about my dog now?”

From that time on, she and Elena talked endlessly about the new dog as they watched the people come and go next door. But Natasha made sure to keep well away from the buyers and their agents.

Chapter 11

Two Saturdays later, Natasha answered the ring of the front door. And there he was! A squirming white puppy with a brown face in the arms of a man she had never seen before. "My puppy! My Happy!" Her squeal brought Papa to the door.

"Jack!" Papa said. "Come, please."

Natasha patted the puppy that licked her fingers and tried again to jump out of the man's arms.

"Better keep the pup outside. Grown, hasn't he?" Jack was a tall lanky man with wind-burned, tan skin.

Mama arrived at the door. "He's lovely." Elena ran up followed closely by Babushka. "It's Jack from the garage," Mama explained. Sonia, left alone in her high chair, began to cry and Mama turned back inside.

Jack squatted down, his long legs folding under him like a collapsible table. Natasha knelt down beside him.

"Your name's going to be Happy," she told the puppy as she felt the velvety softness of his coat. His body was firm and hard with a wiry strength. The skin on his forehead was screwed into a frown, as though he was worried. The name Happy seemed a strange choice for him, but Natasha was ecstatic with joy.

"He likes you," Jack said, winking at her. "Hey, your English is pretty good for a newcomer." He pushed his hat back from his forehead and stood up. Happy circled him and jumped up, his paws barely reaching Jack's knees. "Down, boy, down. You'll have to train him, you know."

Elena extended her hand. "Will he bite me?"

"Not if you're gentle with him. He'll be gentle back."

The puppy sniffed Elena's fingers and gave them a lick. "It tickles," she giggled.

Babushka scrutinized the dog. "Natasha, ask the man if he's sure the dog is Labrador and spaniel. Looks like he has some terrier in him."

When Natasha translated, saying "other kind of dog" as she did not know the word for terrier, Jack grinned and scratched his head. "Probably has some other breed in him, too. His parents are not pure-bred. Do you still want him?"

A full-throated "yes" from Natasha brought a laugh from Jack and Papa. With a clearing of his throat, Papa asked, "Drink?"

"Beer'd be great, mate."

Returning with Sonia in her arms, Mama translated. "*Pivo*."

The two men disappeared inside, the screen door slamming behind them. Happy stopped in his tracks. His whine and scratching at the door brought Jack back. As long the puppy could see Jack, he allowed the girls to play with him. Natasha and Elena chased him and were chased by him around the front lawn. The dog's ears flopped around as he ran and his pink tongue lolled out, so he looked like he was smiling. He seemed totally at ease with them until, fifteen minutes later, Jack put him on a leash, gave it to Natasha and walked back to his car, whistling quietly.

Happy strained against the leash, jumping in the direction of the car and squealing plaintively. When the car drove away, he howled with a heart-tearing intensity that reverberated inside Natasha's body as she gripped tightly onto the leash. "Mama, my dog doesn't like me. He doesn't want to stay with me!"

"It takes time, darling. Don't pull so hard. You'll hurt his neck muscles." Mama was as upset as Natasha, and when the noise would not stop, Elena ran indoors.

Babushka came out, picked up the dog in a no-nonsense manner and took him inside. She distracted him with two soup bones while she set up the blanket that was to be his bed in the storage room off the dining room.

It took three days for Happy to feel at ease in his new home. Natasha rushed home from school to his exuberant welcome. Next he would lie at her feet as she ate her snack. Their ritual became a walk after the snack and then Happy slept at her feet as she did her homework.

In the evening, while Babushka and Mama bathed Elena and Sonia, she sat on the floor beside Happy and confided the troubles of her day. His big eyes followed her movements and she felt he understood everything she told him. He even seemed to grin when she told him jokes, licking at her fingers as she talked and caressed his silky fur. Elena lost interest in him after the dog chewed up one of her dolls, and then Natasha felt he was really *her* dog.

* * *

A month later, the house next door sold, and finally the moving trucks came and carried out the Jenkins' furniture and boxes. Mama and Babushka smiled whenever Natasha or Elena asked about the buyers. "Wait and see," was all they would say.

"Do you think they'll like us?" Natasha asked. Behind her words was the unspoken question; will they like us even though we are new Australians?

"I'm sure they'll like us," Mama answered confidently.

Three days later, Natasha arrived home to find another, larger van parked in front of the next-door house. She had stopped to remove letters from the letterbox when the front door flew open and one after another, girls came out from the house. She counted. Four girls, all with light brown hair. They emerged from the house then stopped. The tallest looked over to her and smiled, and then they all approached the fence. The door opened again and two younger boys appeared, and, from inside, came the sound of a baby's cry.

Natasha couldn't believe it. "How many kids are in your family?'

"Eight," replied the tallest girl. "Six girls and two boys."

"Wow." Natasha's eyes widened. "That's wonderful."

The girls all laughed. The tallest spoke again. "I'm Sally and I'm fourteen. This is Helen—"

Helen completed the sentence. "And I'm twelve."

"G'day. I'm Lizzie and I'm ten," another girl said.

"I'm Susan and I'm eight."

"Wow." Natasha could not stop smiling.

Sally pointed to her brothers. "That's Andrew and Michael. They're six and four. The babies, Mary and Therese, are inside."

"I'm Natasha and I'm ten," she turned to the two younger girls, just as Lizzie climbed the fence. "So I'm the same age as Lizzie, right?"

"Right-oh." Lizzie threw a leg over the top and settled comfortably onto her perch. From her scraped knee and untidy hair, Natasha decided she was the tomboy in the group. "When's your birthday?" Lizzie asked.

"September 24th." Natasha watched Lizzie, fascinated. She had never thought to climb the fence, but now she would as soon as possible, in private first, to make sure she could.

"I'm older than you. My birthday's in June." Lizzie jumped back down onto her side of the fence. "Do you play jacks?" From her pocket she produced a set of green painted sheep knucklebones and flipped them into the air.

"I *love* jacks. Oh, and I have two sisters, Elena who's five and Sonia who's just a year old." She shook her head in amazement again. "I was so worried about who would come to live here. I'm so glad it's your family." She laughed aloud and waved the letters she held in her hand. "This is better than *Little Women* even."

One of the boys sidled in front of his sisters. "I'm getting a go-cart," he told her earnestly, "and I'll let you ride it if you want to. And I've got a slingshot, look." From his pocket he extracted a forked twig with a rubber band tied to the forks.

Susan pulled at her brother's shirt. "Andrew, you'll be in trouble if Mum sees that. And tuck your shirt in, too."

"We like our new house," said Helen, whose hair was secured in bunches on either side of her head. She seemed the serious one. "It's much bigger than the one we had before."

"We sure need it," Lizzie added.

"I was hoping lots of children would move in," Natasha said. "But eight! I never thought there would be eight. It's funny how you are all two years apart."

Sally nodded solemnly. "Mum always says it's the rhythm method, but I don't know why."

Natasha wondered if Lizzie would be in her class. "Will you all go to Lindhurst Public School?"

Helen answered, "We'll be going to the Catholic school."

Lizzie's eyes narrowed. "Where are you from? You're not Australian, are you?"

Natasha froze. Well, there was no hiding it. They would find out sooner or later, so she told them straight out and waited for those terrible words.

Instead, Sally said, "Wow. That's so exotic."

Natasha had never heard the word 'exotic', but from the way Sally said it, she knew it was not something to be ashamed of. She would look it up in her dictionary when she went inside. "Thanks. I'm so glad we'll be friends." A loud bark came from her house.

"You have a dog?" Lizzie's face lit up in a smile.

Natasha laughed. "That's Happy. He's just a puppy."

"Can I play with him?" Lizzie gazed at the front door where Happy was scratching at the screen. "I love dogs, but Mum says there are too many of us already."

Andrew jumped up. "I love dogs, too."

Just then a lady came out of the front door of the house next door. "There you all are. I was wondering why it was so quiet. Well, hello there, love," she smiled warmly at Natasha. "I'm Mrs. Flannery. I see you've met my family." She was short and plumpish with a cheery, happy air about her.

"How do you do," Natasha returned the smile. "I'm Natasha and I'm so glad you moved here."

"Yes. We think this will work out very nicely. I'll come in and meet your parents in a little bit and have a cuppa. Just need to sort through some boxes first. It's a terrible mess inside right now." Natasha liked her immediately. She spoke to her as though Natasha were an equal. "Come on, everyone. I need a bit of help. Cheerio. Nice to meet you, dear."

"See you," Lizzie waved as she turned to go.

With a chirruping chorus behind her, Mrs. Flannery retreated through the front door. "Bye. Bye!" The children called out and waved furiously before disappearing inside.

Natasha stood still. She felt she had just glimpsed paradise. She had never seen so many happy faces surrounding her and wanting to be friends. Even the boys seemed nice.

She could not wait for the weekend to get to know them better. She wondered if they would continue to be so nice. Sometimes you met people and they seemed nice, but after a while…well, she reminded herself, look what happened with Lorraine.

But she would not think of that now. She was thrilled to have all these kids next door, and as long as she did not lose her temper, she was sure everything would be great.

With a lingering smile, Natasha looked down and noticed the letters in her hand. A blue airmail letter with Chinese characters caught her attention. Shanghai, she thought. The sender's name was Popov. "Mrs. Popov," she breathed. "I wonder how she is."

That evening Mama placed the unopened letter beside her throughout dinner. The talk was of the new family next door. Mama admitted that she had known for a while and kept it a secret.

When they had finished dinner and Babushka served cups of lemon tea, Mama said, "Now it's time to read Mrs. Popov's news."

Chapter 12

Mama slit the envelope, and opened the letter. Natasha leaned forward. "Is Mrs. Popov all right?"

"Well, first she asks about us and…let's see." Mama began to read aloud. "'Last month, the doctor discovered a large tumor,' oh dear, 'in Vasa's abdomen.'"

"*Gospodi Bozhe moi*!" Babushka clasped a hand to her mouth.

Mama's eyes met Babushka's. "The poor man." With a shake of her head she returned to the letter. "'Although he has felt no pain so far,'" she read, "'the cancer is spreading rapidly. Olga (you remember my niece?) couldn't take the news. She panicked, packed up and fled in the night. Would you believe she left baby Marina behind?'"

At Babushka gasp, Mama peered up from the letter and nodded. Babushka patted Sonia's leg, as she kicked against the high chair and exposed four tiny teeth in a big grin. "Precious pet," Babushka whispered.

Mama continued reading. "'How could a mother do such a thing? Well, Olga is young. I guess she didn't tell her parents the truth of what happened and didn't want to return with an illegitimate child.'"

Papa tapped his pipe on the ashtray. "Without Vasa, how would Olga have managed? And with a baby, too."

"What does illeg…what was that word?" Elena asked. "What does it mean?"

Natasha thought she knew but waited to hear what Mama would say.

"It means…it just means that the parents aren't married," Mama said and returned to the letter. "Mrs. Popov writes, 'I didn't know what to do at first. I didn't think I could look after that baby, with all the pain her mother caused me. But a few days after I heard the news I went to the shop. Little Marina was there, grubby, hungry and needing someone to care for her. Vasa had tried, but you know how men are. It is not the baby's fault that she was born. Vasa was so glad to see me, and although I can never love him again, I will care for him until he passes.'"

Babushka interrupted. "I wonder how soon?" She crossed herself, and then fingered the gold crucifix around her neck.

Mama read on. "'So I have moved back in above the shop. The baby, dear Marina, has completely accepted me. God has given me a reason to go on living in the life of this precious little one. Every day I watch her growing and learning new things, and her eagerness for life gives me such joy. I no longer care how she entered this world. She is the light of my life and the daughter I could never have myself. Please tell the girls that Shura is well and misses them. He no longer talks as much as he used to. He's getting old, too, I guess.'"

Elena said, "He used to say *zsdravstvuite* whenever I went up to visit."

Mama smiled. "Yes, he was a polite parrot to say 'hello'. The letter continues, 'I miss you all and wish you could see my little Marina. I hope, now God has given her to me, he'll allow me to live to see her grow up. Well, dears, thank you for your concern. I try not to worry, just take it one day at a time. I have employed a young Chinese couple who look after the shop very well, especially since all the customers are now Chinese, very few Westerners still here. I will remain here until Vasa passes. Please pray for him and for me, too, my friends. Knowing you are settled is a great happiness to me. Take care of yourselves, your loving friend, Maria Popov.'"

Mama's gaze swept them all. "What a strange way for their lives to go. I do hope she will be all right. I'll write again and let her know we could find a sponsor for her and

Marina if she would like to come to Australia after…after poor Vasa is gone."

Papa lit his pipe. "I don't know how she'll manage. China's not the same. There's every chance she'll lose the shop. Communists don't believe in private ownership, or in commerce the way we know it."

Babushka sighed. "How will she provide for Marina then?"

"She's an outsider in the land she calls home." Papa grunted. "It's a different world there now. It's not the Shanghai we knew." He took a draw on his pipe.

"Well, I think Mrs. Popov sounds happier," Natasha said. "She has family now and is not alone anymore."

A telephone call for Babushka interrupted them. When Babushka returned to the table, she frowned and announced Agnes was not well. "Poor Agnes. Now *there's* someone who's all on her own with no one to look after her. She has the flu. Having family would make such a difference to her life."

Agnes had visited Natasha's family several times since Elena's birthday party. It was hard for Natasha to imagine Babushka and Aunt Agnes as friends as they were so different. Babushka was soft and round and pink and usually wore housedresses and aprons. But Agnes always wore elegant, if old, dresses of silk or linen with ruby, sapphire and diamond rings, gold bracelets and often a fan-shaped diamond brooch on her lapel.

"Doesn't Aunt Agnes have anyone?" Natasha asked.

"She has us," Babushka replied.

Elena leaned forward. "Wasn't she ever married?"

Babushka replied, "She's buried three husbands."

Elena let out a shriek then hid her face in her hands. "I don't like her anymore!" Sonia began to cry but stopped when everyone laughed at Elena.

"Her husbands died." Mama stroked Elena's cheek. "That's all Babushka meant."

Elena looked up sheepishly. "Well, you didn't say it right. Anyway, I knew Aunt Agnes would never kill anyone. She has such nice rings and bracelets. When I grow up I'm going to have lots and lots of rings and bracelets and," she gestured along the length of her arm, "and I'll wear them all at the same time."

Natasha touched the plain gold wedding band on Mama's finger. "Mama had to sell her jewels."

"Jewels are not important," Papa said and sucked on his pipe. "It's the kind of person you are, and Agnes is a very good person."

"Didn't she have any children?" Natasha asked.

"No children of her own. She's been alone for…" Babushka squinted as she calculated, "ten years now." She began to stack the dishes. "Well, it's Thursday today. Do you think I could go to look after her on the weekend? Someone would have to take me."

"Where does she live?" Natasha rose to help.

Moving towards the kitchen, Babushka answered, "Chatswood. On the north shore. She works for a doctor and has her own place nearby."

It was agreed Papa and Natasha would take Babushka to care for Agnes. Elena was upset she had to stay home and more so when she found out Papa had given Natasha sixpence for her help. But, she cheered up when Natasha realized she would miss out on a whole day with their new neighbors. Lizzie had come in to see Natasha a couple of times already and she was hoping they would become good friends.

They set out at seven o'clock on Saturday morning. Before leaving home, Babushka insisted they all sit in silence, with heads bowed, a Russian custom to ensure a safe journey. When they caught the bus on the corner, Papa said it felt like they were setting out on a big adventure. Natasha agreed.

It was a cool winter morning and Babushka had dressed in her favorite three-quarter-length black coat over a grey skirt, with a black beret covering her hair. Papa wore his brown leather jacket. Natasha had not seen any jackets like it on other people in Australia, and it often drew stares from the people they passed. Since he had begun working as a motor mechanic, Papa had stopped wearing a fedora and now wore a cloth cap, like other working men.

At the train station, Papa stood in line to buy tickets. He had practiced saying "Three to Chatswood," the previous evening, but when the ticket officer asked if he wanted returns, he called to Natasha. Through the grille, Natasha asked the man with the impatient red face for one adult and one child return to Chatswood and one adult single. Papa clicked his tongue as he took the tickets. "Maybe if they didn't speak so quickly I'd have a better chance."

"You'll learn, Papa." Natasha stared down at the slightly too small shoes that were pinching her feet. Her heart ached for her father, while she wished he could again be the strong Papa he had been in Shanghai. She decided not to mention her shoes.

Babushka peered into her son's hand. "Did he give you the right change?"

Papa checked and nodded. He hunched his shoulders as he searched for the platform for the next city train.

"It says Platform 2." Natasha pointed to the slatted sign listing all the station stops that the train would make.

"You'd better check with someone." Papa's gaze swept the station.

"Who?"

"The ticket collector. That man in the blue uniform." When the ticket collector confirmed the platform, they descended the stairs slowly as Babushka found the deep Australian steps difficult after the shallow ones in China.

The stores closed at noon on Saturdays and did not open on Sundays, so for many working people Saturday morning was their only time to shop. Thus, the station was crowded with people setting off to the city. Natasha felt marooned amongst the groups of Australians standing and chatting around them. She sensed how different her family looked.

She yearned to be as casual and confident as the young Australians, like the blonde girl who stood chatting to two young men, flicking back her hair with a quick movement of her hand. Natasha envied the crisp white collar protruding from a pink sweater, wide skirt and matching satin hair ribbon. Her long hair in its tight plaits seemed old fashioned now, and her pleated tartan skirt felt dowdy. If only she had shorter hair so she could wear it loose. Everyone at school had hair so different to hers, and last week Lorraine had again said her hair looked strange. Maybe she should get it cut.

Babushka nudged Natasha. "Look at the boys in shorts and long socks on such a cold day. Their legs are bare."

"The boys at school all dress like that." Natasha answered quietly, so people would not hear them speaking in Russian.

"And look! That girl is barefoot and carrying her shoes."

Natasha glanced at the young girl who happily trod from one to another of the puddles left from the previous night's rain. "She wants to keep her shoes from getting wet."

Babushka laughed. "Shoes should protect your feet and she protects her shoes."

Natasha frowned. "They'll hear you, Babushka." In a way she was ashamed of her grandmother. She sidled a few steps back from her.

Babushka raised her voice. "They can't understand what I'm saying."

Natasha hurried back to her side. "No, but they know you're talking about them."

"You're right." As a group of well-dressed young people walked past, Babushka sighed. "Look at the way the young walk. So carefree, their heads up so high. Few disappointments in their pasts and high hopes for their futures." She nodded and looked her granddaughter in the eye. "Yes, *dorogaya*, the future belongs to you."

"And to you, too."

"I'm old and will soon be gone. I'm at the age when I wonder how I might die."

An empty hole opened up inside Natasha. "Don't say that, Babushka." How could she have been ashamed of her? Babushka was so important to her.

Papa arched his eyebrows. "She'll outlive us both. You've heard of Russian people who live to be 140 years old? That'll be her."

Babushka laughed and said. "You have time to accomplish things, Natasha. I no longer have the time and certainly not the energy."

"Who knows how much time any of us have?" Papa said. "When you're young, life seems so long, the summers are endless, but somehow it all slips past in a flash."

Natasha wanted to accomplish *something* in her life, and although life did seem to stretch out forever, occasionally she felt she needed to hurry up to get started She had thought vaguely she would enjoy being an architect, but getting trained took so long. For other jobs you started as an apprentice at fifteen. "I think I'll be a hairdresser," she stated aloud.

"You can become anything you want, Papa replied, *after* you have finished university."

"But hairdressers have to apprentice and they won't take you if—"

"You will finish your education. That's the one thing no one can ever take from you." Papa looked grim. "That's why we came to Australia."

Natasha's exasperated glance irritated Papa. He barked at her, "You don't know what university will open for you, worlds of literature, art. Pushkin, Chekhov, Shakespeare. Think of all the learning that has gone on through the centuries. A lifetime is not long enough to appreciate it. And you don't even want to open your mind to it."

Natasha was glad to hear the chugging rumble of the approaching train. Papa could go on forever when he started about Pushkin.

Babushka became anxious, grabbing Natasha's arm. "Are you sure it's the right train? What if it goes to Liverpool or somewhere else!" The stationmaster assured them it was the right train, so they joined the surge of passengers ready to board.

The only seating available for three people backed onto the entry porch of the train and meant they were traveling backwards, facing the other passengers. They sat gingerly, aware of the stares of the people facing them. Natasha realized people looked at them differently, in a sideways sort of way. It didn't happen when she was alone.

They sat in silence, swaying in time to the jolts of the train as it traveled through fields of houses with red tiled roofs. Inside the train, there was a steaminess and stuffiness in the air and an odor of wet wool. The old leather seats, with a few slits exposing cream padding, stuck to Natasha's legs. When Babushka spoke in Russian, the other passengers watched suspiciously, as though her family might be plotting against them.

Facing them a few seats away, sat a woman in a green tulle hat, who kept glancing at them and pursing her red lips. The man beside her pulled a pouch of tobacco from his pocket and when he began to roll a cigarette, she rolled her eyes and gazed at the ceiling.

Two stations along, the woman rose and said a loud "Excuse me," to the man beside her. Then, as she passed by Natasha's family, she leaned towards them. In a husky low voice, she hissed, "If you don't even bother to learn our language," her red mouth was just above Natasha's head, "you should go back to wherever you came from."

She straightened and squared her shoulders. "Can't tell you're in Australia sometimes," she added in a half whisper meant to be overheard by the other passengers.

Natasha's thick eyebrows shot up. Before she had a chance to think, she burst out with, "How do you know we're not learning? Just because *you* can only speak one language?"

Around her the whole carriage had gone a deathly quiet. Papa had sprung up while the woman had taken a step backward.

"What a rude child!" she sputtered.

"*Shto ona skazala*? What did she say?" Papa glared at the woman.

"It's all right, Papa. She…she just said we should learn English."

"Tell her to mind her own business!" Papa's body was thrusting forward.

Natasha turned to the woman and smiled sweetly. "My dad says to mind your own business."

"Oh, my goodness!" Her words came out with a snort. She flung her head back and proceeded into the entry porch to wait for the train's doors to open.

Papa, scowled at her through the glass door. When the train lurched to a stop, he was thrown back into his seat. Embarrassed, his hand strained at his collar while a flush crept up his neck.

Natasha sat back, feeling the eyes of the other passengers glued to them. But inside she was angry. Maybe she should have told the woman she was a descendent of convicts. Maybe she should say that to all these people who were still silently observing them.

A young man's voice broke the silence. "Don't let that old bag worry you. Not all Aussies are like that."

Natasha glanced at the speaker. He was a good-looking young man who had been hidden behind a newspaper. He gave her an impish grin and she returned a shy smile. "Your English is pretty good, young lady. No trouble coming back at her." He folded his newspaper. "Where are you from?"

"Shanghai," Natasha answered.

He gave a laugh. "You don't look Chinese."

"No, we are Russian."

His voice turned serious. "Commies?"

"No," Natasha answered quickly, aware of everyone listening.

Papa said in Russian, "Tell him we're White Russian." The word Commies was one he knew too well already.

Natasha translated and the young man nodded wisely. "You'll be a *dinkum Aussie* before you know it. Good luck to you all."

The atmosphere in the train suddenly lightened and people began to chatter amongst themselves again. The man who was smoking his self-rolled cigarette blew out a stream of smoke and added loudly, "That old bag doesn't approve of anyone or anything. See the way she turned up her nose at my ciggie?" He laughed out loud. The young man turned to him and flashed a grin before returning to his newspaper.

Natasha certainly felt better now, but what if they had been Commies? How would these people have reacted to them then? Did she want to be a *dinkum Aussie*? If she wasn't an Aussie, then would she always be a Russian in Australia and never fit in?

Somehow, everyone in the carriage now looked at her family with tolerance and even kindness. Why did being White Russian make them better than plain Russian? She would ask Papa, but it had to wait. The train was pulling into Central Station and she needed to make sure they made the correct connection.

Chapter 13

Central Station sprawled over several platforms under a huge canopy. A few people were seated on the slatted wooden benches, but many more stood around waiting. This time Papa and Babushka relied entirely on Natasha, trailing behind wherever she led. Natasha felt this was the wrong way around, but was grateful they no longer made her ask questions when she already knew the answers.

The next train was less crowded as they were now traveling out of the city. Natasha watched the signs and at Chatswood they got off and followed the directions towards Aunt Agnes' apartment.

The morning sun had begun to warm the day, although a crispness kept the air fresh and bracing. Overhead tall gum trees jutted up into a clear blue sky that seemed impossibly far away. A large white cockatoo abruptly swooshed his wings and burst out of a tree, giving Babushka a fright. She laughed when she realized it was just a bird and paused for a moment to watch its progress.

Natasha pulled a strip of bark from the trunk of a gum tree, and fingered its roughness, thinking about their train trip. Further down the street, one kookaburra's laugh turned into a chorus and Natasha recited a chant from school about a kookaburra sitting in an old gum tree. As she finished, she asked, "Papa, why did the people on the train like us better when we told them we were White Russians?"

"It means we are against communism, like they are."

"I don't want to be a communist because nobody likes them, but I'm not sure what one is."

"Communism is the system of government in Russia and some other countries. You remember how the communists came to power in Shanghai?"

"Yes. But we aren't in the government?"

"If a person thinks communism is a better system of government than capitalism, then people say he is a communist."

They passed a low brick fence with brilliant red bougainvillea spilling over the side. Natasha broke off a leaf and squashed it in her fingers. "Isn't it funny how it's nearly winter and there are still flowers on this?"

"The weather here is so mild, not like Shanghai," Babushka answered. "Ah, the world has changed too much. The war showed the depths of humanity. Who would have ever dreamed of the things that happened. Nazis, the extermination of people. People! Gas ovens. Bombs dropped on cities," she shook her head. "I have lived too long."

"But Papa, why do people hate communists so much if it's just a system of government?"

"Governments affect the way people live. Communists want to spread their influence all over the world. But there is good and bad in every system, just as there are good and bad people in every country."

Babushka scoffed. "You would have good things to say about anyone, anything, about a snake!"

Papa raised his hand. "Wait, Mother. I'm not finished. I doubt that communism can ever work. It's only a theory. Some of its ideals, such as wanting people to live without poverty, are good. *But*," Papa clicked his tongue, "many bad things have happened in its name. A lot of people had their property, things they worked many years to attain, their businesses, their homes, taken from them."

He patted Natasha's shoulder and said, "That's why I always tell you how important education is. Nobody can take that away from you. With communism, there is only one party, so it can't be voted out of office. That's a *very* big problem."

Babushka reached out a gloved hand to steady herself against a fence. "What they did to the Tsar and his family!" Her chest heaved as she spoke. "May God forgive them as I never will. Communists!" She shivered in disgust. "If it hadn't been for that Rasputin, maybe things would have been different."

"It would still have happened, Mother."

"They still haven't buried them properly, you know. The poor Tsar. No one knows exactly where their bodies are. Or I haven't heard, anyway." She closed her eyes, inhaling deeply. "Mother Russia has suffered too much."

Papa frowned. Natasha wasn't sure if it was the conversation or the way Babushka's chest was heaving.

"Let's stop a moment." Papa took her arm. "Are you all right?"

"Yes, yes." Babushka unfastened the top button of her coat

"Are we on the right street, Natasha?"

Natasha pointed to the street sign and said, "Stuart Street." She knew how hard Papa was trying, but she still wished he could read English like, well, like everyone else.

Babushka shook her head. "Vera told me the communists are going to close all the churches in Shanghai. Terrible, just terrible!"

Half to herself, Natasha murmured, "People are talking about communists all the time, on the radio, in the papers."

"The Australian government tried to ban the party."

"Do Australians hate Russians because of the war, too?" Natasha asked.

"We were on the same side in the war. No, it's communism. It pretty much started in Russia. That's why the train passengers were happy we were White Russian."

As they waited for Babushka, Natasha pondered Papa's answers. She decided to mention they were White Russian at school. Most of the time now, the other kids ignored her origins, but whenever anything about communism was mentioned, a few glances slid her way.

Papa said, "One day, when we've lived here long enough, we'll become naturalized Australians."

"Do you want to?" Natasha asked.

"If it is to be my home, then of course I do. And you would be a naturalized Australian too. With an Australian passport and the right to vote."

Did she really want to be Australian? Natasha wanted to be *like* the Australians, to fit in. But would she ever really *be* Australian? She tried on the feeling of being Australian, but it didn't quite fit.

There would always be part of her that was Russian. She knew that already she was not as Russian as Babushka, or as that new family who had just arrived from Harbin, China. She decided she would have to be Australian with the Australians and Russian at home. Thank heavens their new neighbors were nice people who were not worried they were Russian. Lizzie even acted as though it was interesting.

Babushka adjusted her coat. "I'm ready to go on."

"Good." Papa cleared his throat and spat to the side of the road.

"Papa, what are you doing?" Now, Natasha understood how Aunt Vera had felt when she had done the same thing on their arrival in Sydney. In Shanghai, there had not seemed anything unusual about spitting, but here, it now seemed so rude. She glanced around to see if anyone had seen, but they were quite alone.

Babushka smiled at her and nodded. She understood. Her father was striding along, totally unconcerned. Maybe she should tell him that Australians did not do that. It seemed she was becoming Australian without even realizing it.

In a few minutes they found Aunt Agnes' street and began checking the numbers on the shops that lined it. A fish and chip shop had the same number as Aunt Agnes, except hers had an *A* after it. "That's funny," Papa said.

"Look," Natasha pointed, "there's a door between this shop and the shoe shop."

In the narrow doorway were six mailboxes. Papa checked his paper. "Apartment number 5." Natasha read the names on the boxes and there it was, Agnes Thompson.

"This isn't what I expected." Papa took off his cap and ran a hand through his hair. Babushka followed as he led the way up the stairs. Numbers 1 through 3 were on the first landing. On the second landing, Papa knocked at a door with the number 5, as Babushka struggled up the final stairs.

"*Prikhodite*. Come in, it's open." Aunt Agnes' voice called in reply.

Chapter 14

Papa turned the handle and they entered a one room apartment. Aunt Agnes reclined on a bed against the opposite wall. On Natasha's right stood a stovetop with two burners releasing a faint whiff of gas, and beside it was a miniscule laminate table with two chairs.

Agnes lifted a hand, gold bracelets jangling. Babushka rushed to her. "*Kak ti, dorogaya?* My dear, how are you?" A black lacquered Chinese screen served as a headboard, while in shadow under the bed, Natasha glimpsed an enamel chamber pot.

"Luchshe, Galia. Better." Agnes pecked Babushka on the cheek.

Taking off her beret, Babushka collapsed into a gold velvet armchair with fraying edges. Natasha hung back. Aunt Agnes seemed to have shrunk. Her blue tinted hair was still in a net on her head, but now the curls looked flat and matted.

"Natasha, come here, my dear."

Agnes' rings indented Natasha's flesh as they clasped hands. The older woman's lavender scent had a stale odor and her voice trembled as she said, "What a clever girl to bring your Papa and Babushka to me." She winked but without the usual energy.

Natasha smiled. Aunt Agnes always made her feel like an adult, responsible and mature. Aunt Vera, however, made her feel like a child trying to break out of a tight restraint. It was funny, the way she felt her personality changed with different people because of the way they treated her.

"What a lovely cozy flat," Babushka said, taking off her coat.

"You must all need a nice cup of tea," Agnes suggested. "Galia, the cups are in the side cabinet." From her bed, Agnes instructed Babushka on where to find things, and then asked, "How was your trip here?"

"Not bad." Papa exchanged a glance with Babushka. "A silly woman on the train made a fuss about us learning English." He waved a hand as he pulled off his coat.

"She was rude." Natasha pouted at the memory.

"My goodness, what happened?" Agnes asked.

Papa shrugged. "This woman doesn't like immigrants."

"She tried to make us feel awful." Natasha glanced around to see where to sit.

"She had no power over us. It doesn't matter," Papa said.

Natasha turned to her father. "Not like soldiers, you mean? No, I guess not." In her mind she saw again the soldiers on the train platform on the way to Tianjin with their swinging batons, lamps and guns.

Papa nodded as he sat. "That woman only has the power you give her."

"But words can hurt," Aunt Agnes said. "People like that are usually very shallow. It's a shame she ruined your trip."

"I need that tea." Babushka rose.

"Sergei, how is your job?" Agnes asked.

"It pays the bills." He gave a half smile. "You do what you have to do."

"That bad, is it?"

"No, no. They're good 'blokes.'" Papa laughed. "But sports crazy, cricket and football, sports I don't understand. Rowing isn't popular here. I can't hold a conversation yet. It's tough to learn a new language at my age."

Babushka measured tea leaves into a pot. "I can't make that *th* sound. I spit at everyone around me." She grinned at Natasha.

Papa chuckled. "You're the only one whose English is worse than mine."

"It's good that you can laugh," Agnes said. "You'll pick it up, Sergei. You're surrounded by it at work."

"I suppose. I read while I eat lunch, for the moment. You know, I don't know where to buy Russian books here."

"Try the church," Agnes suggested. "Back where they sell Russian food."

Papa nodded. "Natasha should attend Russian classes on Saturdays but without a car, it's not possible. I'd hate her to forget her language and culture." He coughed. "Agnes. The bathroom?"

"Down the hall, Sergei. It should be empty." Papa nodded and left.

Babushka took Agnes' hand. "You're still quite pale."

"While I'm lying down, I'm all right, but when I stand I feel faint. I've missed three days work and need to get back."

"I'll look after you." Babushka patted her hand and shuffled back to the sink.

Natasha asked, "What kind of work do you do, Aunt Agnes?"

Babushka answered. "She works for a doctor."

"I'm a housekeeper for Dr. Wilson, a surgeon. Poor man lost his son in the last days of the war. Got the telegram just as he was about to operate, but he did it anyway. Such bravery. He was concerned about his young patient. Did a brilliant job, too."

"So sad," Babushka murmured.

"Is a housekeeper like an *amah*?"

"No, no," Babushka answered. "She gives the other servants orders."

"What other servants?" Agnes laughed. "A cleaning lady once a week?"

"Well, *you* don't clean, and that's what Natasha means." Babushka filled the sugar bowl. "Do you have milk?"

"It went sour. Maybe Natasha can go to the shops. Galia, dear. My job is quite menial. So my life is different from before, when *I* had servants. But I am alive and can support myself. I'm lucky to still have some beautiful things like that screen. I understand too well how Sergei feels."

"He was so clever at school." Babushka paused. "The way he loved his books, we always thought he'd become a professor."

"Why didn't he?" Natasha asked.

"Your grandfather died," Agnes answered. "Sergei had to work, as Babushka couldn't support the family with her sewing business. Andrusha was already studying engineering and Sasha was too young to help."

"Your father tried business," Babushka gave a laugh. "Head in the clouds, that one. A good man, but not a good business man."

Agnes nodded. "Didn't like taking money from people. Wanted to help people."

Papa's face appeared at the door. "Is tea ready?"

"Sergei," Agnes asked, "could Natasha go and buy a few groceries?" Natasha jumped up. "The shop is across the road and there are lights at the corner."

Seating himself in the gold armchair, Papa waved a hand in agreement. "Careful crossing the street."

Agnes directed Natasha to her purse and counted out money. She gave her a list of items and a string bag to bring them home. Handing Natasha some extra pennies, she said, "Buy yourself something for your help."

"She doesn't need anything." Papa said, patting his pockets for his pipe. "You save your money for yourself."

Agnes winked at Natasha and pressed the money into her hand. "Thank you, dear."

Natasha ran down the stairs to the street. The smell from the fish and chips shop made her mouth water. It was now late morning and she realized how hungry she was. She turned away from the aroma, passed the shoe shop and proceeded to the lights at the corner. The streets had filled with people since they had arrived.

Waiting for the lights to change, Natasha found herself beside a ladies' clothing store. Its window display was breathtaking with beautiful mannequins and elegant clothes like Mama used to wear. She had never seen anything like it in Australia before. The three outfits in the window were simple yet stylish, with seams that molded them to the figures of the mannequins.

Natasha gritted her teeth. Mama would never wear such elegant clothes again. The blue wool suit with the satin piping and wide belt would have made her look so beautiful, just as she had in Shanghai. She could wear her jewelry again, any she had left, and the high-heeled shoes she used to love instead of the "sensible" shoes she always wore now.

A faint scent in the air reminded Natasha of burning incense, and suddenly a wave of homesickness for their old way of life overcame her, a sharp ache for the things she knew and understood instead of the new and unpredictable. Shanghai felt so comfortable, so soft around the edges, while Sydney seemed a jumble of hard corners, jutting into her in unexpected places.

She yearned to go back home but Mrs. Popov's story showed it was impossible. Familiar images sprang to her mind, her bedroom in her old home, the dining room with its open fire, Chang Ma and the old uncomplicated life she had led.

Was it just because she had been younger then? No, it was definitely different. In Shanghai her parents had not worried about money the way they did in Australia. And even though, as she learned English, she was becoming accepted in a way Papa was not, things still happened that caught her totally unaware. Such as that woman on the train and, at school, the talk of mountain devils that had frightened her last week. The other kids had laughed at her fear.

Yet, everyone she asked if there were mountain devils in the Blue Mountains outside Sydney, had said yes, even the teachers. Jan, who was becoming a good friend at school, was at home sick, so she couldn't ask her. Then Ian Jones had shown her one, and she saw that it was just a twig that looked like a devil with horns, dressed up in specially made clothing, nothing to be scared of at all. Silly things like that made her feel like they all belonged to the same club and she was an outsider.

In Shanghai she had accepted herself without thought. But now, she worried constantly about her unusual hair style and how different she looked. If only she could go back, back to Shanghai and her old life, and have everything revert to normal.

Glancing at the coins in her hand, she wished she had enough money to buy Mama the blue suit. But the carefree, laughing Mama of Shanghai would never return. Now, she was a frowning, working woman, with too little time to spend with her children, especially the oldest.

She stared at the window as the lights turned to green and back to red again. The toe of her shoe nudged a pebble in the grass between the window and the footpath. She kicked it hard and watched it skitter into the street. With a deep breath, she straightened up and crossed the road to the grocery shop.

Inside, a young family was being served, the children crying and reaching for the lollies, candies, that filled large glass jars. While she waited for her turn, her eye caught the shine of rhinestone buttons in the display case. There were two larger buttons, which sparkled like Aunt Agnes' diamonds. She gazed at them, comparing them to her favorite lollies which stared back at her, shiny black licorice and creamy white milk bottles. Her mouth tasted their sweetness and chewiness.

When she had purchased the items for Aunt Agnes, she took a last look at the lollies and asked the price of the two larger buttons. She told the shopkeeper she wanted the bigger one for her mother and the other for her grandmother. The man smiled as he took them out.

Her hand hesitated as she reached for them, and the shopkeeper asked how much she could afford. She added up the sixpence and Aunt Agnes' coins. With a grin and a wink at the other assistant, the shopkeeper announced this was exactly the price of the buttons. Natasha bought them and hid them deep in her pockets.

Chapter 15

The midday sun blazed in the winter sky, but the stairwell to Aunt Agnes' apartment, was dusky and dim. As she came through the door, Babushka took the string bag of groceries, noting its hefty weight. Natasha, however, strained to hear what Aunt Agnes was saying.

"*Kakoy syurpriz.* It took us completely by surprise. We'd been to a ball at the Peninsula Hotel on the Saturday night, the sixth of December, it was. You remember the Peninsula in Hong Kong, Sergei? So beautiful! What a foyer, as if it were a palace! Such an elegant evening. Even the Governor was there." Her chin quivered as she paused, remembering. "My dear George looked so dashing in his tuxedo. I would never have guessed what was to come." As her voice trailed off, she saw Natasha.

"Oh, my dear," she straightened up on the bed. "Thank you so much. Did everything go well?"

Natasha nodded. She didn't want to break in when they were talking about the past.

Papa pointed his pipe at Agnes. "*Pochemu ti ne uyekhala*? Why didn't you leave Hong Kong when they were evacuating the wives? It was a mistake to stay."

Unpacking the groceries, Babushka asked, "Did he give you the right change?"

"Why do you always ask that? I want to listen to Aunt Agnes."

"I don't trust them. They'll cheat you if you can't speak their language."

Papa rolled his eyes. "You're imagining things, Mother. And you forget, Natasha *can* speak the language, almost."

"You always think the best of everyone, Sergei. *I* know better." With pursed lips, she opened a drawer and rummaged in it. "I'll make some *zakuski* for us."

Agnes settled back against her pillows. "Maybe I should have left with the British wives and children. Three and a half thousand people left Hong Kong then. The government was criticized for that. Favoritism, racism. That's what they were accused of. But that night, at the ball, we didn't realize the Japanese were so close. Only thirty-six kilometers away, and there we were dancing so happily," she said softly.

"And then on the Monday, it was December 8, 1941 in Hong Kong, just hours after the Pearl Harbor bombing in America on December 7, they attacked. The Japanese troops crossed the river at Lo Wu and their planes bombed Kai Tak Airport. We were evacuated from Kowloon to Hong Kong Island, hoping we would be able to hold that, at least. Looking back, it was stupid to hope, really."

"You should have left when you had the chance."

"In the first evacuation from Kowloon? Well, that was over a year earlier, and we thought it was impossible the Japanese would take Hong Kong. The city was British! I was volunteering as a nurse, so I could choose to stay. I wanted to be near George. And Susan, his daughter from his first marriage, was on her way from England to join us."

Agnes stopped speaking and then gave a small chuckle, remembering. "You know, George's barber, Mr. Yamashita, at the Gloucester Hotel? He turned out to be a spy for Japan." Her tinkling laugh sounded awkward.

"It's funny, now. He had been there for years. He would cut his client's hair and ask simple, friendly questions. 'Not much English,' we all thought. Ha! He reported everything to his master. After the occupation, he became one of the administrators of the camp at Stanley." She sniffed at the memory and raised an arthritic hand to smooth her curls. "No longer so friendly."

"Agnes, it's all in the past now." Babushka busily arranged salami, liverwurst and black bread onto plates. "We can look forward to better times, God willing. It is like it happened in another world, and now there are all these differences to cope with in Australia. It's so different to China, no open-air markets, no servants, no respect for age."

"It's a country for the young," Papa said, "and that's partly why we came, so the children could have a better life."

"I know," Babushka agreed. "But it's easier to think of those virtues when we don't have to live here day to day. You know, in my dreams I'm still living in China. I wake up and can't understand where I am. In Australia I can't go out alone. I can't read the signs. I'd get lost and never find my way back." She shook her head. "Oh dear. And we can never go back home. Sometimes, I think we've given up too much."

"We didn't have the luxury of choice, Mother."

"Of course. I know it."

"But look," Agnes' face lit up as she spoke. "Look how many things you've learned by coming to Australia. And all the new things you've seen: Sydney's beautiful harbor, all the new plants and animals, days of sunshine like today when the air is so clear that it glitters and dazzles your eyes. Can you imagine a life lived all in one place? You could end up too scared to go anywhere."

Natasha perched on the edge of Aunt Agnes' bed. "That's a good way to think about it." Yes, she had learned a lot of new things since coming to Australia. It was fascinating to see how things were different from one place to another.

Agnes continued, "Of course you miss things from your old home. That's only natural. And a new place is frightening at first. It doesn't have the safety of the familiar."

"That's true." Natasha understood perfectly.

"But it often turns out to be a blessing in disguise."

"There's a lot to be said for a stable life," Babushka sounded grumpy. "Here's fresh tea, Agnes. And one for you, Natasha. I'll put the meats on this table. You can all reach it. Do you want some pickled cucumbers, Sergei? Agnes, did you say you had dilled tomatoes? At least there's plenty of food in this country."

"Not like in the camp at Stanley." Agnes' shoulders gave a little shiver.

"What's a camp?" Natasha reached for a slice of liverwurst.

"An internment camp for citizens. We were 'the enemy.' The Allies. So they had a sort of prison for us."

"A prison?" Natasha looked up.

"Prisoners of war."

"But that's awful, Aunt Agnes. You weren't a soldier."

"The Japanese needed to keep us under their control so we didn't undermine their war efforts. They certainly ruined our Christmas that year."

"Did you go in on Christmas Day?" For Natasha this was the most sacred day of the year, even though Babushka always said Easter was a far more important religious festival.

"The Allies surrendered on Christmas Day. We were at the Vasilieffs', remember the Vasilieffs, Sergei? Basil and Sophia? I was grieving for George. I didn't care what happened to me. The days passed in a fog of explosions and gunfire. I did whatever I was told, come here, go there. Luckily, I had good friends. The Vasilieffs were wonderful and took great care of Susan and me. The poor child needed nursing back to health. We mourned George together and in a way, looked after each other. What a sad time!"

"I'll say." Natasha couldn't imagine someone she knew living in a prison, well, camp, Aunt Agnes had called it.

"Yes, the Japanese invaded Christmas Day 1941. When we woke that morning it seemed nothing had changed and we were still fighting. At the Vasilieffs' house, the parents tried to make it a nice day for the children with a few trinkets and gifts in the morning. There were several families squashed in there. Somehow, they managed to scrape together a meal at lunchtime. Then about four o'clock, we noticed the noise had stopped. The noise of gunfire. That's how we knew the fighting was over. A couple of weeks later, we all had to go to Murray Parade Ground and then we were put into Chinese hotels. After that we went to Stanley."

"What happened to your husband?"

"Poor George was killed just before the surrender."

"Killed?" Natasha's hands gripped the edge of the bed. "How?"

Papa cleared his throat. "He died. That's all."

"No, he didn't. She said he was *killed.* How?'

"Can I tell her, Sergei?" Aunt Agnes and Papa stared at each other. "It will help her think about the big issues of life, not to be bogged down with trivialities."

"What trivialities?" Natasha asked.

"Hair styles, clothes. Talking and thinking only about the mechanics of life, how to organize cupboards, things like that." Agnes pointed a finger at Papa. "You complain about how boring people like that are."

Papa's fingers drummed on the armrest of his chair. "Keep the details to a minimum."

Aunt Agnes said, "In a war, Natasha, people are killed in many brutal ways. Your father wants to spare you the horror."

"But, I want to know."

"You're a curious person and that's good." Papa picked up his cup of tea. "But sometimes you might find out more than you can handle."

"I'll be careful," Agnes assured him. "Well, after we'd all been evacuated from our homes on Kowloon, we'd gone to stay with the Vasilieffs. They lived on Stubbs Road, halfway up to Victoria Peak. A large house, lovely views of the harbor.

They had taken in several families, so you can imagine how congested it was. We arrived with a few suitcases of things we had managed to save. Everything else we had to leave behind." Agnes' voice faltered as her fingers plucked at her blanket.

Natasha waited until the elderly woman breathed deeply and continued.

"The weather had been beautiful all December, sunshine every day, but the nights were getting cool. And every day we would hear the bombs and war planes and guns. Then on December 22nd, it was about midnight, there was a knock on the door. We were terrified, you can imagine. Basil went to answer with us all behind him. Soldiers were at the door, but they were Canadian, not Japanese soldiers. They had come to tell us to get to higher ground. There had been explosions all evening but we had become sort of used to them, and were about to go to bed."

"Anyway, we got our clothes back on and were trudging up the winding road to the Peak in the dark. Being outdoors made the noise of guns and bombs far more real. Soldiers were among us. I don't remember whether they were advancing or retreating, retreating probably. George and Susan were behind me, about a hundred feet away, so I didn't see when it happened. I knew as soon as the explosion came. It was too close. I was knocked flat to the ground. People were screaming and crying all around. I lay there, my face pressed against the rocky ground, hardly daring to breathe, waiting for the next explosion, for the next aircraft to go over." Agnes had half risen from her bed.

"I was too terrified to get up. My left arm was in dreadful pain, but there was nothing I could do. When it finally seemed safe, I looked back and…oh dear, dear…" She lay back on her pillow and closed her eyes.

"God bless his soul," Babushka whispered, crossing herself.

Natasha tried to imagine how it must have felt, the sudden blast so loud and so close it ripped a person's body apart. Probably you wouldn't know what had happened and then it was all over. She hoped that's how it was. A picture of George in his coffin flashed into her mind. He must have been put into it in pieces, maybe an arm or a leg placed beside his head, *if* the pieces were big enough. Ugh! How awful. Lucky he was not Russian, so they would have a closed casket. Australian children had never seen dead bodies, and she scared them with stories of how waxy dead people looked and how cold to the touch.

Agnes' voice gained a little strength. "Susan was injured, but not seriously. It was miraculous."

"Come, come." Papa said. "You are getting upset."

"It's hard to stop once you start remembering." Agnes shielded her eyes with her hand. "I know you want to protect the young one, Sergei."

Papa reached out and touched her other hand. "It's not doing you any good, either. Come on. Forget the past. Look at this food. I'm hungry."

Agnes made a noise like a grunt. "It has been so boring for the last three days, lying here alone. And I don't mind talking about the past. It is interesting to the young. They need to learn what happened so it never happens again. But she's your daughter, and if you don't want her to know, I'll respect your wishes."

Natasha's voice was almost a whisper. "What did you do then, when he was killed, Aunt Agnes?" Her fingers caressed the buttons hidden in her pocket.

Papa frowned.

"Papa, it is history. The history of our friends and family. The history in my school books."

Papa concentrated on making a sandwich of his bread and salami. Just before taking a bite he said, "If you had only left when they were evacuating, there wouldn't be all this *history*."

Agnes pulled up her blankets and then smoothed them down with her bejeweled hands. Natasha suddenly realized the rings meant so much to her as they were all she had. Her family was gone.

"We buried poor George at Happy Valley with a short memorial service the next day. Several people had been killed, so the service was for all of them. The others were strangers to me but Basil knew one of the men." Natasha watched the hands with bulging purple veins twist the edge of the blanket. "George was British," Agnes continued, "so I didn't have to worry about the Russian services. Dear George. He was a good man."

Natasha waited through several seconds of silence, and then asked, "But what about you? Were you all right?"

Lifting her left arm, Agnes twisted it around. There was a bend midway between her wrist and elbow. "I had broken my arm. At the time, it was the least important thing on my mind. One of the men carried Susan the rest of the way up the hill. Poor dear was in a dreadful state, almost hysterical. And then to die of dysentery just a few months later. She'd always been a sickly child. Only fifteen years old. I missed her so much."

"Fifteen?" Natasha couldn't imagine dying so young. That was only a few years older than she was, now. It seemed so wrong.

"Yes, fifteen. She suffered so badly with cramps and diarrhea. We thought she'd recover, children usually do, but with her diabetes as well. There was a shortage of sulfur drugs at the time and hygiene wasn't good, however much we tried. And the food! Oh dear. My throat still gags when I think of it."

"What did you eat?"

"Imagine the taste of rice with weevils – tiny beetles." She shuddered. "Rice every single day, usually served as a kind of…well, slop. We would queue up in the morning at ten and again at five. Life was a series of queues, for this, for that, for everything. At first, the conditions were better, at least we could boil water. But later, because fuel was low, we could only do that for a certain time each day. So, even having a cup of tea was a problem."

Agnes wrinkled her nose as she said, "Have you ever heard of pine needle tea? Amazing what you make do with when there isn't anything else. And shoes. " She gave a quick laugh. "I used cardboard to make soles when they wore out. Not just me, everyone. But as they didn't last long, someone had the bright idea of making soles from biscuit tins. That worked better, but they weren't too comfortable."

"You must be strong, Aunt Agnes, to have lived through all that and still be so nice."

Agnes chuckled and a spark flickered in her walnut-brown eyes. "I don't know about strong. We all do what we have to do to cope, although I always knew I would get through it. I had lived through so much, already, I was not going to let them get the better of me. It was all just a temporary inconvenience."

"I know. You 'made do.' Like Mama told me when we were at Aunt Vera's."

"Exactly." She took a sip of tea. "You know, my room at Stanley camp housed eleven people. I had a mattress on the floor, which was a bed at night and a sofa during the day. People are so adaptable."

"Not all people," Babushka interrupted. "I don't feel so 'adaptable' any more, believe me. Age. It's harder with age."

"At least there was sunshine and a beach. Stanley is a wonderful place. Hong Kong is so beautiful, isn't it? The harbor. The trees. The wisps of mist floating up the mountainside" Agnes paused, and then added, "You know, I have some old photographs in the bottom of that wardrobe."

"Can I get them?" Natasha jumped up.

"Yes, dear. Under the folded clothes."

A musty smell of camphor and mothballs escaped as Natasha opened the door to the wooden wardrobe. Beneath Aunt Agnes' three hanging dresses were four carefully folded sweaters and two blouses. These were all the clothes she had.

"Can you see the album poking out under the blouses? Here, bring it to me."

Agnes took the album reverently and slowly opened the heavy leather cover. Sheets of filmy white paper clung to the thick black pages on which old photographs were fitted into small corner fasteners. Her hand trembled as she turned the pages. The stern faces of old-fashioned people stared at Natasha. After a few pages Agnes stopped. "Look, here's your father as a young boy."

Natasha stared. "But he's wearing a dress!"

Agnes and Babushka laughed as Papa leaned over to see. "It's a tunic," he said, "although I believe Babushka did dress me as a girl for a few years."

"You were so pretty with such lovely curls, and I wanted a daughter so badly."

"It never happened, just as I probably won't have a son."

"There's time for you. Tania is still young."

"But there's no money."

Natasha studied the photo of three boys, aged between four and ten, standing stiffly in a garden. They wore dark pants and white belted tunics with wide collars and floppy bow ties. The two younger boys, her father and Sasha, had close-cropped hair, while the older boy, her Uncle Andrusha, wore his longer hair parted on the side. Behind them, stood two women in ankle-length, lacy dresses. Babushka was easily recognizable as a woman of about thirty-five; beside her stood an attractive dark-haired woman.

"That's Babushka and that's me," Agnes pointed to the second woman.

Natasha looked from the photo to the real woman. They were like different people with no connection. *Is this what happened when you grew old*? But Babushka in the photo still resembled Babushka today, just younger and slimmer. Maybe she hadn't had as many problems in her life as Aunt Agnes. Maybe that made a difference.

Agnes turned another page. "Here they are. George and Susan with me between them." Gazing at the photo, she bit her lip.

"Here, dear." Babushka handed her a fresh cup of tea. "You've hardly eaten a thing." She poked a finger at the photo. "I remember that. Your wedding in '38, wasn't it? I'm so glad I met George before you left Shanghai. Doesn't Susan look lovely?"

Agnes accepted the tea. "It seems such a long time ago."

Natasha cast a glance at Agnes. "Were you young when you married George?"

"Not young, no. George was my third husband. I was well into my forties. He was actually younger than me. I was very lucky to find him."

Agnes and Natasha examined the photo in silence. The young girl looked the same age as Natasha was now. Her long hair was pulled back, while a few tendrils had escaped and softened her face. She had a calmness about her that made Natasha wonder if she knew she would die so young. How awful, and yet how romantic. Everyone would always remember you as young forever, and you would never get old like Babushka and Agnes. She imagined Susan in her coffin and was about to ask if she had an open coffin, but then remembered Susan was British like her father.

Agnes traced the outline of George's face with the tip of her finger. His hair was dark and wavy and he had a thick mustache that curled at the ends. "For ages I couldn't believe I would never see him again," Agnes whispered. "Gone. In just a second." She closed the book abruptly. "It's been so long since I looked at this. Leave it here. We'll go through it tonight, Galia. Maybe later I'll bring it to your home, Natasha."

Natasha nodded. She would have liked to see more, but Agnes had had enough. "What happened to your home in Kowloon?"

"I returned to my flat once before the surrender. I should not have gone, but there were so many things. Well, they had disappeared. The flat had been looted. It would have been better not to see. I was lucky to have taken my jewels and best clothes and linens when I evacuated. Later, in the camp, I only sold a few of my own things. You see, I had both George and Susan's things to sell."

She mused for a moment, then added, "That sounds so hard, selling their things to spare my own and yet…well, the times were hard. But I still feel guilty, even today. You know, that I survived and they didn't."

Papa's fingers rubbed at his eyes. "We all feel that. So many died too young."

"The Japanese committed so many horrific acts!"

"It was war," Papa answered. "Both sides committed horrific acts."

Babushka gave a snort. "There you go again, Sergei. You try to see everyone's side, and then you don't know whose side you're on."

"Of course I do, Mother. But no one side is purely good and the other purely evil. Life's not like that."

"You're a good man, Sergei." Agnes patted Papa on the sleeve. "The camp was my penance for surviving George. If I hadn't married a British man and taken his nationality, I would not have been there. Russians were not interned but they had to carry 'third national' passes for identification. Not that their lives were easy on the outside."

Papa stretched his legs. "The war changed all our lives, but at least we are alive and together."

"Except Sasha." Babushka fingered the gold cross at her throat. "May God care for my dear son and bring him back to me."

"Yes, Sasha. I wonder if we'll ever know what really happened to him."

Agnes wiped a little moisture from her cheek and nodded.

Papa checked his watch. "My goodness." He pushed himself up from the armchair. "Natasha, are you ready to go?"

"Papa, I want to know everything else that happened."

Papa turned to Agnes. "Agnes, we'll come for Mother tomorrow afternoon."

"I've run you off with my reminiscing." Agnes gave a wan smile.

"No, Aunt Agnes, I want you to tell me more next time. When you come to our house, you can tell me everything."

"Bless you, child," she laughed and some of the old sparkle returned to her eyes. "Not everything. Life is nicer sometimes if you get a cleaned-up version."

Papa leaned over and kissed Agnes on the forehead. "Get well."

On the way out of the door, Natasha's hand reached into her pocket and caressed the buttons she had bought. She would wait until Babushka came home to hand out her gifts, but somehow sparkling jewels and beautiful clothes did not seem so important any more.

Chapter 16

When Mama returned from work on the following Thursday evening, Natasha greeted her with her hair loosened from its usual tight plaits. Nearly black in color, her hair curled in ringlets around her face and cascaded in waves down her back.

Mama patted the rhinestone button she had sewn onto her gray cardigan. "My new button was quite a hit at work. Pretty, isn't it?"

She kissed Natasha and ran a cool hand across her forehead. "But why is your hair all out like that?"

Natasha followed her mother into the dining room. "Can I cut my hair? I want it short like the Australian girls."

"*Dorogaya.* Darling, why?" Mama lowered herself into a chair. "You have such beautiful long hair. You can almost sit on it. It takes years to grow hair that long."

"It doesn't look right."

"Of course it does. All the girls in Russia wear their hair long."

"But we're in Australia and nobody does here. It looks," she screwed up her nose, "it looks old-fashioned. Lorraine said so."

"Don't be silly, dear." Mama turned to Elena, who had rushed into the room, flourishing a painting with bright reds and blues. Happy ran alongside her and she shooed him away. "Mama, Mama," she cried, hoisting herself onto her mother's lap.

"Hello, my darling. Did you paint that all by yourself?"

Natasha couldn't tell what the painting was supposed to be. "Mama, maybe we can style my hair differently. Maybe I can wear it loose. Or like this?" She held up a strand of hair at each side of her face.

"My picture is a train. See this?" Elena pointed to a streak of blue. "That's smoke?"

"It's a wonderful train and very good smoke." Mama glanced back at Natasha, inhaled deeply and said, "Your hair's too curly. It will get tangled. Plaits are sensible for school." Happy sniffed the painting and then disappeared under the table.

Elena regarded her sister. "You look silly like that."

"That's enough, Elena."

"It looks better this way than in plaits." Natasha scooped her hair up from her neck. "Nobody wears plaits. Only babies have their hair—"

"We've had enough about your hair." Mama sounded both stern and tired.

"But, Mama, please!"

"Subject closed, thank you. Now, Elena, what letters did you learn today?"

Natasha's shoulders slumped. It was so unfair. They didn't even discuss it. Flouncing out of the room, she called, "Come on, Hap." The dog, tail wagging, followed her to her room. She flopped onto the stool in front of her dressing table and stared at her hair in the mirror. It was pointless to ask Papa. He always agreed with Mama. With both hands she lifted her hair up high. Maybe a French twist would be a more up-to-date style. She twisted the mass of hair into a roll and turned her head sideways to see it better.

Happy gave a grunt as he circled a couple of times, and then settled beside her. "You like my hair better this way, don't you, Hap. You understand how plaits make me feel so different, and so plain." The puppy's ears twitched in response.

The next morning, Natasha argued with Babushka about her hairstyle. Babushka usually parted her hair down the center and plaited it so tightly that her scalp ached, but the hair stayed in place all day. Today, however, Natasha wanted a softer style. She wanted her hair loose, with a few strands near her face held back with a clip. Babushka finally convinced her to wear her hair the usual way one more time, and then, over the weekend they would both discuss it with Mama.

When Natasha arrived at school, gray clouds jostled to cover the last patches of blue sky. The dreariness matched her mood. Although it was winter, the gum trees that rimmed the edge of the asphalt playground were still laden with leaves. Clusters of three or four children perched on the wooden benches that fronted large hydrangea bushes.

Natasha had learned that in Sydney, most winter mornings were cool, but usually by lunch time a warm sun would strip the sweaters from the students, who ran around in shirtsleeves. This morning was cool, windy and damp. The wind blew in quick gusts, billowing the girls' skirts and rustling the leaves on the trees, spreading eucalyptus fragrance. Natasha was grateful for the thick woolly cardigan Mama had knitted for her.

Jan was waiting at their special bench. Jan's friendship had made all the difference at school and she was such a *nice* girl, nice in a way Natasha knew herself not to be. Jan always seemed grateful for her little space in the world and surprised when others did anything kind for her, as if she didn't deserve to put anyone out or take up their time.

As Natasha arrived, Jan ran up, her broad face radiant. "Guess what? There's going to be a new girl in our class. She's really pretty. I saw her and her mother go in to see old Nosey." Their nickname for Mrs. Wilkey was a secret between then. "I can't wait to meet her." Jan danced little steps as she spoke.

A thrill leaped through Natasha. What would the new girl be like? Maybe she would be a new friend for her and Jan. And now she, Natasha, would no longer be the newest member of the class.

Jan continued in a rush, "And you'll never guess! Lorraine said she's from Italy and can't speak English, just like you before!"

Abruptly, Natasha's feelings changed. She could not quite decide why, but she no longer felt so welcoming. Somehow, this new girl was intruding on her position, taking away something of what made her, Natasha, special at school. She did not like the way she felt. Well, she would give this new girl a chance and see what she was like.

"Aren't you excited?" Jan gazed into her face.

"I hope she's nice," Natasha answered evasively. "What's her name?"

"Don't know yet."

"What does she look like?"

"She has short, dark hair, but not as dark as yours. It's shiny and bouncy, really pretty. I only saw her from a distance."

Natasha did not think she was going to like this new girl after all. Hoping that Jan could not see how she was feeling, she forced herself to smile. "Yes, it's exciting."

Jan's face suddenly saddened. "She'll probably end up a friend of Lorraine's. That's what usually happens."

This time Natasha did not mind the thought of Lorraine getting a new friend, even if she did act like a satisfied cat, licking its whiskers.

Mrs. Wilkey, her long nose pointing the way, entered the classroom with the new student close behind. A buzz whizzed around the class. The teacher placed a hand on the new girl's arm, and introduced her to the class. Then she wrote her name, Gina Tucci, on the blackboard. Gina smiled shyly while her liquid brown eyes tried to find a safe place to rest, often settling on the painting of gum trees on the back wall.

When she had finished speaking, Mrs. Wilkey seated Gina near the front. "Natasha," she said, "you can show Gina around the playground at recess. I expect you understand how our new classmate is feeling."

Natasha nodded and squeezed a smile onto her face while Gina watched her with a worried frown and bit her lip. Jan, smiling broadly, nudged Natasha. "I'll come with you," she whispered.

On the other side of the room, Lorraine raised her hand. "Mrs. Wilkey, can I help? I could show her Australian things better than Natasha." She was smiling brilliantly at the newcomer, swishing her head so that her abundant peach colored hair flowed out around her head. Natasha glanced at Judy, Lorraine's current best friend, and felt momentarily sorry for her. Her days in Lorraine's orbit were definitely numbered.

Why did Lorraine need to constantly change her friends? It was as if only new people were interesting. Natasha thought about how Lorraine knew all the Australian rules of life and broke them whenever she wanted, while she, Natasha, was still struggling to learn the "right" thing to do so as not to stand out.

"Thank you, Lorraine," Mrs. Wilkey said, raising one eyebrow, "but I think Natasha might be more sensitive than anyone else to Gina's predicament. Now," her cloud of dark hair floated around her head as she turned and wrote several math equations on the blackboard, "these are simple division, so please complete them as quickly as you can." As the rest of the class worked on the math, Mrs. Wilkey bent over Gina's desk to watch her attempts.

The equations were easy for Natasha and she found herself staring at the new girl as she completed them. Gina had removed her thick wool jacket and now sat upright in her seat, her slender body tapering into a small waist banded by a wide leather belt. She wore what Natasha considered old-fashioned clothes by Australian standards, but there was no question that her teal colored dress was beautiful. Made from a soft draping fabric, tiny pleats ran from a high yoke all the way to the hem.

Mrs. Wilkey read the correct answers and then her voice droned on, explaining for those who had errors. Natasha forced her eyes away from Gina but now they focused on her name on the blackboard. Gina Tucci. It was so light, bright and friendly. Not at all like her long and heavy name. She glanced at the new girl and had to admit that Gina's hair was exactly as Jan had described it, soft and pretty and bouncy.

Scanning the other desks, Natasha realized everyone seemed to be mesmerized by Gina. An Italian girl was so much more glamorous than a Russian girl could ever be. There was not the anti-Communist feeling intermingled with their reactions, even though Italy had fought on the opposite side of the war to Australia, America and England.

When Natasha thought back truthfully, she realized her anger about coming to Australia must have shown when she arrived at school. She had not been friendly at first, nor smiled like Gina did when she was introduced. Natasha had glared at everyone in the class and scowled. She hated being new and different, and now, suddenly, she didn't want Gina to be the new and different girl.

At recess, folds of gray clouds entirely covered the sky and Natasha kept hoping rain would cut short her tour of duty. She and Jan escorted Gina around the playground, making sure she understood where the restrooms were and where the class lined up when the bell rang. She was glad to have Jan along. The new girl was shy, trying hard to please and nodding her head so much Natasha wondered whether she really understood. Natasha forced herself to stop staring at the way the breeze lifted Gina's hair, ruffled it and then let it fall gently back into place. Her own hair felt stiff and unmoving in its tight plaits.

It was a surprise, however, to see Gina's nails, which were bitten down to little moons on the soft pillows of her fingers. She wondered if Jan had noticed, but Jan was happily teaching Gina the word *tree*. Did bitten nails mean this pretty girl was nervous or lacking in self-confidence? She would have to ask Mama.

Other classmates ran up, wanting to be introduced to Gina and teaching her their names. They would laugh and tell Gina how well she pronounced the few words she knew, in a way that had not occurred when Natasha had first arrived. Lorraine, however, gave them a wide berth, not even looking to see where they were. She sauntered around the playground with Judy, whose smiles indicated to Natasha she thought the danger of being dropped as Lorraine's friend was over. But Natasha knew better.

As recess ended, Natasha breathed a sigh of relief. She was now free of Gina. Let Lorraine claim her or anyone else who wanted her for a friend. But when the lunch bell rang, Gina turned and smiled at Natasha, obviously expecting to eat with her. Natasha remembered her own first day when she had eaten alone and nearly cried because of the fuss made over the unusual smell of her sandwich. She returned Gina's smile and nodded as Gina fished a brown paper bag from her satchel.

At lunch, just as at recess, Natasha became even more aware of how fascinated the students were with Gina, who tried to be friendly to everyone. Her thin eyebrows tilted up in the center, making her look as though she was always on the verge of smiling. Her dark smooth curls bounced in time with her tossing head when she turned to face yet another classmate who wanted to befriend her.

Although the air was dense and heavy, the rain continued to hold off. Natasha glanced curiously at Gina's lunch, which consisted of thick bread with a tomato paste. When John Williams came up and wrinkled his nose at the aroma, Natasha quickly let him know how much tastier Gina's sandwich was than the vegemite sandwich he held in his hand. Gina's eyes widened. Unsure what had happened, she realized Natasha had somehow stood up for her. Natasha endured lunch until the bell rang to resume classes. In the late afternoon, the rains finally came, and after school, Gina's mother was waiting to whisk her away.

On the slippery wet bus trip home, the talk was exclusively about Gina. Raincoats and boots squelched as children leaned over each other to pass on bits of information. Natasha received a lot of attention, as she had eaten lunch with her, but she had nothing to share. Students speculated on where Gina lived, what her father did, and whether she had brothers and sisters. Natasha was tired of hearing her name when her stop arrived.

Chapter 17

In her room at home, Natasha was about to start her homework when she caught sight of her reflection in the dressing table mirror. Immediately, she compared herself to Gina, and did not like the comparison. She hated her plaits. She wanted to be more modern, lighter and brighter. If she had short hair, hair like Gina's, her life would be better, more interesting and exciting.

It was quiet in her room. Happy was snuggled asleep beside her and Sonia and Elena were in the kitchen with Babushka. Seated at the dressing table, she cradled her chin and gazed at her reflection. Holding up one plait, she imagined how she would look if she cut it, right there, about three inches below her ear. Then she slid her fingers up the braid. *What about here? No, too short.* She smiled, imagining her hair short, soft and wavy, exactly like Gina's.

Natasha thought of the scissors kept high up on the bookshelf where Sonia could not reach them. She'd get them down. Not to use right away, but just in case she needed them, for her homework. Climbing up on her chair, she felt around on the shelf until her fingers touched the cold steel and closed around them. She brought them out and gazed at them in awe, fingering the blades lovingly as she climbed down from the chair.

For a quick moment, she glanced out of the window at the softly pattering rain outside. Then, once again she sat in front of the mirror and held up her left plait. The scissors were poised in her right hand. For several minutes she sat, gazing at herself with the blades ominously open and pointing at the ceiling. Mama would be so angry if she cut her hair, as she had said 'no' just yesterday. But she and Papa did not understand. They did not have to go to school every day and feel so "wrong" and different. They hardly had time for her these days anyway, probably would not even notice that her hair was cut, maybe for a week or even more.

Outside, the rain clattered more insistently against the window. It reminded her of the day in Shanghai when Papa told them they were moving to Australia. They had not asked whether she wanted to go, did not take anything she said into account. If she did it, if she really cut her hair, she would just have to put up with their disapproval for a while. They would be shocked, but then they would get over it.

Could she really do it? She had never disobeyed them before, but she was older now, nearly a teenager and they did not treat her like one at all.

Her room seemed stuffy and airless around her. All she could focus on was the need to cut this hair, to cut it off and be more a part of the world outside her home. Almost in a stupor, she forced the blades of the scissors together and began to chop through the thickness.

Oh dear, I've really done it! I've started now and I can't stop.

It was a lot tougher than she had imagined. The scissors were too blunt to cut easily and she needed to concentrate to chop through the braid. She squeezed the blades together and apart, together and apart, and finally, the plait lay cupped in her hand. It looked so sad and lonely, like an orphan. Somehow, it did not seem possible that this little sausage-looking-thing had been the long plait attached to her head. Then she looked up into the mirror and froze.

Oh no! She stared at herself in horror.

The cut hair was not at all the pretty, soft kind she had imagined. The formerly plaited hair had come unraveled and frizzed, standing up and out, away from her head.

How terrible!

If it had been at all possible, she would have stuck the braid back on. At least long hair was something she knew and understood. This other hair, this stuff around half her head. Oh heavens!

What could she do now? Her face crumpled in despair. A quick flare of lightning followed by a faraway rumble of thunder heralded a new splash of rain against the window. Well, she thought, drawing in a deep breath, there was no going back. Maybe, just maybe it would look better when both sides were the same. She gritted her teeth and, with steely determination, pumped the scissors and hacked through the second plait.

There. It was done!

But it looked nothing like she had imagined. She sat looking at her new hair and a tear staggered down one cheek. The frizz that encircled her head was not like anyone's hair she had ever seen. It did not look like hair at all. It looked like a lion's mane! What would the kids at school say, now?

Somewhere in the background she heard Elena's voice, and then the door opened. Elena ran in, jumping onto her bed with both knees. "Did you know Babushka made a—" As she spoke she turned towards her sister. Her eyes widened in alarm and her hand flew to her mouth. Her scream reverberated through Natasha's head. But still Natasha sat and stared at herself in the mirror.

Babushka came rushing into the room and seeing Natasha, began crying and crossing herself, calling on the Lord above to explain what had happened. "*Gospodi Bozhe moi*! Natasha, Natasha! What will your parents say? How could you do this?"

The commotion around her did not seem real to Natasha. She sat in a trance. It was as if everything was happening in a movie and although she could see it acted out in front of her, it really had nothing to do with her. She felt quite calm, as though it would only take for her to shut her eyes, and then, when she opened them, her hair would be the way it had been for as long as she could remember.

Elena gingerly moved towards her and tentatively reached out to touch the new frizzy locks. Natasha swatted her hand away, and with the movement came the realization that this was the way she was going to look from now on.

A wail burst out of her throat. "Babushka, I hate it! It's so horrible. It's not like I imagined it. I wanted it to be pretty and soft like Gina's, and it's…it's…the most horrible hair I've ever seen!" Her sobs contorted her face.

"You shouldn't have disobeyed your mother." Babushka ran a hand over the springy locks.

"I know now, but it's…it's too late."

"How could you, Natasha? How could you?"

"I'm sorry. I…I wanted to be like everyone else." Her voice dropped to a whisper. "I wanted to be beautiful."

"Being pretty is all very well." Babushka sat on the edge of Elena's bed. "But it's not enough. It goes, you know. Disappears. It's your mind you should be cultivating. It lasts your whole life long."

"Who's going to notice my mind when my hair looks like this?'

"Oh dear, dear," Babushka murmured sympathetically. "You know, it looks like your second cousin Vasia's hair."

"But he's a boy!"

"Of course. All the girls have long hair."

"It's nothing like I wanted. Nothing like Gina's."

"It's new for you. It's a shock. And who is this Gina?"

"A new girl at school. She's Italian and so pretty and her hair…" Suddenly, the tears erupted and she cried until her throat hurt and her head began to ache. Every time she glanced up, the frizz around her head looked more untamed, and she became even more upset and unhappy. Now, she would be in trouble with her parents for something she wished she had not done. Babushka and Elena quietly left the room, closing the door.

Lying on her bed, her face in her pillow, Natasha waited for her parents to return home. She was quite sure she would be given a terrible punishment, months and months jailed in her room. If Mama was really angry, as she would be, she might even smack her.

When she heard her parent's voices as they came up the path, she froze. Then she heard voices murmuring inside the house, which must be Babushka explaining. Finally, loud footsteps clattered down the hall to her room. She wanted to scream when the door burst open and Mama rushed in.

"What have you done?" Mama's high-pitched voice sounded panic stricken. "After everything I said yesterday! Natasha, I can't believe you did this!"

Papa and Babushka followed Mama into the room. Natasha screwed up her face and the tears flowed again even though she tried to stop them.

"She's so upset," Babushka said.

"But I told her just yesterday!"

"She knows she shouldn't have."

Mama's voice turned sharp. "You deserve a hard smack. You're not too old, young lady!"

Papa spoke next. "How could you disobey your mother? Now, sit up straight, Natasha, and let us see."

Slowly Natasha uncurled her body and straightened up, her eyes squeezed shut against the world, holding back a new outbreak of tears. She heard a quick gasp from Papa, who added, "Poor Natasha. Well, there's your punishment."

"I can't believe it," Mama whispered.

"It's so awful," Natasha wailed. "I'll never ever do it again. I'm so sorry!"

Mama let out a deep breath. Bending over, she stroked her daughter's back. "You always learn the hard way, don't you? Let me have a good look." Mama's hand, patting her matted hair, felt like it was yards away from her head.

"It's not so bad," Mama murmured.

Natasha plunged back to her pillow. "It's terrible."

With gentle coaxing, Natasha sat up again and Mama brushed her hair. She had no more tears to shed and watched sadly as Mama's slender hands tried to tame the wild frizz around her head. The hair was just long enough to pull back tightly into a bunch at the back of her head. "There," Mama said. "I think that's the best we'll be able to do."

"It's ugly and it doesn't look any better than plaits."

"Perhaps if we had spoken to a hairdresser, we would have known what to expect."

"You wouldn't let me."

"Shush, Natasha. Nobody's happy about this. Now, we have to make the best of it."

The rain stopped overnight and Saturday dawned a bright cloudless morning. The freshness in the air entered the room through the half-open window. Natasha stayed in bed late, thinking, mainly about her hair, but also about Jan and Gina and even Lorraine. She was glad to have two days at home with her new hair, but was worried about how the kids at school would react on Monday. Would Jan still be her best friend? She was quite sure that Gina would soon be Lorraine's newest friend.

She turned over onto her side, away from Elena's breathing in the next bed. Mama had already taken Sonia out of the room. Good riddance to Gina, Natasha decided. She was never really a friend. I never liked her much anyway.

But the thought of Gina turning to smile at her at the lunch bell replayed in her head, and when she was finally honest with herself, she admitted that, yes, even though she was a little, just a very little bit jealous of Gina, she did like her. She would like them to be friends. She twisted onto her back.

'That will never happen," she said aloud. "I know Lorraine too well."

For the entire weekend she played with her hair. Lizzie, from next door, came by and together they tried out as many styles as they could dream up. By Sunday afternoon, her hair had, to her relief, settled down a little. However, she agreed with Mama, that pulling it back into a bunch at the back of her head was the best for school.

On Monday morning, Natasha dressed carefully and Babushka again combed back her hair as severely as usual. But what would the kids say? Now, instead of plaits, she had a round ball of fuzz on the back of her head. If only no one laughed at her, that was all she wanted. Then there was Gina. What would she say to the new Natasha?

When the bus stopped at school, she got off last, slowly. So far, no one on the bus had mentioned her hair. It seemed almost as though they had never looked at her properly before. Then she saw Jan and Gina running towards her.

"Hello, hello," Jan sang happily.

"Hello," Natasha said and held her breath.

Gina smiled and echoed the greeting. Neither of them seemed to have noticed anything new about her.

"My hair," Natasha said, glancing enviously at Gina's bouncing curls. "What do you think?"

"Your hair?" Jan stopped and regarded Natasha seriously. "Oooh, my goodness, it's cut! Oh, wow!"

Gina, too, stared at the ball of fuzz on Natasha's head. She tentatively put up a hand to touch it. Natasha nodded her approval, and Gina felt the coarse strands.

Natasha swallowed hard. "Is it all right?"

Jan sized her up from several angles. "It looks pretty much the same," she said. "It's all pulled back and, well, it's sort of different. You'll always be a bit different."

Jan's right, Natasha thought. *I will always be different. Never quite Australian and no longer Russian, either.*

Natasha looked up to see Lorraine on her way towards them with Wendy, a quiet girl whom Natasha rather liked.

Wendy looked stunned and seemed unsure whether to say hello. Natasha smiled and greeted her and she was about to reply when Lorraine pulled her away.

"Poor Wendy," Natasha whispered to Jan, "she doesn't know whether she's pleased to be Lorraine's new friend or not."

Suddenly Lorraine spun around. "Your hair!" She burst into high-pitched laughter.

Natasha froze.

"It's like a bush on the back of your head. Bushy, bushy Natasha!" Now, her laugh sounded false.

A chill radiated through Natasha's body. She held her breath, waiting to see who else would take up the chant. Wendy looked away, embarrassed. A few others looked towards them, but then turned away. When there was no obvious support for her, Lorraine flicked her own hair and pulled Wendy away with her.

At first Jan frowned, but suddenly a smile lit up her face. "That's a great new nickname for you. Let's call you Bushy." Natasha was unsure whether she liked this name, but Jan squeezed her arm. "Isn't it nice we're all friends? Before you got here this morning, Lorraine tried so hard to get Gina to go with her, but Gina couldn't understand what she wanted—" she stopped, then added slowly, "or *pretended* she couldn't understand."

Gina smiled shyly at Natasha. "Bushy," she said with a lilt in her voice that made the name sound so jolly and happy.

Natasha nodded. "Yes, Bushy."

"Friend, yes?" Gina added.

"Yes," Natasha agreed, "friend."

She smiled at her new friend, even though she felt a slight twinge inside. She warned herself that she was not going to be jealous of Gina's hair. She was a very nice person and that was all that mattered.

Chapter 18

A week after Natasha cut her hair, school let out for the spring vacation, which in Australia came in September. The rain had passed and the weather was cool in the mornings and evenings, but sunny throughout the day. Natasha and Lizzie from next door had invented a new game. They were dressing up to be prospectors in Alice Springs, ready to dig for gold.

"You'll look too much like a bush-ranger if you let your hair out," Lizzie told Natasha. "We're gold diggers."

They rummaged in the box of old clothes the Flannerys used for dress-up. "Here's a good shirt!" Lizzie struggled to pull an old shirt over her head without undoing the buttons. As her head emerged, she sputtered, "We'll…we'll go around the edge of the bush and then come back."

"We can leave the hose on outside, and when it floods, it will be our—," Natasha struggled to find the right word, "you know, when water is running down?"

"River? Stream?"

"Yes, stream. We can look for gold in the stream." Natasha donned another of Mr. Flannery's cast-off shirts. He was an accountant and wore shirts every day, whereas Papa wore overalls to work and saved his shirts for "good." She loved rooting around in this box of old clothes in the Flannerys' playroom, trying on one item after another. It was amazing that the family, with so many children, should have a room just for playing. Their bedrooms, however, resembled dormitories with double bunk beds along the walls. The playroom was nearly bare, a wood floor with no rugs to worry about and only a desk and two chairs beside one wall.

Australian furniture was light colored and plain, not at all like the dark heavily carved pieces that Natasha's family had brought from Shanghai. So much in Australia seemed plain to Natasha. The homes, inside and out, the landscaping, (not nearly enough trees, Mama always said), even the clothes people wore.

"Now, let's see." Lizzie checked their supplies. "We've got pots to scoop the dirt and bags to carry the gold, but you need a colander, like I've got. Mum doesn't have another one." At Natasha's blank look, she held up a metal colander. "Like this. Something to sift dirt to see the gold."

"A colander. Sure. We've got one. I'll be right back." Natasha raced from the Flannery house, down the drive, over the fence and ran to her own home. Happy, barking excitedly, jumped up. She patted him quickly and slipped inside.

Babushka stood at the kitchen sink peeling potatoes. She glanced up. "Natasha, *dorogaya,* bring me my apron from your bedroom. I left it when I put Sonia down. Be careful not to wake her."

Natasha wished she had not come across Babushka, but it would not take a minute to get the apron, so she hurried to her room, quietly opened the door and entered. Before she knew it, the breeze from the open window slammed the door shut behind her. Natasha froze, expecting an immediate wail from Sonia's crib. But there was none. No noise at all. Maybe Sonia wasn't there. Natasha tiptoed to peer inside the crib. There she was, lying still and quiet. At the window the sheer white curtains billowed and rustled with the breeze.

She stood, motionless. Was Sonia breathing? Something was not right. Holding her own breath, she thought she might suffocate as she watched for some movement from her sister: the flick of an eyelid, a rising of the chest, anything. The baby lay still, her eyes closed, tiny silvery veins visible on paper-thin lids. Strands of curly black hair clung to her forehead. She looked incredibly tiny and fragile.

Natasha stared at Sonia who had celebrated her first birthday in June. She prayed with all her might that her sister was alive. Leaning forward, she gently brushed the back of her finger along the small arm that lay over the top of her lacy blanket. Sonia twitched and pulled her arm away.

Natasha let out a long breath. Sonia was alive! Everything was all right. But somehow, deep down inside, she still felt uneasy. Suddenly, Natasha clapped her hands hard. Sonia sucked in her sleep, a few tiny bubbles appearing at the corners of her mouth. She slept on, completely undisturbed.

Natasha spoke aloud. "Sonia." Was there a flicker? A small response? Not really. Still the baby slept. Maybe if she picked her up, Sonia would react normally. She reached over to get a grip on the baby when the door opened and Babushka entered, wiping her hands on a towel.

"What are you doing?" Her voice was a harsh whisper. "I just got her to sleep." She gently closed the door behind her.

Natasha's mind reeled. "I was just checking…"

Babushka would be worried sick if she told her what had crossed her mind. Her grandmother had been worried about Agnes and still cried over the letter about Uncle Sasha. Of all her family, Babushka seemed the least happy and least like her old self since their move. Natasha did not want to upset her if she did not need to. She would tell Mama first. "Isn't she beautiful?" she whispered. "I couldn't help watching her."

Babushka nodded. "I thought she must have woken when I heard the door slam. The little one needs sleep and I need the time to get dinner." She moved closer to the crib and peered in. "Thank goodness. Still asleep. Now, let's go and leave her to rest."

Natasha handed the apron to Babushka, and slipped away to the back garden. Happy ran to catch her, his ears flapping as he jumped up to be petted.

Behind the garage, Natasha stepped into the chicken coop. The dog sat outside the wire-link fence, giving short whines to be let in. No one visited the coop in the late afternoon, so she could think for a few minutes in peace. She shooed the chickens away and leaned back against the garage wall that formed one side of the enclosure. The chickens squawked and spluttered and then marched around, peering at her sideways. The rooster's black-green feathers glistened in the brilliant sunlight as he preened and strutted.

Occasionally, Happy barked and the hens squawked and scattered, but mostly they ignored him as he paced the fence. Warm against her back, the fibro garage wall had faded from the full force of the sun.

She needed to think about Sonia.

Could it be that her sister could not hear properly? At Aunt Vera's, Babushka was always relieved that Sonia slept through so many of Aunt Vera's scenes. Maybe Sonia just slept heavily. Maybe when she was awake she would hear the noises around her.

"What do you think, Hap?" The dog stopped pacing and sat down, watching her with his worried frown. "Do you think Sonia might be—" but she couldn't say the word, not even to Hap.

"She didn't wake, Happy. Not when the door banged, not when I said her name. Is she all right?" The chickens, used to her stillness, moved nearer, pecking closer to her feet. "I don't know what to think, Hap. She's so little. It just doesn't seem right." The smell of the coop began to irritate her. Then Lizzie's voice floated over the fence.

"I'm not waiting any more, Natasha."

"I'm in with the chooks." Natasha brushed at her clothes.

"The game's over."

"Wait. Please. I'll get the col—col— that thing and be right there." Quickly she let herself out of the coop. Happy chased her back to the door, nipping at the back of her heels.

Colander, colander. Another word she would have to learn. For the moment she forgot about Sonia, but when she returned next door, Lizzie would not speak to her. She had taken off her old shirt and now squatted in a corner of the playroom, knees drawn up to her chin, her head bent over a book.

"Please, Lizzie. Something important happened and I couldn't come right away."

Lizzie looked up. "What?"

Natasha bit her lip. "I can't tell you. Not yet." How could she tell Lizzie what she suspected when she had not yet told anyone in her own family? And maybe it was not even true.

"Well?" Lizzie thrust out her jaw.

Maybe Natasha could give her a little hint? Swear her to secrecy? But no hint that would not bring more questions would come to mind, so she just stared down at her friend with sadness. Poor Sonia, she thought. The news was too important to throw out for a game, even with Lizzie.

When it was clear Natasha was not going to tell her, Lizzie snuggled down into herself and resumed reading. No matter what Natasha said, Lizzie would not look up. Finally, Natasha gave up and returned home. Sonia could be deaf and Lizzie was not speaking to her. Happy raced toward her but she ran past him, her face reflecting her feelings.

Babushka glanced up from the cooking pots. "What's wrong, my little *golubka*?"

"Nothing." Natasha veered into the living room as Sonia still slept in the bedroom. Babushka followed. "You can't help me, Babushka. This is between Lizzie and me."

"Just tell me what's wrong?"

Natasha shook her head. Babushka clasped her hands and peered into her face. "Did she hit you?"

"No!" Natasha pulled her hands away. "Of course not."

"Then what's wrong? Maybe I can help." Babushka rubbed her back the way she used to when she was little.

Natasha took a deep breath. "I took too long to get the colander so she is angry with me. That's all."

As soon as she had finished speaking, Babushka turned and marched out of the door. Natasha ran after her. "Where are you going?"

Babushka didn't answer but kept going. Soon Natasha saw her marching up the drive to the Flannerys' house, the strings to her apron fluttering behind her. Natasha collapsed into a chair. "Oh, no." She hid her face in her hands. "What will she do now?"

A few minutes later, Babushka returned down the path, holding a bewildered Lizzie by the hand. How could Babushka do this to her? Lizzie would think she was a child, complaining to her grandmother and expecting things to be fixed for her. As the back door opened, Natasha looked up. "I'm sorry. I didn't know she was going to do this."

Lizzie, her face pink with embarrassment, glanced at her and then back at Babushka.

"Come here, Natasha," Babushka ordered.

"What for?"

"Do as I say, please."

Natasha stood and came forward.

Babushka reached towards her. "Give me your hand." Natasha stretched out her hand and grandmother took it quickly. "I need your little finger."

Now, Natasha knew what Babushka was doing. Years ago, when she and Elena had fights, Babushka would hook their little fingers, make them look into each other's eyes and then they would be friends again. But she was not little anymore.

"Babushka. *Nyet.* You can't do that. I'm not a baby and poor Lizzie doesn't have a clue what's going on."

"Your finger, Natasha."

With her hand caught in her grandmother's steely grasp, she had little choice. Babushka wagged Natasha's little finger at Lizzie. "She wants your little finger, too." Natasha stared at the floor.

Lizzie stuck up her little finger and Babushka smiled as she joined the two. "Hook them around each other, Natasha. You know what to do. Now, tell her to look into your eyes."

Natasha translated, but added, "You don't have to if you don't want to. We used to do this when we were small."

Lizzie giggled. "Babushka's so funny. I really like her."

Natasha smiled. "Will you be my friend again?"

"Of course." Lizzie unhooked their fingers. "Do you still have the colander?"

Babushka's shiny pink face was beaming. "It worked."

"*Spasiba*, but please, never, ever again. Let's go, Lizzie."

Chapter 19

That evening dinner proceeded quietly as the sun set outside and lights were switched on indoors. To Natasha, the calm around her was like the soothing stillness preceding a storm. Her parents were tired. They did not speak much but encouraged their daughters to talk about their day's events.

Elena recounted a school visit to National Park and how she had seen a kookaburra fairly close, how big it was and how she had not been too frightened. Natasha listened. Having finished her story, Elena bit into her *vatrushka* cheesecake. At the head of the table, Papa let out a sigh, his body slumping forward as he stirred strawberry jam into his tea. Happy waited under the table for leftovers.

Sonia jiggled in her mother's arms and smiled at anyone who paid her attention. Natasha reached over to waggle a finger near her. As she expected, Sonia grabbed the finger and used it to hoist herself up and down. When she tired of the game, Natasha stood up and walked around behind her sister. She waited until Babushka disappeared into the kitchen with a stack of dishes. If she were just imagining the problem, it would be wrong to cause her grandmother extra concern. After a slight hesitation, she called Sonia's name. Her little sister did not respond, although Elena looked up from her cake. Natasha clapped her hands. Still the baby did not turn, but her mother picked up the morning's newspaper and muttered, "What are you doing, Natasha?" She juggled the baby from one knee to the other, head bent, concentrating on the front page.

Natasha returned to the table and sat down beside her mother, placing a hand on her arm. "Mama," she steeled herself to say it, "I don't think Sonia can hear properly."

Mama glared at Natasha for a second, then laughed aloud. "Why are you trying to frighten me? That's not a nice thing to do."

Natasha bit her lip. This was so hard. "I'm serious, Mama. Something made me realize this afternoon."

With a look of alarm, Mama glanced at her youngest daughter and then back at Natasha. "What happened? What do you mean?"

"Watch." Again positioning herself behind her sister's back, Natasha called to her and then clapped her hands. Sonia gazed serenely into her mother's face.

"No," Mama shook her head. "It can't be. I…I just don't believe it could be. That could mean anything, surely?"

With his mouth open, Papa stared at his wife. Silence shrouded the group at the table. Finally, Mama said in almost a whisper, "Why are you doing this, Natasha? Why are you trying to scare us?" She closed her eyes and crushed Sonia to her chest. After a minute, she brushed her lips against her baby daughter's hair. "I just don't believe it. It cannot be true."

Papa sat up straighter. "What happened to make you think this?"

Natasha clasped her hands and related how she had gone to the bedroom during the afternoon and the door had slammed. Sonia had not awakened. Nor had she turned around after dinner when Natasha made a noise behind her back.

Glances full of unspoken words passed between her parents. Papa leaned forward. "Do it again." His Adam's apple jiggled as he swallowed hard. "Let's see."

Again standing behind Sonia, Natasha clapped her hands while everyone watched. Sonia smiled at Papa, and then stuck her thumb into her mouth.

Papa cleared his throat. "Let's not rush to any hasty conclusions. This could all be a mistake. We've never suspected anything before and surely we would have if…" His voice broke and trailed off. He ran a hand over his chin and cleared his throat again.

They all stared at the happy baby in her mother's lap. Then Elena whimpered, hiding her face in her hands. Papa spoke again. "Let's wait for a doctor's diagnosis. It might be something temporary, or something that can easily be fixed."

Babushka returned from the kitchen, carrying a tray. She paused as she entered the room. "What's wrong? You're all sitting here like you've seen a ghost." Her cheeks were rosy and shiny from the humidity of the kitchen.

For a moment nobody spoke. Papa clicked his tongue and said, "We're a little concerned about Sonia."

"What's wrong? Look at her." Babushka tickled Sonia under the chin, who giggled, drawing in her chin and scrunching up her shoulders. "She looks absolutely fine to me."

Papa looked down at the table. "She doesn't seem to hear too well."

"Hear? What do you mean? Hear!"

Papa flicked a hand towards the baby. "Natasha, show her." Again, Natasha called Sonia's name and clapped her hands. Her sister continued to chew the hem of her bib.

"She's just playing," Babushka's eyes sought Mama's. "Isn't she?"

Mama and Papa again exchanged a look. Natasha stared hard at the back of Sonia's head. Babushka stared at everyone in turn. "*Gospodi Bozhe moi*. I don't understand. I just don't understand."

"She didn't wake," Natasha began. "This afternoon, when the door banged shut while she was asleep. I've tried all sorts of ways to try to see if she can hear."

"We can't be sure," Mama paused, closed her eyes and sighed. "We can't be sure, but there's a suspicion, now. Maybe there's a problem."

"*Nyet!* Surely not!" Babushka sank into a chair, her hand covering her mouth. "*Bozhe moi, Bozhe moi. Pozhaluista eyo spasi,*" she chanted to the Lord, her eyes shimmering like pools of rainwater. Her body began to sway in the direction of the lampada as she crossed herself, praying in a loud whisper.

Elena, crying, wiped at her eyes with her sleeve. Seeing the distress of everyone around her, Sonia's mouth worked into a pucker and she let out a wail. Mama hugged her, murmuring, "My baby. My little, little baby."

Papa rubbed at his chin. "She's so small. Only fifteen months old. So tiny."

Babushka reached for her handkerchief and blew her nose. "Are you sure, Sergei? Are you sure?"

"Of course we aren't sure. We aren't doctors." He stood and moved nearer his wife.

"God must have his reasons. He must be planning something we don't understand yet." As Babushka carried on, Papa raised his eyebrows while Mama sat oblivious to everything, hugging and rocking Sonia. Babushka continued, "It was all the worry about leaving Shanghai. Too much was happening. You weren't eating right, Tania."

"It probably is my fault." Mama's voice faltered.

"Hush." Papa placed a hand on Mama's shoulder. "No one knows the reason and it's too late to worry about that now. We have to look to the future, to what we can do. That is, *if* there is a problem."

Babushka bowed to Mama. "*Ya izvinyayus.* I'm sorry. I didn't mean to suggest it was your fault, Tania."

"I know you weren't accusing me." Mama sounded tired. "But I can't understand how I didn't notice anything before, if it's true."

"We've been so preoccupied," Papa said, "so busy getting settled."

Babushka sighed loudly. “I thought she was so good at sleeping through noises. Remember, at Vera’s? And I never once thought anything of it.”

“She’s so bright, so smart, so happy. Who would have thought?” Mama rubbed her nose against the baby’s head. “Anyway, we could all be wrong.”

A silence settled on the family and Natasha did not want to break it. She felt as though the family’s unhappiness was her fault. If she had not pointed out what she had noticed, this would not have happened.

After several minutes, Babushka pulled herself up and then lit the silver icon and lampada in the dining room. With her back to them, she bowed low to the Lord, hoping they were mistaken and Sonia could hear perfectly. Finally, she added that God knew best and would look after the baby he had brought into the world.

Elena left her seat and sidled up to Mama. She patted Sonia’s head gently. “Will she be all right? Will she be able to walk and talk?”

“Of course she will,” Mama assured her. “You must treat her the same way as before. She’s still the same Sonia she was yesterday. The doctors will tell us if we have to do anything special, but she’s a normal little girl, okay?”

Elena nodded, her head drooping onto her mother’s shoulder. “I love her,” she whispered.

“I know.” Mama smoothed Elena’s sweater. “We all do.”

Papa sat back down and was picking at his nails when he asked, “She’s later than the other two to walk, isn’t she?”

“Maybe a little. But that wouldn’t have anything to do with her hearing, would it?”

“When did the others walk?”

Mama frowned. “They were standing at ten months and walking at twelve.”

"She's not saying anything yet either." Papa leaned forward, dropping his hands between his knees. "But Elena was late to talk too, wasn't she?"

Babushka turned around. "She makes noises. Some are hard sounding, but she definitely can make noises. Nothing wrong with her vocal chords."

"She used to make more noises than she does, now." Mama looked from Papa to Babushka. "Have you noticed she's quieter, now?"

They were silent until Babushka suddenly spoke up. "She hates the vacuum cleaner. That must mean something. She must hear something!"

Mama smiled. "That's true. Some noises must get through to her." A glimmer of hope shone in her eyes.

"Thank God." Babushka's body relaxed. She swiped the backs of her hands across her cheeks to smooth away the moisture. "What do we do now?"

Mama straightened up. "Tomorrow, I'll take a day off and take her to see Dr. Horowitz. He'll tell us if it's true and what we should do next if it is."

"I'll come too." Papa leaned over and took hold of Sonia's hand.

That night Natasha could not sleep. Her parents talked late into the night. At first Mama wondered if Sonia would be able to learn to speak and how her schooling would be affected. Then Papa spoke about the problems of taking her for special treatments. The cost would be difficult, but of course they would find a way. Babushka could hardly take her to doctors or treatments, so one of them would need to take time from work which would mean less money coming in.

Mama whimpered. "Maybe I didn't eat enough while I was pregnant." Papa shushed her, saying that she had taken as good care of herself as she could. Food had not been as plentiful as when she had been pregnant before. It was not her fault. These things happened just like, just like Matvei. They had to look to the future, not the past.

"I feel so guilty, as though it's a punishment." Mama's voice was muffled and Natasha found it hard to make out all the words. Papa hushed her again, saying this would not help Sonia. Mama's voice grew louder as she wished she could take the deafness on herself. She would be able to bear it better than her precious baby. Such a young innocent child! How could this happen?

Natasha pulled the covers over her head. Maybe it was *her* fault. She remembered one time when Mama was pregnant with Sonia, and Papa had been reading to her and Elena. They sat on either side of him, and it seemed so perfect and right, that she wondered where the baby would sit. She thought that three children might be too many. Now, she knew that three children was a perfect family. Three girls especially.

But would Sonia's problems affect Natasha? Would she be laughed at for having a sister who could not hear? Would Mama and Papa spend all their time with Sonia and leave her and Elena to fend for themselves? Then she felt guilty for thinking of herself when Sonia had so much to contend with.

She tried to pretend that she was deaf. What would the world be like? She covered her ears, but nothing seemed different. It was easier to pretend she was blind. With her eyes closed, the darkness was something she could comprehend. But being able to see and not to hear was more difficult to act out. Maybe it felt like not being able to understand a language. When they first arrived in Australia, people around her talked, but it was all gibberish.

Luckily, Sonia would still be able to read, to see the sun and the birds and animals. She could run and play. Surely, she would be all right. Then she realized she was glad it was Sonia and not she who had this problem, and once again, felt guilty at this thought that had sneaked into her head without her permission.

What would the doctor say tomorrow?

Chapter 20

The next day, Natasha and Elena did not spend time with their friends or neighbors. A quiet, misty rain added to their feeling of solemnity. They tried to read but could not keep their thoughts from Sonia with her parents at the doctor's office.

Everyone had risen early that morning and waited for the doctor's surgery to open. Both parents had called work for their first day off. Finally, on the dot of nine, Mama called and set up an appointment for eleven o'clock.

It seemed an impossible wait at home. Babushka prayed constantly, asking God his reasons for this calamity. Hadn't they suffered enough, what with Sasha's disappearance? Nothing more had been heard about him but she still believed one day they would be reunited. She tried to clean house, but gave up as she found herself polishing the same piece of furniture over and over.

At lunch time, Babushka placed salami, teawurst sausage and black bread on the table. The three sat, hardly speaking, each lost in thought. Every noise outside brought the girls to the door until finally, at one-thirty, they heard the unmistakable sound of a taxi. As her parents entered the front door, Natasha reached to kiss Sonia in her mother's arms. Sonia cooed and blew bubbles for her sisters as Elena patted her leg.

Babushka crossed herself. "Pray God the news is good. What did the doctor say?"

Papa clicked his tongue. That was not a good sign. Babushka sighed as Papa pulled at his jacket. "We have to take her to a specialist. Dr. Horowitz says there's definite hearing loss but we won't know how much until we see Dr.

Simpson on Macquarie Street. The good news is that he thinks there is some hearing still there."

Babushka covered her mouth with her hand, her eyes filling with tears. Natasha turned away. It was so hard to see her little sister smiling happily, unaware of the problems facing her.

Elena asked the question that was also on Natasha's mind. "Can they help her?"

Mama released Sonia into Babushka's arms and unbuttoned her coat. "She'll probably have hearing aids when she's bigger. Dr. Horowitz says Dr. Simpson's very good. The best in the field for children." Hanging her coat on the hall-stand, she stretched to remove her hat.

Babushka nuzzled Sonia's cheek. "My poor baby. Maybe there will be an operation that can help." Removing Sonia's coat, she handed it to Natasha. "Is this doctor on Macquarie Street expensive?"

Natasha rubbed her cheek on the coat, taking in its baby smell. "This coat used to be mine."

"And mine, too," Elena reminded her.

Mama brushed a smudge from the felt pile of her hat. "All the doctors on Macquarie Street are expensive."

Papa picked up three letters that had come in the mail. "We have to see him and we'll find a way to pay whatever he charges."

Babushka continued, "You know, Vera told me the government will pay part of the medical bills for people, even immigrants, who can't afford the costs."

Papa set down the mail. "I said *we'd* pay. I don't ask anyone else to pay for me." He lunged along the hall through the dining room, swung open the back door and left. The door slammed hard behind him.

Babushka frowned and turned to Mama, who shrugged and said, "You know how he is. He's upset about the baby, too." She picked up the letters and shuffled through them. "Mortgage, electricity bill, and, oh, from Mother in Russia!"

Babushka said, "It's silly if he won't even consider it."

"He feels it's his responsibility. You're the one who brought him up that way."

"It's the way men are. They feel they have to provide for their families with no help."

Mama took Sonia back into her arms. "He's gone to the garage. You know what that means."

"He may be upset, but if the government passed a measure to help us with our bills, then God means us to use it."

Mama rolled her eyes. "God doesn't get the government to pass measures to help us."

Babushka pursed her lips. "Look. Natasha needs shoes, Elena needs a coat. How can we pay for everything on a mechanic's salary. I know, I know," she gestured at Mama, "you work hard, too. But the money does not reach as far as it needs to."

Mama strode down the hall. "We'll manage somehow. We can always sell some of the silver if we have to." Natasha and Elena followed her into the dining room.

"Here? In Australia?" Babushka hurried in behind. "No one has real silver here. You won't get what it is worth."

Mama's shoulders drooped. "We'll manage somehow. Did you see I have a letter from Russia?"

"Yes, I noticed the stamps. I'll get some tea while you read it. Are either of you going back to work?"

"No. It's too far for me." Mama settled Sonia into her high chair. "And Sergei's too upset."

Babushka continued to stand between the dining table and the door to the kitchen. "Did the doctor say how it could have happened?"

"He asked about illnesses I had while I was pregnant. But that was such a terrible time. I didn't pay much attention if I wasn't feeling well for a few days."

Babushka sighed. "It's going to be so expensive. I don't like it that you support me, too. Maybe I should talk to Vera, see if I can live with her."

Her words jolted Natasha. She encircled her grandmother with both arms. "*Nyet.* You belong to us, Babushka. You've always lived with us. You are *our* family."

Mama's voice sounded tired. "Don't be silly. How could I work if you weren't here with the girls. Then where would we be?" She placed her letter on the table and poured a glass of orange juice from the jug left over from lunch. Leaning over, she held the glass to Sonia's mouth and cupped a napkin under her chin.

Babushka patted Natasha's back. "Your Papa should listen to reason. He's always been stubborn when he's made up his mind about something." She gave Natasha a squeeze. "It's all right, *golubka.* I'll stay here if you all want me."

"Of course we want you," Mama stated with finality.

Natasha kept her vice-like grip on her grandmother. "Say you'll never, ever leave us, or I won't let go."

Babushka laughed, her stomach shaking against Natasha's body. "*Dorogaya.* My darling, I can't say that. At my age, I might die tomorrow."

"You're not allowed to die. I won't let you."

"Hush." Babushka peeled Natasha's arms from around her body and drew her hands towards her. "Only God knows when we will die. We mortals toil until our time comes. But thank you for wanting me." Kissing Natasha's palms, she turned to Mama. "You must be starving. I'll get that tea."

"Something for Sonia, too. It's been hard on her." As Sonia finished drinking, Mama placed the empty cup on the table and sat down wearily.

Natasha pulled a face. "Babushka wouldn't live with Aunt Vera, would she?"

"It may not be as easy as she thinks." Mama smiled. "You know, Dr. Horowitz said how good it is that we realized about Sonia's hearing loss while she is so small. Some people don't realize there is a problem for quite a while longer. The sooner it is discovered, the better. We can help her use the hearing she does have and that will help her start speaking." She held out a hand to Natasha. "Thank you for noticing for us."

Natasha clasped her mother's hand. She had felt so guilty, yet it appeared that she had helped her sister. "I'm so glad she'll be able to speak," she whispered, squeezing her mother's fingers. Sonia, too, suddenly smiled and banged her doll's head against her high chair.

Mama returned the squeeze, then gently withdrew her hand and raised the letter from Russia. "Let me read this," she said as she tore at the envelope. Reading quickly, she suddenly let out a cry. Her head in her hands, Mama sat deadly still.

Natasha turned from her school bag, "What's wrong?" She stared at her mother. "What is it, Mama?" Elena began to suck on her fingers.

Closing her eyes, Mama answered, "It's my father. He's not at all well."

"Grandpa? What's wrong with him?"

"He has to have tests…oh, dear." Her voice rose as she called to the kitchen. "Galia, come here."

Babushka returned quickly. "What's the matter?"

"My father. He's in the hospital. He's been having dreadful headaches and has to have tests."

Reaching behind her for a chair, Babushka chanted to God, "*Gospodi Bozhe moi, Gospodi Bozhe moi*. Can't you see we are already suffering, dear Lord? Bad things always come in threes. Sasha, Sonia, and now this."

Natasha raced to the garage to fetch Papa. The door slammed as he rushed back in. "Tania, my dear." He hugged his wife to his side.

"If only I could go to him, Sergei."

"I know, I know. Does it sound serious?"

Mama swallowed hard. "Mother is probably putting the best face on things, you know, not to worry us."

"Let's phone," Papa said. "We can at least do that. Where's that neighbor's phone number? Let's see if we can get to them."

The telephone operator in Australia tried several times to call Russia, but finally gave up, saying that there were no lines available and to try again later.

Papa said, "We'll try again in an hour. Will you tell them about Sonia?"

"No, no. There's plenty of time for that."

An hour later they phoned again. Mama kept murmuring, "They are so far, so far. If only I could do something." In the dining room the girls and Babushka waited.

Again, there were no lines and they were told to try later. They phoned several more times that evening and every evening after that, but on the few occasions the phone call got through to Russia, there was no answer.

Frustration showed in Mama's quick temper, and her worried frown kept Natasha and Elena from disturbing her. Mama wrote to Gran to be kept informed of her father's condition, but letters took such a long time.

* * *

Dr. Simpson on Macquarie Street could see them in three weeks. They waited impatiently, although Sonia reveled in the extra attention she received.

Mama borrowed several books from the public library about deafness, but she seemed unable to concentrate. She would settle with a book but her eyes wandered from the page into the garden. Or she would come into a room and forget what she had come for. She would cuddle Sonia for long periods and not notice the baby had started to cry.

Natasha read the books also, looking up difficult words in her dictionary. "Listen, Mama," she said and read aloud, "'The affected child should be treated as normally as possible. The family members should speak to the child more than to hearing children, and it is a good idea to face the child when speaking to en-en-courage lip reading.' But Mama, what language should we use? English or Russian? Will she get them mixed up if we use both?"

After some thought, Mama decided that Natasha and Elena should speak to her in English. The adults would use Russian. "That way she will learn both." Starting right then, they all chatted to Sonia whenever they were near her, touching her arm for her attention and using exaggerated facial expressions.

Every day Natasha checked the mail for letters from Russia. She was to phone Mama at work the moment a letter arrived. But day after day, no mail from Russia appeared. Papa worked as much overtime as possible and often did not return home until after nine o'clock, smelling of grease and soap. On his arrival, they immediately phoned the emergency number in Russia but had nearly given up hope of getting through to an answering voice.

Then Papa would stand at the bathroom sink, scrubbing off the grease that outlined his fingernails. Stripping off his greasy overalls, he would spend a half an hour in the tub. He had invested in two sets of overalls and every day Babushka washed the dirty one and hung the clean set on the hall stand for him to wear.

School was back in session when Sonia's appointment day arrived. Mama made an eight o'clock appointment in hopes of getting to work for half the day, but to get to the city so early, they had to leave at quarter to seven.

To Natasha, the day seemed much longer than usual, as her mind stayed with her sister and the events occurring in the doctor's office. Maybe there would be a wonderful new treatment and Sonia's hearing would be restored. When she returned from school, her parents and Sonia had just returned from the doctor. Sonia whimpered as she sucked on a crust of bread.

"What's wrong?" Natasha asked as she dumped her school bag.

"She's just tired," Mama answered. "We're all tired." Her lipstick had gone and her hair hung limply around her face.

Papa furiously stirred his tea. "I feel like sending that man a bill for my time. Two hours. How can he justify keeping us waiting two hours? We have to work or none of us, including him, will get paid."

"But Sonia. What did he say about Sonia?" Natasha asked.

Mama sighed as she answered. "He gave her a few tests. There is definite loss in both ears. She'll need more tests and special education. It looks like a long drawn-out process. But he said we've done all the right things and need to keep stimulating her."

Papa added, "All these tests before a final diagnosis, and only then will they work out a plan to help her. With his prices, you'd think he'd have a diagnosis on the spot. I don't know how to make it clear to him that our time is valuable, too."

"Sergei, we cannot afford to alienate the man. We'll be seeing him many more times."

Babushka asked, "I wish there was an operation to fix it."

Papa shook his head. "Nothing easy like that. But, I guess we'll take turns to take her to see him."

"You cannot understand what he's saying." Babushka pointed out.

Mama said, "I'll explain at work. I'm sure they'll give me time off without pay. But Natasha, dear, I won't be able to come to your Education Day Program."

"You missed my concert already," Natasha began, but the look on Mama's face stopped her. "It's okay. I understand."

"I'm sorry. You know I want to come. I do envy Mrs. Flannery being able to stay home with her children and go to all their events. But life here is so expensive."

"We'll manage," Papa said.

"There's something else," Mama said with a glance at Babushka. "This will be hard for you, Galia, and for Sergei, but we talked about it on the way home and think the doctor is probably right."

"Hard, hard for me?" Babushka gestured with one hand.

"The doctor said we can't speak to her in two languages. She may have to learn to lip read, you see. So because English is the language spoken here, he thinks we should speak to her only in English."

"But I can't speak English. Neither can Sergei. How are we supposed to talk to her?"

Papa answered, "We have to learn as much English as we can. All the simple things a child needs."

Babushka turned her body away from them. "I don't think I can."

Mama placed a hand on her shoulder. "This is a sacrifice you and Sergei have to make for Sonia. Not for me or the doctor, but for the baby."

Babushka began to speak but instead started to cry. Papa cleared his throat. "It's hard for me, too." He took hold of Sonia's fingers and stroked them.

"What about sign language?" Natasha asked.

"Yes, we have to consider that too," Mama replied. "But lip reading would be a lot more natural, and with some residual hearing, she should learn to function better."

Papa added, “It’s been a long hard day. Thank heavens Sonia is a clever—” He stopped speaking as the telephone rang.

Mama rose to answer it. She listened silently for a few seconds and then let out a whimpering cry. Papa ran to her as she leaned back against the wall. “My father. He’s gone.”

Chapter 21

"May God bless you and give you strength in this time of sorrow."

Mama bowed her head as Father Dimitri blessed her. "God be with you," he murmured to each of the family members in turn, raising his hand in blessing.

Papa had arranged the seven o'clock service immediately after the phone call from Russia as, in the tradition of the Russian Orthodox Church, prayers for the deceased had to be offered on the day of death. He had also phoned Agnes and Vera but stressed he did not expect them to come. Now, he also bowed his head to the priest as he muttered a prayer for his father-in-law. Sonia, cradled in his arms, burrowed her face in his neck at the priest's approach.

Natasha had seen the priest previously at the Russian Orthodox Cathedral, when his passage through the church had resembled a robed emperor expecting the worshippers to part for his progress, as the Red Sea parted for Moses. This evening, however, he was dressed in simple black robes instead of the gold embroidered chasuble he wore for Sunday services. His gray hair, worn long like many Russian priests, was pulled back into a ponytail. His single ornament was a jewel-encrusted crucifix that bumped against his chest as he moved. To Natasha, he suddenly seemed like a simple old man instead of an emissary from God.

Mama's face contorted and her shoulders shook. She swiped at her eyes with her handkerchief and then crushed it to her chest. The priest bent his head to hers and Natasha heard him speaking of God's will, and how Grandpa was reunited with his Lord.

Suddenly, there was a commotion outside. They spun towards the door as Aunt Vera, trailed by her sons, clattered in on high heels. She wore a tight black dress that, to Natasha, made her look like a stack of car tires. A wide black hat with a veil completed her outfit.

"What's she so dressed up for?" Elena hissed to Natasha. Mama and Papa wore the clothes they had worn to see the doctor and Babushka had changed from a housedress to her only black dress.

"Probably wants to find another husband," Natasha whispered.

"Here?" Elena glanced around the nearly empty church.

"Anywhere."

Aunt Vera headed towards them, her voice ringing out in the silent church. "My dear, my dear." She flung her arms around Mama and cried out to the priest, "Father, only you can give her true comfort. Oh, what a tragedy! What a tragedy!"

Taking a step backward, Father Dimitri's eyes darted to Aunt Vera and away. "Let us pray for the repose of his soul," he mumbled and slipped behind the altar to prepare for the service.

Inside the church, a few dim lights cast a soft glow into the cavernous interior. A collection of candles flickered in a brass stand near the altar where an elderly man bowed in prayer. The light glowed on the gold halos of the saints painted on screens shielding the inner sanctum. A trio of old ladies, their hair hidden in babushka scarves, huddled on one of the few benches that fringed the edges of the church. People stood for the Russian Orthodox service.

"I can't believe Aleksei is gone," Vera moaned, "and you are so far away." Mama nodded but could not speak. "Where is everyone?" Aunt Vera hissed to Papa over Mama's head as her gaze swept the empty church.

Papa raised his eyebrows. "What did you expect?"

"You know," she jerked her head towards the empty interior, "people."

"I phoned only you and Agnes. This is a private time for us."

Aunt Vera ignored his tone and reached up to Sonia, "Oh, another tragedy! The poor baby. The good Lord has certainly marked you out for problems. What did the doctor say today?"

"More tests. It will all take time, but right now we are here to pray for Aleksei."

"Of course," Vera agreed and crossed herself quickly.

The priest's attendant, who had been waiting discreetly, now advanced to give them each a small candle set in a cardboard ring to catch the wax drips. Vera sighed as she took hers and said, "Just think, this child will never speak."

"Of course she'll speak," Papa growled at her.

"Do you think so? Well, I guess you have to hope. What bad luck to have a deaf child!"

Mama jerked upright, emerging from the fog of her grief. "Vera, Sonia is a precious gift. Stop this talk."

Vera shrugged. "She can't hear what I'm saying anyway."

"*We* can hear what you're saying." Mama's voice turned hard and sharp like splintered glass as she took Sonia from Papa's arms. "She's a very special little girl. Please treat her that way. Now, shush. Please!"

Natasha felt so proud of Mama. Aunt Vera's words made Sonia seem less than a whole person. She patted her sister's fat baby leg. Elena nudged closer to Natasha, "She's made Mama even more unhappy."

An uneasy silence settled as Mama gave Sonia to Babushka and lit her candle at the candle stand. Sheltering the flickering flame, she lit Papa's candle. He in turn lit Vera's and Natasha's candles and they passed the flame around the others. The priest appeared from behind the screen swinging the censor, which released incense fumes as he passed before them. He chanted prayers to the Lord and the attendant led the responses for the family. Slowly the atmosphere changed and calm settled over them.

Vladimir had glanced at Natasha and smirked as she lit his candle, but she ignored him and concentrated on the priest. The luminous glow around her seemed spiritual and holy, and the scent of the incense brought an inner peace. She thought of Grandpa as she last saw him when they said goodbye at the train terminal. He had not wanted to return to Russia, but had agreed to his wife's wishes. With the help of photographs, Natasha recalled his facial features, but she could remember better the feel of her hand on his whiskery chin and his tobacco scent.

She now tried to think of him as dead, but somehow it did not seem possible. He was just far away in Russia and someday he might visit them. She thought of his velvety brown eyes and how they would crinkle into a smile when he looked down at her. When she was small, he would read to her longer than anyone except Papa.

As the priest moved toward the altar, Natasha's eyes settled on the large icon of the Mother and Child with Mary's serene face circled by a gold halo. The baby Jesus was half sitting, half standing and raising his hand. How could they have let Grandpa die? Both their faces seemed so calm and peaceful, their blue eyes wide and unblinking, and yet such a sad fate awaited them, too. Jesus would be crucified and his mother would watch him die. Mama always said that the hardest thing in any woman's life was to lose a child, even if the child were an adult, like Jesus, or like Uncle Sasha.

Both her parents were engrossed in prayer, their bodies bowing before the altar. She turned to look at Babushka, who sat on a side bench. Sonia was on her lap and had taken off one shoe and was now trying to take off her sock while Babushka tried to force the shoe back on. Natasha smiled. Suddenly, Sonia's deafness did not seem such a major problem. She was alive and healthy. So what if she could not hear! They would work around it and she would have a good life. Natasha smiled and waved to her sister.

After the service they drifted out of the church together. A feeling of acceptance had settled over the adults. They had done all they could according to their faith and would leave the rest to God. The priest promised to telephone for taxis as he accepted the contribution from Papa. To Natasha, Strathfield Cathedral resembled the one in Shanghai. Both were imposing white structures with blue and gold domes. The Shanghai one, however, fronted immediately onto a city street, whereas the Sydney one was set in spacious grounds with gum trees and buffalo grass struggling to survive the feet of worshippers.

While they were inside, darkness had spread over the landscape and the street lamps were few and sparsely placed. The two families stood together and waited. The lingering aura of the church at first surrounded them. A few cicadas began a chorus and the smells of food drifted from the surrounding homes, reminding them of their hunger. The boys began to fidget and respond to each other's jibes. The adults talked above their chatter, at first solemnly discussing the finality of death and then about their taxis. Peter complained about his empty stomach, but Vera silenced him with a flap of her hand, "Go over to the others."

"But I'm hungry. I need food." When Peter frowned, his small features drew together in the center, reminding Natasha of the photo of his father.

"You always need something to eat. No one else is complaining."

Peter scowled at his mother but swung around and proceeded towards Natasha standing nearby.

Vera apologized. "Growing boys. Always hungry. But, Tania, what will your mother do? Will she manage on her own? I know how hard that is."

Mama gazed up the empty street. "It would be wonderful if we could bring her here. I'll never see my father again, but pray God I'll see my mother."

Papa added, "It's not easy to get out of the U.S.S.R. I heard the Molotoffs waited three years to get permission for their father to come."

"They were lucky," Vera told them. "But if you like, I'll sponsor her for you, as you haven't been here long enough to sponsor her yourselves."

"Would you really? That's very kind, Vera," Mama said, embracing her.

Papa cleared his throat. "We'll start applying immediately."

Natasha felt grateful to Aunt Vera for the first time in her life and it was a strange feeling. Maybe she did have some good points after all. She turned back to the boys and Elena as they drew away from the adults.

Peter said, "They never think of food when they come to the cathedral. When Dad died, we never had food here except for that stupid sweet rice. But right now I wouldn't mind even that."

Natasha said, "Babushka said we'd have that at the next service."

Vladimir stuck his hands into his pockets. "My Mum made this great rice once with licorice and red jelly beans making the shape of the cross. Sweetness is supposed to lessen the sorrow, she said, but it sure helps the stomach." He giggled behind his hand.

"We know all about Russian services," Peter said. "The first, the ninth and the fortieth days, you have services, besides the day of the funeral. Gets pretty boring. Everyone felt so sorry for us then, even at the first anniversary service. Like we couldn't survive without Dad." His foot kicked at a stone and he watched it skitter into the darkness.

"But we've shown them," Vladimir said. "Mum gets lots of sewing work, some cooking and translating, too. No problem."

"Yeah, we've shown them," Peter repeated softly.

Natasha felt pity for the boys and their mother. It seemed as though they always had to prove something and could not just exist. She moved a little closer to Vladimir and tried to heal the breach between them. "I'm sorry about your dad. When did he—"

Vladimir interrupted her. "You don't have to be sorry for us." His eyes narrowed. "I've said we've done all right. We're not orphans and Dad left lots of money. Anyway, you don't have any grandfathers left now, and we still have one."

About to say they still had a father, Natasha stopped herself. Calmly she answered, "Well, we have three kids, Babushka, and Happy, so there are lots of people to care for."

"Fancy including a dumb dog," Peter said.

"And all the kids are *girls*," Vladimir said girls in a demeaning way. "You think you are great just because you have a dog."

Natasha knew how desperately Vladimir wanted a dog but his mother would not allow it. When he had come over to meet Happy, Natasha had been upset at how well the dog had taken to the boy. He continued, "Your hair is dumb and Sonia is supposed to be deaf, but I don't believe it." He stared at Natasha with eyes like black marbles glinting in the darkness. They reminded her of the eyes of a mouse she had once glimpsed in the kitchen in Shanghai before it scurried away.

"Why don't you believe it?"

"She's just pretending she can't hear to get more attention. Too many girls."

Natasha snorted. "You might do something so silly, but Sonia's too young to pretend like that."

"Look at her," Vladimir commanded. Sonia straddled her father's hip and chewed on a rusk Babushka had brought. "There's nothing the matter with her at all."

"You don't know what you're talking about," Natasha said. "You can't *see* if someone's deaf. Surely you understand that."

"Don't you laugh at me!" Vladimir's voice had risen and Aunt Vera and Babushka turned in time to see him give Natasha a hard poke, straight in the breast. Natasha cried out and Babushka gasped. Her parents' backs were to them, but Aunt Vera had seen. In no time she was beside him with her handbag raised and, with all her strength, she whacked him over the head.

"Disgusting boy," she screeched. "What made you do something so rude?"

"Don't hit me!" Vladimir returned her blow with one of his own aimed at her arm, enraging her further. The two struggled together, like an elephant battling a mouse. Aunt Vera's hat slipped and she grabbed at it just as her son attacked her stomach.

Natasha wrapped her arms around her chest. She felt confused and outraged. For a few seconds Mama and Papa stood watching. Vladimir hit out at his mother with all the strength he possessed, in a whirl of energy. Then Papa came to life, handed Sonia to Mama and took hold of Vladimir's flailing arms. Aunt Vera caught her breath, slammed on her hat, and then yelled at her son, "How can I hold my head up if you behave like that!"

Papa intervened. "Come on, Vera. He's still young."

She turned on Papa. "Don't you tell me how to deal with my sons."

Vladimir struggled in Papa's grasp, yelling at both Papa and his mother. When Papa let go, he launched himself at his mother again. Once more Papa reached for his arms as the first taxi rounded the bend. With great relief, Papa placed a wriggling Vladimir into the front seat beside the driver, and then helped Vera into the back seat next to Peter. The sound of their voices raised in argument drifted back as they drove away.

Mama wiped at her red-rimmed eyes. "What did he do to deserve that?"

"You didn't see?" Babushka asked. "Dreadful boy."

"He poked me," Natasha answered. "Here."

"What?" Papa spun around in the direction the taxi had gone, his face reddening. "I'll speak to Vera about this."

"Are you all right?" Mama asked.

Natasha nodded. "I thought she never got angry with her precious boys, but, wow!"

Papa punched his fist into the palm of his other hand. "She'll hear about this. I can't believe the way that boy fought with his own mother."

"Boys are much more physical than girls. We're lucky to have three daughters." Mama nodded at her family.

"Of course, we are," Papa agreed, "but if we should have a son next, he'd behave better. I'd be sure *our* son—"

"Sergei, not now," Mama said.

"You know how important it is for me to—"

Mama's voice shattered the quiet evening. "How can you even think, with my father, with us in this country, with everything the way it is! Please, Sergei!"

"Tania, I just–"

"Stop it." A sharp clear command. Mama turned away from them and stood alone, lamplight spilling down her back.

Nobody spoke. Natasha looked from Papa to Babushka. Both seemed bewildered. "*GospodiBozhe moi, Gospodi Bozhe moi,*" her grandmother murmured.

The silence bothered Natasha more than all Aunt Vera's family's noise and fighting. They stayed this way until the second taxi turned the corner and stopped in front of them.

Chapter 22

The silence of their trip in the taxi continued into the house. When Elena spoke to Mama, she stood rooted to the spot, staring at the wall. Then, after a pat to Elena's head, she retired to her room.

After that day, Mama settled into a deep depression. She dragged herself to work, but at home she distanced herself from her family. If Natasha spoke to her, she would glance at her blankly, and then wave a hand and say "speak to Babushka," or "ask Papa."

Only Sonia could rouse her, but even then she would sometimes hold the baby too close and burst into tears, and Babushka would rush in to take over. In the evenings, behind the closed door to their bedroom, Papa murmured softly to her, but his influence with her had disappeared.

When Sonia's next doctor's appointment came due, Mama dressed in her best clothes and resembled her old self, but on returning home, she collapsed like a deflated balloon. When Papa returned from work, he followed her into the bedroom. From the hall, Natasha listened to the murmur of his voice. Babushka took in a cup of coffee and a sandwich on a tray, but soon came back out. Glancing down at the untouched food, she muttered, "She'll starve if she keeps this up."

"Is she all right?" Natasha asked. Happy sat waiting patiently at her feet.

Babushka shrugged, frowning. "Only God knows how much her heart can bear."

"And Sonia?"

Babushka heaved a great sigh. "Oh, God has let me live too long." She leaned against the wall. "They said something about a special school for deaf children." The tray shook a little in her hands. "But they've agreed Sonia's smart. She should cope well."

Just then her father's raised voice rang out clearly. "How long can this go on? What about our other children?"

"I can't," Mama's voice was barely audible. "I just can't. Please let me be."

Natasha and Babushka exchanged a glance, and then Babushka hurried to the kitchen. Papa seldom raised his voice, so Natasha knew how frustrated he felt. Once again his voice traveled to her, "I know how you feel, but Tania, this is going on too long!"

Noisily, Papa emerged into the hall and swept out to the garage. Natasha had the barest glimpse of her mother's body, prone on the bed, her head burrowed into her pillow. Returning to her bedroom, Natasha flung herself on her bed. Elena was curled up in a ball on her own bed.

"Sonia might have to go to a special school. And it will probably cost a lot of money." Happy circled around and settled in his favorite spot between the beds.

Elena picked up a book and stared at it.

"I wish I could help Mama somehow," Natasha said. "Maybe we should get her some flowers or something."

Again Elena did not respond. Natasha watched, but as she did not turn any pages, she spoke again. "Elena, I can't ever talk to you about anything. You ignore me when it's something real."

Elena threw her book in Natasha's direction. "Can't you leave me alone? Talk, talk, talk. You think you can fix everything just by talk." She ran out of the room.

Natasha closed her eyes. Everything was wrong and they all felt it. Again, Shanghai seemed like a paradise, and although she knew things had gone wrong there, too, while she was in Shanghai she had been a protected child, whereas in Australia she had suddenly been transformed into an adult.

* * *

Two days later, Natasha munched on an afternoon snack, Happy under her feet and Sonia in her high chair gnawing on a rusk. Babushka entered the dining room carrying a wooden board covered with a floured cloth and a bowl of risen dough.

"Are we having *pelmeni*?" Natasha looked up from her history book. They were studying Bourke and Wills, and she loved the explorers and bushrangers of Australia's early days. "You make the best *pelmeni* dumplings, Babushka. And, Happy, you'll get your favorite soup bone!" The dog growled as though he understood.

"Maybe you'll wash your hands and help me," Babushka suggested. She shuffled back to the kitchen in her old Chinese slippers and returned with a bowl of cooked minced meat and sautéed onions, a rolling pin and a glass. When Sonia banged on her high chair, she said, "I have a nice slice of apple for you."

As Babushka rolled out the dough, the soft flesh under her arms swayed gently and looked like the dough she was working. "Shame Elena is not here to help. She'll be back in an hour from her little friend Lynne's house." When the dough was thin enough, she carefully pressed down the open end of the glass and then twisted it.

Natasha said, "Lynne loves dolls almost as much as Elena. Maybe, she'll talk to her. She never talks to me"

Babushka lifted the circle of dough and passed it to Natasha, who filled it with a teaspoon of the minced meat mixture. "It's good they've found each other."

The back door was ajar, allowing a soft breeze to freshen the indoor air. After midday showers, the sun splattered the garden with afternoon light that glittered on the thick lush grass. Eucalyptus, hydrangeas and rubber trees now camouflaged the fence. Natasha marveled how quickly everything had grown, and then she realized that in one month it would be a year since they had arrived in Australia.

She folded the dough over the meat and sealed the edges, then brought the two ends of the diagonal together to complete the dumpling. Just as she placed it onto the tray, Happy scampered up and ran to the door. Immediately, they heard footsteps coming up the side path.

Mrs. Flannery arrived at the back door, smiling and calling out, “Yoo-hoo. Anybody home?” Her wispy brown hair looked disheveled and her clothes looked like she had not had time to iron them.

Babushka wiped her floury hands and quickly smoothed her hair into its bun.

“Hello, everyone. I’ve come to ask—” Mrs. Flannery began as Babushka opened the door, but Happy leaped up at her. “Good dog,” she said smiling. “He certainly has grown, hasn’t he?”

“Come in, please, come in,” Babushka said in Russian and Natasha translated.

As Mrs. Flannery entered, her gaze settled on Sonia. “Look at that beautiful baby,” she took Sonia’s outstretched hand. “How are you, sweetheart? I do love babies.”

She turned to Natasha. “How is everything? You know, since your grandfather passed away.”

“Fine, thank you.” Natasha suddenly felt shy.

Babushka grabbed her arm. “Ask if she’d like a cup of tea.”

Mrs. Flannery shook her head. “No, no. That’s very kind but I can’t stay. I was worried about your mother. I can’t imagine losing my dad and being so far away.”

“Mum’s okay. She’s at work right now.”

“Best for her to keep busy. I do envy her the independence that her job gives her, you know, her own money. I tell all my girls, you must—” As if she had said too much, she suddenly confronted Natasha. “And you? Are you all right, love?”

Natasha loved the way Mrs. Flannery’s voice lilted upwards at the end of sentences, especially when she said 'dear', or 'love'. She smiled and nodded. Mrs. Flannery placed a hand on her shoulder. "He's just up in Heaven watching out for you."

Babushka could wait no longer. "Translate, Natasha."

"She's being nice about Grandfather."

"I'm sorry, dear." Mrs. Flannery took a deep breath. "Let me tell you why I've come. Now, I don't want you to be offended," her face reddened a little. "Well, we can see you have several hens and we wondered…you know, maybe you have more eggs than you need? Could we buy your extra ones? We'd know they were fresh, you see, and it seems a shame to waste them. But, if you aren't interested, it's quite all right."

Natasha translated for Babushka, who grinned broadly and patted her neighbor's arm. "*Spasibo*. Tell her thank you, we would love to sell her eggs. What a good idea." She nodded and bowed, her pink face shiny with delight. "Tell her we'll sell them cheaper than the stores."

When Natasha translated, Mrs. Flannery sighed quickly. "I'm so glad you don't mind."

"How many would she like right now?" Babushka asked.

"You can't imagine how much food we all consume. How many do you have?" She bought nine eggs and left with a wave. "I'll send the girls in next time."

Alone again, Babushka rolled out a fresh batch of dough. "That worked out well. Good for them and good for us. Here's another apple slice, Sonia. How do I say 'apple' in English?" Natasha told her and she repeated it a few times, then said, "Maybe we can get a few more hens and sell to other neighbors. And vegetables. I've been thinking of planting vegetables. Things grow so easily here."

Happy again settled under the table near Natasha's feet. "Do you think selling the eggs will be all right with Papa?"

"We won't tell him." Babushka glanced quickly at her granddaughter and then back down as she cut out some more rounds of dough. "*Gospodi Bozhe moi*, goodness knows we need the money. Tomorrow, go and ask Mrs. Adams and Mrs. Wickes, and if you sell to them, you can keep half the money."

"Can I? That would be great. The kids at school get pocket money, but I didn't like to ask Mama." Natasha worked on another dumpling.

"Your parents pay for what you need."

"I know. But I can understand what Mrs. Flannery meant about having your own money. It's funny, she envies Mama her job and Mama envies her being able to stay at home with her children."

"A woman's life is complicated. But Sonia's special needs will cost a lot, and if we bring Gran out to Australia, there's another mouth to feed. No wonder your father is worried."

"Whenever a bill comes in, Papa goes around switching lights off and muttering. I hate it. And the fruit he buys!" Natasha made a gagging noise.

"If you cut off the bad bits, you can eat the rest. It's a lot cheaper."

Natasha's voice dropped lower, "I hate it when he says he wants a son. It's as if—"

"What? As if what?" Babushka sounded almost angry. "He loves his daughters as much as any man could. Look in his wallet. There's a picture of the three of you. It's with him all the time. No more of this talk."

The two worked in silence until Babushka asked, "And how was school today? I worry about you."

"Don't worry about me. Worry about Mama. How many more *pelmeni* do we have to make?"

Babushka gathered up the strips of leftover dough and rolled them into a ball. "Just this," she said, and then added, "Your mother lets things upset her too much. She's not like Gran. Now, there's a feisty one."

Natasha said, "Mama said I was like Gran, but Gran's so little. And I remember that she never let me touch her hair."

Babushka laughed. "That would be true. Did you ever hear about how she and Grandpa got married and ended up in China?"

Sonia finished her apple and let out a wail. "Here's a book." Natasha passed a cloth book that Sonia loved to chew. "Tell me," she said to Babushka.

"Grandpa's family had a shoe business in a small town in Armenia. It was successful and they hired Lilla, your grandmother, to work for them. She was tiny, dark haired and very beautiful, and your grandfather, who had lost his first wife two years before, fell in love with her."

Natasha's hands stopped working. "He had been married before?" What if his first wife had not died and he had not married Gran? What if Mama had not been born? Their family, and she herself, would not have existed.

"His first wife died giving birth to a baby who also died. It was not uncommon in those days." Babushka patted Sonia and continued. "Grandpa wanted to marry Lilla, but the family said no. You see, he was Armenian but your grandmother was Russian."

Natasha completed her dumpling and placed it with the others on the tray. "So what did they do?"

"Grandpa's parents told all the churches in their area to refuse to marry their son to this Russian woman. It was the winter of 1918. They hired a sleigh and had to keep going further and further to find someone to marry them. But after they left Armenia, war broke out in the area where they had lived. They decided it was too dangerous to return, so they continued by train all the way to China.

"Didn't they have any of their things? You know, clothes, furniture?"

"In those days we didn't have all the things people have today. In China, Grandpa couldn't find work and decided to start his own business. Shoes, of course. So Gran sold the few pieces of jewelry she owned, but not the ring Grandpa had given her. I remember that ring, so beautifully set, a single diamond in a scroll-like gold setting. Just beautiful."

She stopped for a moment, smiling, and Sonia smiled back with a gurgle, and then threw her book to the floor. "Here, *dorogaya*, you can have a little bit of dough. Anyway, Grandpa used the money to set up a business, but it is one thing to buy supplies and make a few pairs of shoes. You need customers and that can take time."

"So what did they do?"

"Well, with a bit of…um, sacrifice. Well," Babushka stopped, and then spoke quickly. "As I said, Gran is a feisty woman and she got them out of a tight spot." Sonia began to cry as the dough got stuck between her fingers. "Oh, I knew I shouldn't have given you that."

"But what did Gran do?"

"She found some…uh, work, and helped until Grandpa could support them." Babushka stood up. "I need to get these into broth."

Natasha wondered what tiny Gran could have done that Babushka found hard to admit to. Could she have been a spy, or maybe she was the mastermind of a burglary ring? No, Gran wouldn't do anything dishonest. Or maybe she decoded enemy messages. Yes, it must have been something like that.

As Babushka returned from the kitchen with a wash cloth, Natasha asked, "But what about Mama? How are we going to help her?"

"I don't know," Babushka answered. "But I'll come up with an idea in the next few days. Here, Sonia, give me your hands. What is the English for 'hand.' "

Natasha had faith in Babushka. At home, she seemed to Natasha to be the same that she had been in Shanghai. But when "Australia" intruded into their lives, when they left the confines of their house, she became the new Babushka, who could not understand the strange world they now inhabited. But at home she was fine.

And right now, Mama was just the opposite.

Chapter 23

After school the next day, Natasha visited Mrs. Adams, who had just been shopping and didn't need eggs, but vowed she would buy from her in the future, and Mrs. Wickes, who bought half a dozen eggs right away.

Natasha placed her half of the money in a special purse which she hid in her underwear drawer, and dreamed about saving enough for a gift for Mama. As she passed through the dining room, Babushka warned her about selling too many eggs as they needed some for themselves. "But maybe I can cut down the number I use. I wonder if anyone would notice." The two grinned at each other.

No sooner had Natasha sat down than the front door bell rang. Babushka was nearest the door and opened it. A tall man tipped his fedora and spoke in Russian. "My name is Basil Leonidov Gasparov. I am passing through Sydney on my way to the Russian Embassy in Canberra. Aleksei Sarroyan was a neighbor and friend, so I have come to pay my respects to his daughter, Tania, and her family."

"Come in, come in," Babushka said as she ushered the visitor into the dining room. "How kind of you to visit. I am Tania's mother-in-law, Galia Ivanova, and these are her daughters, Natasha and Elena."

"*Zdravstvuite.* How do you do?" The man took off his hat and unbuttoned his coat. "Winters here are not like in Russia." He had shiny pink cheeks and a habit of pulling on his nose as he spoke.

"Thank heavens," Babushka said.

Natasha added, "It's nearly spring."

"Please sit," Babushka said. "Let me take your coat and I'll get some tea."

The man sat in Papa's seat and rubbed his hands. "Your grandfather spoke of you both often. He was very proud of you." To Natasha the man's clothes looked wrong, as if he had bought them many years ago when he was fatter and forgotten to wear them until now. "Whose dog is that?" He pulled at his nose again.

"That's Happy and he's mine," Natasha answered proudly. "He's usually friendlier. I think he's tired."

"Good looking dog. Yes, a good looking dog." As he spoke, the man's eyes wandered, lingering for a moment on the silver icon and lampada in the corner of the room.

Natasha said, "I wish Mama was here to speak to you."

"Ah, yes. What a shame I have to leave tomorrow for Canberra." He patted his pockets and took out a packet of cigarettes.

Babushka bustled back into the room with a tray of almond cookies, a bun loaf and poppy seed cakes. "Please forgive us. I would have made something special if I had known you were coming.

"But this is splendid, splendid. Please, do you have an ashtray?" He lit his cigarette. "The food looks delicious. I would never have known I had left Russia."

"Natasha, get an ashtray. The kettle is on for tea. But I wanted to ask, did Aleksei suffer? We have so many questions."

"It was only a few weeks that he was ill. Lilla was wonderful with him," he stopped and drew on his cigarette, "but he went down very quickly and, well, he was not a young man."

"And the funeral?" Babushka asked.

"You were all missed. Of course, it was not a religious service. He was cremated and his ashes are in the cemetery near their home. Lilla visits every day, sometimes several times. I miss him also. We didn't see each other as often as I would have liked because of my postings to other countries, but he was a man I respected and could talk to about the world."

"He was a kind man with good words for all of God's people," Babushka crossed herself. "There's the kettle." She hurried off to the kitchen.

"What do you mean?" Natasha asked. "About it not being a religious service."

"It was a normal state-run funeral. In Russia we are very modern and no longer believe in God."

"Nobody does? That can't be right. I'm sure Gran does."

"Some old people find it hard to change." He glanced at the icon in the corner. "But the young know the state is right about atheism. There is no God." He flicked the ash from his cigarette into the ashtray.

Natasha glared. "Well, what happens to Grandpa, if he's not in Heaven?"

"To be honest, I have my own view." The man seemed to be taking her seriously. He pulled on his nose and said, "I think that when a person dies, his influence is felt for as long as there are people who remember him or his works. Sort of like when you throw a stone into a stream. It makes a big splash, that's the man's life. Then the ripples are what is left and slowly, slowly, they spread out and disappear."

Natasha stared at him. Could there be some people, in fact, a whole nation, who did not believe in God? Papa had always said that he did not know if there were a God, but even he had never said that God did not exist. Mama and Babushka were adamant that there was one.

"What about Grandpa's soul? Doesn't it go to Heaven or somewhere?"

"Why should it have to?" The man tugged at his earlobe and asked, "Do you remember what it was like before you were born?"

Natasha shook her head. Was this a trick question?

"Well, that's what I believe it's like when you die."

Elena's voice asked quietly, "Are you a communist?"

Natasha felt as though she had jumped into a pool of ice-cold water. She could barely breathe. Communist was almost a dirty word. It was as if Elena had asked if he were a traitor or a spy.

"Of course," the man answered quite matter-of-factly. "That's our system of government. It treats workers with utmost fairness. Not like capitalism."

Babushka entered with the tea on a silver tray. "What silly questions are they bothering you with?" she asked. "Girls, leave the poor man alone. Basil Leonidov, can you wait for Tania to return from work? I know she'll have questions for you."

He glanced at his watch, and then took a card from his wallet. "I'm afraid I don't have time. Here's the Embassy's number. She can call and ask for me. However," Mr. Gasparov leaned sideways as he reached into an inner pocket of his jacket and took out a small package, "I have something for Tania from her mother. She said I was to be sure to give it only to the family."

Natasha leaned forward and took the package. "What is it?"

"That I don't know, except I am sure it is very special. Ah, this tea smells so good, just as I like it."

After the man left, all three waited impatiently for Mama to return from work. When they saw her walking from the bus stop, the girls raced to her with the package. "A man came, from Russia," Natasha said. "He knew Grandpa. This is for you. From Gran."

"From my mother," Mama murmured as they traipsed back up the drive. "Who was this man?" As they entered the dining room, she sank wearily into a chair.

"What did he say about my father?"

Babushka told the little she knew. "He'll be at that phone number after tomorrow."

"He said he was a communist," Elena said, nodding seriously.

Mama frowned. "Well, I wouldn't tell anyone outside this house."

Natasha asked, "Was Grandpa a communist, too?"

"Grandpa never joined the Communist Party. But I'm sure he had many friends who did. The whole country is communist, and not all bad people like the Australian newspapers would have you believe."

"The man didn't believe in God," Natasha added, "but he talked to me like I could understand."

Mama sighed. "Really? We better talk about that."

"Later. Let's do the package first."

They crowded around Mama as she pulled off the wrapping and a purple velvet box emerged. "So pretty," Elena breathed. When Mama opened the box, they gasped at the ring. A large diamond nestled in golden swirls.

"Your mother's engagement ring. The one she wouldn't sell even when they were so poor that she…well, she wouldn't sell it." Babushka glanced at Natasha. "Isn't it beautiful?"

Mama's eyes glistened as she gazed at the ring. "But why is she sending it to me?" Mama slipped the ring on her finger and stretched her hand out to admire it. "I've always loved this ring. It's part of my family's history." Turning back to the box, she looked for a note. Inside the base of the box, folded many times, was a small slip of paper. She smoothed it out until the writing was legible.

"My dear Tania," she read aloud. "Here is the most important piece of jewelry I have ever owned. Important because your father defied his whole family to give it to me and marry me. It has meant so much to me for many years, but now when I look at it, I break down and cry." Mama's voice softened as she continued.

"I cannot see it without wanting him back so badly," she stopped for a moment and wiped at her eyes, "so I have decided to send it to you. Wear it and enjoy it as it is meant to be enjoyed. I am not young and one day soon I, too, will pass on. Wear this ring for your father and for me. We were so lucky he was part of our lives. This ring will remind you how much he loved us and how he loved life itself. Mama."

No one spoke. Mama's shaking hand held the note to her heart. Natasha felt like crying but felt happy, too. As though Gran had given her a gift. The words of the note were more meaningful than the ring itself.

Sonia broke the silence, grunting to get her mother's attention to lift her. When no one paid any attention, she pulled herself up, holding onto the leg of a chair, and took two steps towards her mother. Babushka noticed first. "She's walking! God be praised. She's pulled herself up and she's walking!"

Mama jolted out of her reverie. "I can't believe it! She did it all by herself." Lifting her youngest daughter, she hugged her hard. "Too much has happened. But thank goodness for new life." She nestled her face into Sonia's shoulder, then kissed her cheek.

"Your grandfather loved life," she turned to Elena and Natasha. "He loved to sing, to read, and to smoke his cigars. He was so kind and good to everyone. That's why I loved him so much. But I can't bring him back. I must pass on to you the kind of love he gave me, but I haven't been doing that lately, have I?"

She reached out to her daughters. "This ring is a symbol of our everlasting love. My father and my mother too, will always be in my heart, as I hope I will always be with my girls. Well, I've learned a hard lesson." She hugged them in turn.

A huge weight evaporated from Natasha's heart. Sonia grinned at all the hugging and spread out her arms to try to embrace everyone. Mama laughed and placed her on the floor. “Let’s see you walk again, darling.” Sonia promptly sat on her padded rear and giggled at the faces peering down at her. Babushka beckoned her and, with steely determination, she pulled herself up and this time took four steps toward her grandmother, who scooped her up and held her high in the air.

“I knew you would be fine, even if you have trouble hearing.” She jiggled her granddaughter in her outstretched arms. “You know, you are going to be famous.” She lowered Sonia and hugged her. “I feel it in my bones. I don’t know what you’ll do yet, but somehow I know you will be famous.”

“Will I be famous too?” Elena asked.

“Not everyone can be famous.” Babushka placed Sonia into her high chair. “You, my dear Elena, hmmm, you, I somehow feel, will be rich.”

Elena’s face lit up. “I’d like that.”

“And me?” Natasha asked.

“Hmmm.” Babushka’s index finger poked at her chin. “Fame and riches won’t do it for you.” She stopped and frowned, thinking for a moment. “You are intelligent and feisty,” Babushka paused. Natasha thought of how Gran was both of these things. Maybe she would be a message decoder or spy, like she might have been.

Then Babushka nodded. “I know. You will have an *interesting* life. You will live in all sorts of places around the world, meet many different people and find out about unusual cultures and ways of life.”

Natasha felt as though a lot of pieces suddenly fell into place inside her. *An interesting life*. Maybe she would do something brave like Anne Frank, or sacrifice her life like Sydney Carton in that Dickens book Papa had read her. And definitely she wanted to travel all over the whole world. “Oh yes. That’s exactly what I’d like and I didn’t even know until you said it.”

Chapter 24

Later that evening, Natasha helped Mama bathe Sonia. They dressed the baby in pink flannel pajamas and after kissing her damp, curly hair, Mama lowered her into her crib. Pulling Sonia's stuffed koala bear from her mouth, Mama whispered a Russian lullaby. Sonia struggled up twice, and finally settled down on her pillow.

Natasha leaned into her mother and asked, "Mama, what did Gran do in Shanghai when she and Grandpa eloped? Babushka wants *you* to tell me."

Mama placed the koala bear at the edge of the crib and ran her fingers over Sonia's forehead. "Gran has always been unhappy about what happened, but it wasn't anything illegal or bad that way." Abruptly, she glanced around them. "Where's Happy? That dog follows you everywhere. I love the way he wakes you in the mornings."

"He's in his bed. He's slow today. Hasn't got any appetite. Babushka thinks he ate something from the garbage yesterday."

"Dogs do that, I'm afraid."

"Tell me about Gran, and then I'll go and check on him."

"Yes, Gran." Mama pulled the baby's blanket up to her chin, patting it absent-mindedly. Sonia's large eyes gazed fixedly at her mother. "You know, there are certain things in a family that you don't talk about to outsiders."

"Like Katya and how she became an amah."

"Like that. Gran never speaks about what happened and would be very upset to hear that you were telling her secrets."

"I won't tell. Promise."

Mama flicked her hand. "All right, but never repeat it. Treat this story the way Babushka has."

Natasha nodded solemnly. In the amber glow of the baby's lamp, light outlined Mama's head almost like a halo, but it also edged the frown marks between her eyes. Mama cleared her throat and began.

"It was a very difficult time for your grandparents when they eloped from Armenia to China. They had nothing, only the clothes they wore. So Gran sold everything she could, her white kid gloves, the little jewelry she had worn. She even cut her long hair," Mama reached out and pulled gently on Natasha's fluffy pony tail, "which she sold to a wigmaker. But she wouldn't part with that beautiful ring."

"You can wear it now," said Natasha, "instead of that ring you sold to pay our way to Australia. Remember?"

"Our life is different here. We don't go to dances or balls any more. One day this ring will be yours; then you will pass it on to your oldest daughter."

"I'd like to have girls. Better than boys." Natasha fondled Sonia's foot.

"Boys are wonderful, too. You like the boys next door."

"Yes, but not Aunt Vera's boys, or Aunt Vera."

"Natasha. It is hard raising children alone and making ends meet. Yet, she has sponsored us and has agreed to sponsor my mother. She even let us stay with her. Maybe if she meets a nice man, she will settle down a bit. By the way, Vladimir will come home from school with you tomorrow. Aunt Vera will come for dinner and pick him up then."

"Why?'

"She's working, translating for some people who are applying for a mortgage. It gives her extra money, and, goodness knows, we could all use that."

"And Peter?"

"He's going to Mrs. Vadim's place."

Natasha nodded. "He likes her cooking. Vladimir likes Happy."

"So let him play with Happy. And please note how Aunt Vera's helping people."

"Okay. Tell me about Gran."

Mama straightened and arched her back. "So, where were we? Grandpa opened a store. With the money from the sale of his pocket watch plus what Gran had sold, he bought leather. He made shoes, but until someone bought them, they still had no income. When they had eloped like that, they could hardly ask his parents for help."

"What about Gran's parents?"

"Gran was an orphan. That's why she had taken the job in Grandpa's parents' store." Mama smiled at Natasha, her eyes glowing in a way they hadn't since her father had died. "Although she wasn't well educated, she was independent and supported herself. In China, though, most people had live-in help. Gran couldn't speak Chinese and there were no openings in the few shops for Westerners. So there were not many ways for her to earn money."

Sonia's eyes had closed, her outstretched hand still clutching her koala. Mama smiled down at her, and then continued softly, "Well, Gran heard of a job working for a group of European artists. They needed a model to pose for them so they could paint her." She glanced at Natasha but quickly averted her eyes. "The problem was they needed to paint her without any clothes."

No clothes! Natasha felt as though a hot stick had been thrust down her spine. Her own grandmother. In front of other people. *Maybe men*! She heard herself take in a loud breath. No wonder Babushka would not tell her.

Mama continued. "Nudes, these kinds of paintings are called. And that is what Gran did for a few months until Grandpa's business began to make money." Mama's fingers toyed with Sonia's blanket.

In Natasha's mind, an image of Gran's face became superimposed on the body of a nude in a painting she had seen in an art gallery. The flesh glowed smooth and pink and the breasts and pubic hair drew her eyes like magnets.

Mama continued speaking, "There really is nothing wrong in what she did, but still, she never speaks of it."

Natasha blinked to banish the image of the nude. "I can understand that. I wouldn't like to do anything like that either. What did Grandpa say?"

She wondered if she, herself, could ever do anything so outrageous. Could she be brave enough to go against what people, especially her parents, would want? Well, she'd cut her hair, but that hadn't turned out all that wonderful. Poor Gran! How embarrassing for her. But if it were the only way to keep from starving, what would anyone do?

"I believe she told Grandpa only that she was posing for artists. He found out the rest after she had stopped working. Of course, he was upset. Anyway, soon his shoe business became successful and Gran helped him out in the store. And then she was expecting me."

Even though Natasha felt a surge of sympathy for Gran, she remembered how this grandmother made her feel inadequate, somehow. As if she was not quite smart enough, not quite pretty enough.

"Gran's not as easy to be with as Babushka. She expects you to do things quickly…and her way all the time."

"You've lived with Babushka since you were born. She accepts you totally as you are. Gran loves you, too, but she wants you to be the best you can be. That's harder to live up to, but you might be grateful to her later. Look, Sonia's asleep. I have to speak to her doctor tomorrow. He's contacting the John Tracy Clinic in America. They say a deaf child can learn to talk, lip read, can even get a university education."

"Great. Papa will be pleased."

"All depends on the right education for the child. You will have to help."

Natasha smiled. "I'd love to help Sonia."

"I know you would. But it's not just a one-time thing. It's again and again and again." Mama gave her youngest daughter's cheek a soft caress. "It will be a long time until we know what she will be able to do." She switched off the lamp. "Shh," she warned as they tiptoed out of the room.

"We don't need to be quiet," Natasha said, "she can't—" Her voice faltered. Mama closed her eyes briefly and nodded as Natasha left to check on Happy.

When she entered the tiny storage room, Happy woke and slowly opened his eyes. She crouched beside his bed, smoothing a hand along his soft white fur, and although he lifted his tail in a quick salute, he kept his head down. After a moment, his eyelids closed and he shivered as though he had a chill. Natasha gazed at him fondly as she caressed his bony head with its worried frown.

I hope he gets over whatever he ate, she thought, as Happy gave a short cough. *Or maybe he just caught a cold.*

* * *

When Natasha awoke, she sat up quickly. Happy had not come in to wake her. She jumped up and ran to his room. Silence greeted her and she looked down in fright. Happy lay in exactly the same position as she had left him the previous evening. One touch of her hand showed the heat of his body, and his nose was not cold and wet as it should have been. As she ran from his room, he gave a sharp cough.

"Mama," she pounded on the door to her parents' bedroom. "Mama, Happy is sick!"

"Come in, dear." Mama was leaning towards the mirror of her dressing table, applying lipstick. Next, she dipped two fingers into her pot of rouge, rubbed it onto the heel of her hands and smoothed it onto her cheeks.

Usually, Natasha loved watching her mother apply her makeup, but today she didn't even notice. "Mama, he's so sick!"

"I can't do anything now," Mama leaned back to get a better look at her reflection, then pressed her lips together, "but we'll see how he is tonight. I'm sure it won't last long, whatever he's come down with." Quickly she gave her cheeks a final rub then glanced around the room. "Where are my keys?" She hurried into the dining room. "I really can't be late today."

Natasha trailed after her mother. "Do you know a vet we can take him to?"

"We'll talk about it tonight. Be nice to Vladimir when he comes home with you," Mama hurried out of the door. "Puppies often get sick," she called back. "Don't worry."

Natasha stood still, feeling abandoned, gazing after her mother as she turned down the driveway. Hurrying back to the dog, she called to Babushka. The two leaned over him and watched his heavy breathing.

"He's worse today," Natasha said. "I'm so worried about him."

"He must have caught a cold or something. I thought it was something he had eaten, but he would be over that by now and yesterday he didn't eat a thing." The lines around Babushka's mouth set more deeply than usual. Gently she stroked his ear. "Poor Happy. But puppies often get sick for a day or two and then they get better. He will probably be over it by the time you get home from school."

Natasha felt a flutter of anxiety in her stomach. "Can we take him to a vet? Do you know one?"

"Let's give him a little time. You need to start getting dressed or you'll be late."

"I'll see if anyone at school knows a vet or maybe the Flannerys do. If he's not better when I get home, then we definitely better do something."

At school Natasha found her mind constantly returning to Happy. When she told Jan and Gina about the dog's illness, she found herself fighting back tears. The long day finally came to an end and she raced home, Vladimir tagging along after her.

By then, Happy's condition had worsened. Babushka said he still had not eaten and had shivered as though he had chills several times during the day. Natasha dropped to her knees beside him and ran her fingers down his back. "Poor baby. Dear little Happy."

Vladimir followed her into the store room and kneeled down beside her. "He looks awful. His eyes are so red. What'd you do to him?"

Natasha threw him a scornful look. "What do you mean? I've been worried sick about him all day."

"If I had a dog, he wouldn't get sick like this. I'd do *everything* to look after him."

Babushka spoke up. "Natasha looks after her dog as well as anyone possibly could."

Elena arrived at the storage room and, seeing Vladimir, stopped at the door.

"Stop it, Vladimir." Natasha hissed so softly that he had to lean forward to hear. "I can't put up with any of your nonsense today." She decided, from now on, to ignore him and maybe he'd go outside and leave her alone with her dog. Wrapping her arms around herself, she said to Babushka, "Look, he's shivering again. Do you think he's cold?"

"It's quite warm in here. No, it's part of whatever's wrong with him. I'll get some fresh water and maybe you can feed it to him with a spoon," Babushka suggested.

"Is he going to be all right?" Elena asked.

"I hope so," Natasha whispered.

They all waited quietly with the dog. Vladimir didn't seem to want to leave. Instead, he gently stroked the dog's fur. "I'll help," he said.

At first, Natasha couldn't believe he'd said it. He seemed to like the dog better than he liked any person she'd ever seen him with, but she continued to ignore him. For the first time, when he looked at her, his shiny button eyes did not mock her. They were so close to each other in the small box room that his "boy" smell, wet grass mixed with perspiration, overpowered the usual musty odor of the room.

When Babushka returned with fresh water in a bowl, Natasha said, "At school I found out the names of two vets." With a spoon filled with water in one hand, she tried to force open Happy's jaw with the other. "Come on. Take a little of this. It will help you." A trickle of water ran down Happy's chin and he buried his muzzle into his blanket.

"Ohhh! What are we going to do?" A jumble of feelings, frustration, love, helplessness, raced through her. "Happy needs a vet. There's one not too far away. We could walk and carry him or take the bus. I'm sure the bus driver would let him on if he's not going to run around."

Babushka rubbed her forehead. "You'll have to ask Mama when she gets home. She'll be early today."

"But what can we do *now*?" Natasha felt so powerless. She looked to Babushka for reassurance, but her grandmother's mouth creased downward. She was worried, too.

"I have to check on Sonia. Come with me, Elena," Babushka said as she left.

Natasha sat on the floor and after a few minutes, reached for her school books and began her homework. Vladimir sprawled beside the dog's bed, stroking Happy's fur and murmuring to him. She listened to the dog's breathing as she worked, starting up when she couldn't hear it and worrying when it seemed too shallow. She knew they had to get him to a vet. Mama would have to agree. A vet would know how to cure him.

Finally, Mama returned home and came immediately to see the dog. "How is he?" she asked. "Oh, Vladimir, how are you?"

"Happy's so sick, Mama. See how red his eyes are? We have to take him to a vet."

Vladimir supported her. "He really is sick. I've watched him all afternoon."

Mama pulled her arms out of her cardigan and crouched down beside the dog. "He's not too bad. He'll probably get over this all by himself. Natasha, you are getting far too upset by this."

"No, I'm not. Oh, please, Mama. We *have* to do something!" Her throat felt as though it was clogged and it was getting harder and harder to breathe.

Mama sighed as her fingers trailed along Happy's spine. "Let's give him one more night. I'm sure he'll be better by the morning."

Natasha's voice bulged with tears. "Mama, I have the names of two vets. One isn't too far away. A vet would know what to do, what medicine he should have."

"Darling, vets' fees are so high. I talked to Sonia's doctor today. Her special schooling is going to be expensive." A pink flush spread from her neck to her cheeks, so that her face looked splotchy, like Sonia's when she had been crying a long while. "We want the very best doctors and teachers for her and they all charge so much. We must be so careful with our money right now." She swiveled her gaze away from her daughter. "I am sure Happy will get over this by himself in no time at all."

The words dropped like heavy balls into Natasha's heart. They grew and grew until they filled her chest. When she spoke her voice escaped as a whisper. "He doesn't look like he's going to get over it. Babushka said he'd be better when I got home from school, and look, he's worse."

Mama's nostrils dilated as she took a deep breath. "One more night and then we'll see." Her knees creaked as she rose to her feet. "Darling, I've had such a long day. Let me go and change. And where are Elena and Sonia?"

Chapter 25

Natasha, her gaze still locked on her puppy, remained quiet and still after her mother left the room. Vladimir watched her silently, and for once she was almost glad of his company. Notebooks were scattered on the floor, one page caught under the dog's water bowl. She felt that she could not move, could not get up and return to the rest of her life. Happy moaned softly and her eyes welled up in response.

Somehow, she had to help him. He depended on her and she was letting him down. She had to be brave. For Happy. She had to do whatever was necessary, just like Gran had to when she posed for the artists.

It all boiled down to money. Money was terribly important when there wasn't enough. In Shanghai they had plenty and so it wasn't important at all. Well, she had a little money, not much, but some. Maybe she could go out to sell some eggs. Maybe Babushka would let her have all the money this time, when she knew what it was for.

Rising slowly, she patted Happy and made her way to the kitchen. Vladimir followed close behind. Babushka was chopping carrots for dinner when Natasha opened the refrigerator and counted the eggs. There were only eight.

Babushka glanced at her. "What are you doing?"

"I want to sell some eggs."

"There aren't many there. Why do that right now? It's for the dog, isn't it?"

"I need some money." Natasha strained to keep her intentions inside, but it all became too much and she blurted out, "I have to take Happy to the vet. Somehow!" Despair resonated in her voice. "I have to!"

"What did Mama say?"

"I just can't keep waiting to see how he is later and later! We should have taken him this morning. It's always money. I have to take him *now,* no matter what Mama says. He's *my* dog. Do you understand?"

Babushka nodded sadly.

"Can I have some of the egg money, please?"

Babushka's watery grey-blue eyes stared at her for a moment. She blinked and said, "I'm sorry, but I gave all the money to Papa for Sonia."

"I thought he didn't know about the eggs."

"I had to tell him. How could I keep it when the baby needs it?"

"Can I get it back? I need it for Happy."

"Natasha, Sonia's needs are too important. Happy is just a dog and dogs usually recover all on their own."

Anger rushed through Natasha. How would Babushka or Mama like it if they were sick, and no one would take them to a doctor? Mama had looked almost guilty when she had left the storage room to change her clothes. Right now everything was being done for Sonia while poor Happy was left to…to die!

There! It was no use pretending anything else. So she *had* to help him. Happy always listened to her, always understood her problems, not like Sonia, who cried if she wasn't getting enough attention and took all of Mama's free time. Happy was so sick, and Sonia was sound asleep in her room. She was healthy even if she couldn't hear. She wasn't dying like Happy might be.

At this thought, Natasha felt huge waves of guilt. She didn't want anything bad to happen to Sonia. She loved her little sister desperately, but she loved Happy, too! "I have to get some money. I just have to."

"How much does a vet charge?" Vladimir asked.

"I don't know. I'll get as much as I can and hope it's enough. If it's not, maybe the vet will let me work for him cleaning up or something to pay off the rest."

Vladimir reached into his pocket. "I have some money."

"How much? Maybe we'll have enough." Oh please, let it be enough!

He pulled out two crumpled notes. "Two pounds. One is mine and Mum gave me the other one for emergencies. I have to give it back to her when we go home. You can have mine, but not the emergency money."

"I'll probably need it all," Natasha said. It was one thing to take Vladimir's money, but Aunt Vera's? She would do anything not to be in debt to her. But today she had no choice. Somehow she would repay it. Perhaps she could sell the braids of hair she had saved. Like Gran had sold hers. Right now, though, she had to borrow it. "Together with my money this should be enough. I'll pay your mother back as soon as I can." She snatched the notes from his hand and ran to her room, rummaging in a drawer for her purse.

Elena sprawled on the floor coloring in a picture book. "What are you doing?"

"Nothing, "Natasha murmured, stashing her own money into her pocket together with Vladimir's.

Elena pointed the crayon at Natasha. "I'll tell on you if you don't tell me what you are doing."

"I don't have time right now. I promise I'll tell you later. It's really important."

Quickly, Natasha ran back to her dog, squatting down beside him. "We're going out, Hap," she said, gathering his leash. "I'll put this on just in case. Don't worry. I'll look after you."

Babushka came back to the storage room. "Are you leaving now?"

Vladimir grabbed for his jacket. "I'll come with you."

Natasha turned to him. “No, you can’t come. It’s bad enough that I’m going. Worse that I’ve taken your money. If you come, I ‘d be in loads more trouble.”

“It’s my money you’re using, so I can come if I want to.”

“Don’t, Vladimir, please.”

Babushka gripped his jacket. “You stay here. Your mother’s due to arrive at any moment. Natasha, what about dinner?”

Vladimir stamped his foot. “It’s not fair. How come she can go and I can’t. I’ve helped with the dog all afternoon and it’s my money that’s going to pay for the vet.”

Babushka took hold of Vladimir’s arm. “Yes, you’ve helped with the dog and we thank you for the money. Now, if you want to help Happy get to the vet, you’ll let Natasha go. Much more noise and Mama will come out to see what’s going on.”

“Give me back my money.”

Natasha stared at him. “Do you mean it, Vladimir?”

“It’s your mother’s fault if he doesn’t get to a vet, not mine.” He began to say something else but a soft whine from Happy interrupted him. “All right. You can have it for Happy,” he switched from Russian to English, “if you do my homework for a week.” Speaking Russian again, he added, “But I’m going to tell my mother you wouldn’t let me go with you. She knows you’re spoilt and always get your way.”

“I’ll do your homework,” she agreed.

Babushka flicked the jacket she still held. “Go ahead. You tell your mother.” Vladimir stalked out of the room. “Natasha, you’d better hurry, but what on earth am I going to tell Mama?”

“The truth, I suppose.” Natasha’s eyes met her grandmother’s.

“I’ll put off serving dinner as long as I can.”

Natasha bundled Happy into her arms, the blanket falling open around him. Leaning over, Babushka tucked the blanket in and muttered a quick prayer. "And may God protect you both," she ended. "But will the vet be open?"

"Has to be. The kids said animals stay there while their owners go away, so someone has to be there." The dog did not feel too heavy, not yet, but she knew her arms would be very tired before she reached Blackheath Road. Happy hardly struggled at all as she jostled him into a more comfortable carrying position.

"Cross the roads carefully," Babushka warned.

Natasha nodded as she hurried out into the gloom of evening. William Street was quiet and still, but as she turned the corner into King George's Road, several cars and buses thundered past, full of workers returning home. Already the dog's weight dragged his body down in her arms. Her feet kept to the unpaved path, as she strode as quickly as she could towards the vet.

Headlights swept rhythmically over her as the traffic flowed past, lighting up Happy's face and outlining the shapes of the homes fronting the road. Inside one house another dog barked frantically as Natasha passed, and Happy's body twitched in response. Gradually his weight grew more and more heavy. She battled onwards, willing her feet to continue and her grip not to loosen, until she felt her arms aching and straining more than she could bear. "I have to stop a minute," she whispered, crouching and gently placing the dog on the ground. "We'll rest, just for a second."

Happy let out a whimper as his body made contact with the hard rocky surface of the path. Natasha let her arms dangle by her sides to restore the blood circulation. Mentally she pleaded with God to please let her get Happy to the vet and let him fix whatever was wrong. She would be good forever, if God would just let this all be over and the two of them back at home and healthy. She'd do anything God wanted. Anything! Finally, she felt strength returning to her arms and knew she had to move quickly to get to the vet before he closed.

"Okay, Happy. We're on our way again." She lifted him and, balancing on one foot, braced him with the other knee. Carefully, she adjusted him to a stable position. Happy settled against her when a violent shiver ran through him and he coughed deeply.

Oh dear, oh dear, Natasha thought. *Maybe it's only a cold. Maybe that is all it is.*

On she went, stumbling over stones, once stepping on and crunching some large insect. Occasionally Happy slipped a little in her grasp and she needed to hitch him up again. Finally, after crossing two more streets, the sign to Blackheath Road came into view. "There it is, Hap. Not long now."

When she turned the corner, she saw a rectangular sign protruding from a house three doors away. In the gloom the letters became visible. 'A. Silverside, Veterinarian.' But the front of the house was totally dark. "Oh no," she murmured. "We have to see him. We've come so far."

To unlatch the gate from the street, she placed the dog on the ground, and then, holding the gate open with her body, she picked him up and ventured up the porch steps to the front door. With one finger, she pressed the bell. She pressed it a second time, just to be sure the vet would hear.

A woman's voice rang out, "We're closed. Sorry. Come back tomorrow, after ten."

Natasha's heart sank. This could not be happening. No. She would not return home like this. She squeezed her finger hard into the button. They had to help her. Despair filled her and escaped in a heartbreaking cry. "Please," her voice shattered the evening quiet of the street. Happy struggled in her arms and she caught him before he slipped from her grasp.

Footsteps sounded inside the house making for the front door. Heavy, loud footsteps. This time a man's voice said, "Could you please allow us to have our dinner?"

"Please," Natasha repeated. "I've carried my dog all the way from William Street. Can you please help him?"

Chapter 26

Lights blazed on inside the house and the door locks rattled vigorously. The large body of the man who opened the door crowded out much of the opening, the glare behind him keeping his face in shadow. Farther inside, a parrot squawked noisily.

Natasha choked on a sob. "I'm sorry about your dinner, sir, but my dog…my dog's so sick." She swallowed hard. "Please help him. I've got money. I can pay."

The man bent down and took Happy from her, leaving her arms suddenly empty and slightly cool. "My goodness, he's just a pup." The vet stood aside to let her into the hall. "Come on and let's have a look."

The front door banged shut as she followed him through an eerily still waiting room lined with wooden chairs and a fish tank beside the receptionist's desk. In the next room, which was the surgery, the vet switched on bright lights and set Happy down gently on the large examining table in the center. Three stools stood haphazardly around the table.

The low ceiling and antiseptic smell pressed in on Natasha. In one corner a white terrier scratched and whined sadly in a metal crate. In the opposite corner stood a huge birdcage draped with a brown scarf. Somewhere in the house, dishes rattled and voices rose and fell in conversation.

"What's his name?" A wisp of dark hair fell onto the vet's forehead as his fingers stroked the side of the dog's head. Happy's body slackened and with a deep breath his body relaxed.

"His name's Happy and I'm Natasha Kiranovsky. I live on William Street."

"How do you do? And I'm Alan Silverside. So you carried him all the way here? Hmm. How old is the pup?"

"Seven months."

"He's big for seven months. You must feed him well." Happy quivered and gave a dry cough as the vet ran an expert hand over his body.

"He loves soup bones. They're his favorite. But do you think he'll be okay?"

"How long has he been sick?"

While the vet unbuttoned the cuffs of his blue flannel shirt and rolled up the sleeves, Natasha related the events of Happy's last few days. "His nose isn't wet like it should be and he has this cough, too. My mother thinks he'll get over it by himself, but I'm too worried." The frown on the vet's face worried her even more.

"Has he had his immunizations?"

"Immunizations? For dogs?" Natasha had only ever heard of children receiving immunizations.

The vet picked up an instrument. "This is an ophthalmoscope. It helps me look into his eyes. It won't hurt him." Carefully he lifted Happy's head, opened one of his red-rimmed eyes and began his examination. Happy wriggled his head and whined pitifully.

Putting the instrument down, the vet said, "We give puppies immunizations to prevent diseases."

"What diseases?"

"Puppy diseases. Distemper, for instance."

"Does he have it?"

"I hope not, but I wish you'd brought him in as soon as he—" The front door buzzer shrilled. "Now, who can that be?" Gently he set Happy's head back down and set off through the waiting room.

Natasha stroked Happy's soft coat as she waited. The palpitations of his heart rose and fell quickly against her hand. When the vet opened the front door, Natasha started at the sound of her mother's voice. She tensed, straining to hear her mother explaining who she was. In only a moment the vet returned with Mama behind him. Natasha's anxious glance met her mother's.

Mama spoke sharply. "I was so worried about you. You should have told me what you were up to." The bright light illuminated the top of her head, leaving deep shadows under her eyes and a look of bitterness to her mouth.

Natasha took a half step backward. "I didn't know if you would let me come."

Mama clutched at her gray cardigan. "I probably would not have." Glancing down at the dog, she asked, "How is he?"

Tears sprang to Natasha's eyes and she shook her head.

Dr. Silverside bent over the dog again. His prodding brought another whine from Happy. The sound brought all of Natasha's attention back to her dog. She wanted to pour her own strength and energy into him. Even her own life. Anything to make him better.

The vet spoke to Mama. "Your daughter tells me the dog has not had any immunizations."

"Immunizations? Whatever for?"

"Distemper, for instance."

"No, I've never heard of such a thing."

"Maybe Jack took care of it?" Natasha suggested.

"We bought the dog from a man named Jack," Mama explained. "But he didn't mention anything about immunizations. Does Happy need these?"

"I'm afraid so." The vet glanced at the mother and daughter and back at the dog. In a soft voice, he added, "Distemper could be the problem."

Natasha's heart clenched. Already she could tell it was a very serious disease. She felt herself trembling as her mother's arm encircled her.

Dr. Silverside rubbed his thumb against his forehead. "He's obviously well fed and strong. Leave him with me tonight and phone me in the morning. Early is okay."

Natasha staggered back onto a stool just as Happy opened his eyes and sought her. A deep gnawing pain spread through her stomach. She couldn't meet Happy's gaze. It hurt too much.

Mama spoke softly. "He knows how much you love him, Natasha."

The vet placed a hand on her shoulder. "I promise I'll do everything possible. I'll look after him as well as you do."

"We have to go home now, dear," Mama said.

"Soup bones," Natasha whispered as she stood to go. "Remember he loves soup bones."

* * *

The night was cool but not cold. Blue-black velvet, the sky seemed far away, distant and totally uncaring. Even the Southern Cross, clear and brittle bright, seemed to turn away from her. For several minutes Natasha and her mother strode along in a silence that was heavy with recrimination. They turned into King George's Road and cars and buses jostled past them.

Letting out a deep breath, Mama said, "You shouldn't have gone out like that without asking me."

Natasha whirled around to face her. "Why didn't Happy get any immunizations?" She wanted to hit out at her mother, bash hard at her with both fists, to make her as unhappy as she felt herself. This was Mama's fault. No immunization and waiting so long to see a vet.

"I didn't know he needed any." They stood facing each other as headlights glared into the night around them, lighting them up momentarily and then plunging them back into darkness. "We never did anything like that in Shanghai. Dogs were just dogs. Sometimes they got sick and then they got better."

Natasha kicked at a stone. "Did they *always* get better?" Her voice sounded like it belonged to an embittered old woman.

"Well, sometimes I suppose they did not."

"What if something happens to Happy?" There was a catch in her throat now. "What if he doesn't get better?" She couldn't say the word "die" out loud.

Mama clasped both her wrists firmly, her fingernails making small indentations in the heels of her daughter's hands. "He'll probably get over this. He's young and strong. And Natasha, you know it wasn't because we didn't want Happy to get better. Our family has lots of worries right now, Sonia's deafness, bringing Gran out to Australia. Our money can only go so far."

"Money! I hate money!" She yanked her hands away. "It's all you think about these days. Just money and Sonia!" As soon as she said these words, guilt made her glance into Mama's face. Tears glistened in her mother's eyes. Her lips parted but no sound came out.

Natasha stammered, "Well, that's what it seems like to me."

"You know I love you. You're older and can take care of yourself."

"I still need a mother."

Mama's lip quivered. "You've always seemed so capable. Sometimes, I forget you are still so young."

Natasha didn't want to be thought of as "so young". Although still angry, she couldn't help but respond to the way her mother looked, so dejected, so sad. Deep down, she understood the reasons for her mother's behavior. There were too many things she had to take care of.

Mama pulled her close. A horn sounded near them as one car overtook another. Mama was breathing deeply. "Dr. Silverside seems to be a good vet. I'll pray that Happy will be all right."

An image of Happy alone and ill at the vet's settled into Natasha's heart. She yearned with all her might, with all her being, he would recover and return to live with her. In the evening darkness she felt the warm dampness of her mother's lips on her forehead. "Let's get home. Everything that can possibly help Happy will be done."

They resumed walking, but now their arms encircled each other. Natasha had done what she could for Happy, and in her heart she could no longer blame her mother.

She understood now why her mother had been so distant after Grandpa's death. A hole erupts in your soul, in the same way that death blasts a hole in your life. But the hole hurts. It hurts so badly that you cannot speak. And the awful thing is that you cannot *do* anything to make it better, for the person or pet who is sick or died, or for yourself. You are so helpless.

Natasha's thoughts returned to the problem of payment. "Dr. Silverside didn't say how much it is going to cost."

"Babushka told me about the egg money you saved and the money you borrowed from Vladimir."

"Some of the money is Aunt Vera's. It's still in my pocket."

"Give it to me and I'll return it. Somehow, we'll pay ourselves."

Years ago in Shanghai, Natasha was amazed that Papa always had money, always had a few *yuan* for an ice cream cone or a lollipop. Now, she knew that even in Shanghai, a few *yuan* were not enough. "I wish I could earn more money, so I wouldn't have to ask you for it."

"Your job right now is to do well at school. You know how important Papa and I think education is."

Natasha nodded. "I know. But right at this minute, all I can think of is Happy."

* * *

Warm heated air engulfed Natasha as she and Mama entered the house. The overhead light blazed and the smells of cooking and food threatened to overpower her. Papa rose from the table and came towards them. "How is the dog?"

Aunt Vera and Vladimir, sitting with half-eaten dinners, remained silent and for once were not the center of everyone's attention. The blue-black of Aunt Vera's hair stuck out coarsely on her head and the pink puffiness of the flesh under her eyes made her look like a piglet to Natasha. Her aunt and Vladimir stared at Mama as she related what the vet had said.

Babushka, her face glowing in the harsh light, listened attentively while she served up the stuffed cabbage leaves she had kept warm for them. When Mama finished speaking, Babushka reminded her that Sonia and Elena were ready for bed and waiting for their goodnight kiss.

Natasha picked at her food. She kept her eyes on the starched white tablecloth that glowed bright and clean. Vladimir kept glancing at her and even his mother seemed to be concerned for her. However, Aunt Vera's appetite had not left her and she was obviously enjoying Babushka's cooking.

"I didn't think to tell you about the immunizations," she said, still chewing. "Everybody here knows about them. You should have…never mind." For a moment she seemed about to say more, then stopped and swallowed, a look of concern crossing her face. With her head tilted sideways at Natasha, she murmured, "Poor old Natasha."

Although Natasha was grateful that her aunt did not criticize her or her parents, she still did not want her sympathy. She wanted her and Vladimir to just go home. "Mama has the money to pay you back," she began, but her aunt interrupted.

"Hush, now. There's no problem there."

"It's my money, too, don't forget." Vladimir's pointed nose and small teeth reminded Natasha of a fox. Aunt Vera shushed him, too. He poked his knife into a bread roll. "Will Happy get better" He held the roll up as though he had just killed an enemy.

Natasha shrugged. "Don't know."

"Put that knife down. You know better than to play with your food. I've told you often enough what good manners are at the table." Aunt Vera's voice droned on in Natasha's ears. The same familiar phrases, the same battle between mother and son. How could it all go on the same when Happy was so sick and could be dying?

The warmth of the room crowded in on her. While the talk continued, Natasha just wanted to get away to her room where she could cry if she wanted. As soon as she could, she asked to be excused and cleaned up in the bathroom for bed. Babushka beckoned her as she was entering her bedroom. "Come with me, Natasha."

Reluctantly she followed her grandmother to her room.

"I heard what the vet said." Babushka sat down on her bed and motioned for Natasha to sit beside her. "I will pray for Happy, but maybe things will not work out for him." Natasha leaned into Babushka and hid her face. Babushka's soft hand stroked her hair. "You need to be prepared in case he doesn't make it." A flame flickered in the corner, glowing red in the lampada under Babushka's golden icon.

"I couldn't stand it if…if…" The house was so empty without him. Tears filled her eyes and spilled onto her cheek. She swiped at them with the back of her hand and then stared hard at the photo of her missing uncle on Babushka's dressing table.

"When I was a little girl," Babushka began, "we used to believe animals had a wonderful heaven where they could speak and live the way people do on earth, and nothing could harm them." Her fat fingers squeezed Natasha's hand.

"Now, there comes a time in every family's life when there has to be a death. Death is just sitting and thinking about which member of the family he will choose. We used to say animals could feel this in a way that humans couldn't." Natasha rubbed her head against Babushka's arm. "You know, Sonia is having all sorts of tests and things. What if something more should go wrong for her? Just think how terrible that would be."

Natasha prodded the leg of the dressing table with her toe. When the image of her little sister's determined face came to her, she shuddered at the thought of something else going wrong for her. It would be so unfair.

Babushka continued, "Well, Happy has decided himself, if something else has to go wrong in our family, it should be him. He's getting ready to protect the rest of us."

Natasha frowned. "That can't be true." She rubbed the sleeve of her pink chenille robe against her eyes as the tears threatened again.

"Who knows? I used to think it was. Animals can really sense some things before people can. And I believe in a Heaven for us, so why not for dogs?" Babushka smoothed down the eiderdown they were sitting on. Thick knotted veins crawled up her wrists and disappeared into her sleeves.

"Just think. On earth a dog's life is very limited. They can't speak, can only eat what we give them, don't have such nice soft beds like this to sleep on. Wouldn't Happy love a heaven full of beef smells? There'd be huge bones to chew, so huge he could never get through them. Large fields where he could run and run, and never be penned up in a yard again. There'd be cats and birds especially for him to chase, and maybe he could do other things, things he sees you do but he can't. Something to think about, isn't it?"

Natasha nodded and chewed on her lower lip. It probably was not true. But maybe…who was to say? She thought about how Happy acted around her. "Happy would like to read. He likes stories." It would be great if there was a Heaven for dogs.

"There you go. Now, you need to get to sleep." Babushka rose and adjusted her apron. "I know it won't be easy to sleep, but you won't help Happy if you cry all night." With a kiss, she let Natasha return to her bedroom.

A large moon cast a bright glow against the curtains of her room. The shadows of the furniture loomed huge in the semi-darkness. She climbed into bed quietly so as not to wake her sisters. As she lay in bed, she listened to Aunt Vera and Vladimir leave, then Mama and Papa getting ready for bed. Happy's face kept appearing no matter how she tried to settle down. All the feelings of guilt she had managed to put to rest on her walk home with Mama, now resurfaced. She had let Happy down by not getting him immunized. She hadn't known, just as Mama hadn't known. Maybe Jack should have told them. But again she realized, there was no one to blame. Maybe just God.

What would Babushka say if she told her she blamed God? Maybe there was no God, like that man from Russia said. Things just happened and that was that. But Babushka would say that God cared and was watching out for her. It was certainly a nicer feeling, but why would God let Happy get sick? She would ask Mama.

Sonia stirred in her sleep and gave a whimpered snore, then settled down again. It would be terrible if anything were to happen to Sonia. She already had to deal with being deaf and that was nobody's fault, too. Poor Happy was suffering and maybe he would…maybe he would die. She forced herself to say the word out loud in the darkness. "Die." It echoed back to her in the stillness of the house.

Finally, exhausted, she searched for a handkerchief and blew her nose. She had to admit that there was nothing, absolutely nothing more she could do for him. Wouldn't it be great if there was a dog heaven? Could Happy have really known about death waiting to strike someone in her family? What if death was after her? Would she still want Happy's life to save her own? Probably none of it was true, anyway. She'd think about it all tomorrow, in the daylight. Everything always seemed worse at night.

When Natasha finally fell asleep, she slipped into a dream. Healthy again, Happy quivered with joy at her touch, nudging her cheek with his cold wet nose. Happiness welled inside her. Her puppy was fine. Laughing, she cradled his wriggling body in her arms as she had so often, ecstatic to find that it had all been a terrible mistake.

But the smell of the veterinary surgery seeped into her dreams, and then an army of masked doctors advanced towards her and her dog. She writhed and thrashed, trying to escape, tangling herself in sheets and blanket. Sweat covered her as she woke and the image of Happy on the vet's examining table, unable to pull his body up, brought back what had really happened.

Natasha checked her watch. Three o'clock. She had a long wait until the morning.

Chapter 27

The gray light of a cloudy day spread along the curtains of Natasha's bedroom. The long night had finally crept to an end. Another year seemed to drag by until she heard the creak of her parents' bed and then Papa's slippers shuffle into the hall. With an eye on her sisters, she dressed quickly, a knot in her stomach reminding her constantly of Happy.

When she entered the dining room, Papa patted her shoulder and smiled. "He'll be all right," he said. But his smile did not reach his eyes and his jaw clenched. Natasha's anxiety increased. She thought of how Happy *should* have wakened her and how he should now be under the table, nudging her foot with his snout. Today her porridge was too lumpy to fit down her throat, but Babushka insisted it was the same as every morning. Natasha's spoon toyed with her food while she watched the steam rising from her plate.

After Papa left for work, Natasha heard Mama getting ready for the day. She knocked and entered her bedroom just as Mama was checking the seams of her stockings.

"Natasha, dear," Mama twisted around to check the second leg. "I know you want to phone right away, but we have to give the vet a chance to check on Happy."

"He said early." Natasha threw herself on her parents' bed and muffled her head in a pillow. "I've been up so long already."

Mama bent over to adjust the top of her stocking in its suspender. "We'll phone him the last thing before I leave, okay?" She stood upright and straightened her skirt. "Let me get my coffee first."

Natasha trailed her mother to the dining room. At the table, her eyes focused on her mother's moves, watching how she nibbled her toast as she scanned the newspaper's headlines, how her lips left red marks on the rim of her cup, and how the coffee cup hung suspended in the air when an item in the paper caught her attention. Natasha wanted to scream, to rush her along so they could phone. Mama tended to Elena's note for her teacher and to Sonia's cry for more milk, while Babushka packed their lunches.

Finally, on the way to the front door, with her handbag already on her arm, Mama stopped in the entrance hall and picked up the phone. Suddenly, Natasha felt rigid with anxiety. She wrapped her arms around herself as she scrutinized her mother's face for clues to what the vet was saying.

"No change." Mama repeated the words for Natasha to hear. "We will check with you again this afternoon. Thank you." The phone clicked as Mama hung up.

Natasha gave a soft sigh. Happy might not be better, but at least he was not worse.

Mama kissed each daughter and turned to leave. "We'll see how he is this evening. I'll come home early again. Are you ready for school?'

* * *

"Poor Happy!" Jan extended an arm around Natasha's shoulder in the playground at recess. "I wish I could do something to make him better." Jan smelled of soap and shampoo, such a vibrant, alive smell. Natasha wanted to rest her head on her friend's square shoulders and never have to face the world again. Gina walked beside them, frowning and patting Natasha's arm. Her friends formed a protective shield around her, keeping away anyone who came too close.

The three sat down on their favorite bench. The morning had dragged on and on, the lessons occurring at a distance from her as though her mind was encased in cotton wool. Nothing seemed real, only the knot deep in her stomach, and Happy.

Natasha sniffed. "There's nothing any of us can do. The vet doesn't know if he'll get over it. It's a terrible disease."

"He's a good vet, you know," Jan said. "Brian, my cousin, took his cat to him when no one else could help poor Tabby. Dr. Silverstone cured her." She unwrapped her snack. "Have my chocolate cake. You'll feel better."

Natasha shook her head and smiled. "Thanks, but I don't feel like eating." Jan loved chocolate cake more than anyone she had ever met.

Seeing Lorraine saunter towards them, Jan muttered, "She's lower than a snake, that one. What does she want, now?"

Natasha straightened up to face her.

Lorraine tossed her hair to one side. "What's wrong with you? Looks like you've lost your best friend, or something."

"What do you mean?" Natasha stood up, but Gina raced forward, took Lorraine's arm and led her away, making gagging noises to suggest her friend was not well. Natasha smiled, but then remembered poor Happy and her throat constricted.

Jan stared after Lorraine. "She's never recovered from you telling her off that time. No one else has ever done that. I hate to admit it, but I'm still not game to try to be on one of her teams."

Natasha's eyebrows rose. "You mean when I told her that she didn't know how to be a true friend?"

"You only said what was true. *You've* been a true friend to me, and to Gina, too."

Natasha gave her a quick hug. "You don't need to be on her teams. The three of us will always go onto a team together."

When Gina returned, she glanced back to where she had left Lorraine, rolled her eyes and giggled.

"Thanks." Natasha nodded to her. "I don't know what I'd do without you two."

At the end of the school day, Mrs. Wilkey brought the class to attention. She tapped some brown envelopes against her long nose and called three girls, including Natasha, and two boys to her desk. She dismissed the rest of the class, and then turned to them with her wide smile. Handing each an envelope with an official government seal, she told them to take it home to their parents. They were to return one of the notes inside with their parent's signature after the weekend.

"This is very special and I'm very proud of all of you," she said. As they turned to leave, Mrs. Wilkey reached out and stopped Natasha. "Is something wrong? You don't seem yourself today."

"My dog's sick. He's at the vet."

"I hope he'll be all right. I have a dog, too, so I know how you feel." She lowered her eyes and picked up her pen. "Don't forget to bring an answer to the note on Monday, and I'd like to know how your dog is then, too."

Natasha nodded, stuffing the brown envelope into her pocket. Jan and Gina were waiting outside. Jan pointed to the envelope. "What's that?"

"Don't know. Old Nosey said it was something special. She told me she has a dog, too."

"She's not too bad," Jan decided. "For a teacher. Listen, I'll pray for Happy. Phone me if there's any news."

"Hope," Gina said, holding up crossed fingers. Then one more word she knew, "Okay."

"Oh, oh," Jan nudged Natasha. "Here comes 'Her Majesty' again."

Lorraine sauntered their way as though she needed to go somewhere beyond them, but as she drew level, she paused. "I heard about your dog. He's sick, isn't he?" She fiddled with a strap on her brown leather school case, and then dropped it to the ground. A small puff of dusty earth rose around it.

Natasha nodded and looked away, hoping Lorraine would leave.

"You'll get over him. He's just a dog."

Natasha swung back to face her. Her voice low, she said, "He's not 'just a dog,' Lorraine. He's so important to me, just like my friends are. I keep my dog and my friends for life, not just until someone else comes along."

"I can have any friend I want," Lorraine declared. Her foot edged her suitcase closer in towards her. "I don't need to have 'New Australians' for friends, either."

"Gina and I are so terribly deprived."

Lorraine flipped back her hair. "You'll be sorry. Just wait. You'll want to be my friend again. Everyone does."

"Jan and I have been your friend, but now we have found true friends."

Lorraine didn't answer, but picked up her case and strode towards the bus stop, her hair swinging in one direction as her hips swung in the other.

Natasha took a deep breath. "She makes me so angry. Boy, if she had needed to get out of a country like we did, if she had seen the soldiers and the shooting and—" She stopped. It was a long time since she had thought about Shanghai. Especially at school. Her old life and the trip to Australia were receding in her mind.

Jan shrugged as she watched Lorraine retreat. "You know, I think, in a funny way, she was trying to make you feel better about Happy."

"But he's not *just* a dog." Natasha kicked at a pebble. "He's Happy."

Jan nodded. "We understand. She knows it's too late to be your friend. She always wants what she can't have."

Natasha saw everyone turn as Lorraine joined the bus line. "She makes lots of enemies. There are so many girls who used to be her best friend. Guess she'll have to change schools one day to start on a new lot."

As her mother's car pulled up, Gina leaned over and gave Natasha a hug. "Happy better soon," she said. "Bye bye, Bushy. Bye, Jan."

The mention of her nickname prodded Natasha to reach up and touch her unruly hair. Even now, Gina's pretty curls brought out a hint of envy. Gina had proved to be a caring friend, she reminded herself, and she couldn't help marveling at how quickly she was picking up the English language.

* * *

At home, Elena kept her distance from Natasha and even Sonia realized something was wrong and stayed close to her grandmother, banging slowly on the kitchen floor with a wooden spoon.

Natasha curled up in Papa's big armchair with Ivan. At school, her mind kept returning to Happy, but at home it was worse. There were so many places she was used to seeing him. She shivered at the thought of him being even more ill than he was this time yesterday, but convinced herself that, as he was at the vet's, he should be improving.

Once, when her eyes were closed, she thought she heard him panting and sprang up. His tail seemed to disappear around the doorway. For a second, she stood rooted, totally confused. Then, with her heart beating furiously, she slumped back into her chair, knowing it could not have been true. But, an idea made her feel better. As tomorrow was Saturday, she would visit him. When they telephoned the vet, she would ask. Still, she could not go into the storage room to see his cold and empty bed.

As the shadows lengthened, her dread grew. With every sound, she raced to the window to see if Mama was home. Finally, Mama's heels clicked up the driveway and she rushed to meet her. Their eyes met briefly and Mama motioned her to follow. "Come. We'll phone right away."

"Ask him if I can visit Happy tomorrow."

Mama nodded. Natasha could hardly breathe as Mama dialed, each rotation seeming to last an hour.

Natasha listened hard, leaning into her mother, trying to hear the voice on the other end, but only registering the urgency of the tone. At intervals, Mama murmured, 'I see," and "Yes, please take care of it," and finally, "Thank you for all you've done."

Why was she thanking him like that?

When Mama replaced the receiver very slowly and turned towards her, Natasha's whole body tensed. Her heart lurched and she knew, knew with total certainty that the worst thing possible had happened.

"I am sorry…" Mama began.

"No!!!" Natasha heard a scream and realized it was her own. Mama reached for her but she twisted away and ran, ran straight to her room. The door banged behind her as she flung herself onto the bed. Her hands shook as she reached for Ivan.

It couldn't be true. No! How could it have happened!? She had taken him to the vet, hadn't she? It was not possible. But then a small voice inside told her that yes, it was possible and it had happened. Her dog, her dear little Happy, was gone.

She cried until her throat hurt. Her chest ached and her nose was clogged. In her mind, she could feel Happy's scratchy tongue licking her fingers. She could see his furrowed brow that made him look worried. Once again, when she closed her eyes, she was sure he was snuffling beside her bed. But these things were over. Happy was gone.

She should have taken him to the vet earlier. It was her fault. And it was Mama and Papa's fault for not knowing about the immunizations. It was the vet's fault for not saving him. Her whole family was at fault for hoarding money for what Sonia might need instead of what Happy did need. She hated them! Hated them all. And she hated herself most of all!

She felt so terribly alone. Through half-open eyes, she saw the curtains quivering as though they were under water. Happy had been there for her when had she needed him. He asked for so little and she let him down.

The sun melted away and the evening gloom crept into the room when she heard Papa arrive home and Mama whispering to him. First, Papa with his car oil smell, then Babushka, and finally, Mama, all came to her room. The palm of Papa's hand felt like a padded, callused paw as he squeezed her hand. He brushed her hair with his lips before leaving to clean up for dinner. Babushka followed him out, but Mama perched on the edge of the bed, murmuring about what a good dog Happy had been and how much he had added to the family.

Abruptly her voice changed. "What's this?"

Natasha glanced at the edge of the brown envelope sticking out of her pocket. "It's something," she hiccupped, "something Mrs. Wilkey gave me. To give to you. I forgot." She closed her eyes and turned her head away.

Mama slotted the note into her own pocket and Natasha felt her hand massaging her back. Softly her mother's voice began, "Happy is no longer in pain where he is now."

Natasha turned on her, her cry rising to a wail. "It's my fault," she sobbed and hit out at the headboard, "and it's your fault, too, Mama. We should…we should have…" Sobs overtook her. Mama tried to embrace her but she broke free. "Did you hear? It's your fault, too! He was just a little puppy!" Flailing out, her fists attacked her mother.

Mama grabbed at her and took her by the shoulders. Natasha collapsed against her mother, her body melting until she was clinging like a baby. She whispered, "I hate you, I hate everyone!"

Now, Mama began to speak quietly, telling her of a time before Elena was born. Before Natasha turned two, something terrible had happened to their family. "Have you ever wondered why there is such a large age gap between you and Elena?"

Natasha nodded. She had often wished there was someone closer to her own age to share things with. Even though her heart still seemed to be pounding in her ears, she quieted down enough to listen.

"We had another baby. A little boy."

Natasha's eyes sprang to her mother's face.

"Your brother."

"I had a brother?" The news overwhelmed her and for a second everything else faded. She had had a brother! Now, long-forgotten memories of a sadness in her family surfaced: a time when everything seemed to happen slowly and quietly, and people forgot she was there.

"Yes, you had a brother." The skin around Mama's mouth slackened and her voice quivered a little. "A dear little boy. We called him Matvei. Matthew in English." She intertwined her fingers and stared at them.

"But what happened? I should remember."

"You were very little. It's better that you don't." Mama shook her head. "Matvei became ill." She lifted her gaze, her eyes empty. "It didn't seem anything major at first. But then, suddenly…well, Papa grabbed a rickshaw and raced him to the hospital. It was just two streets away, not far. I had taken you to a birthday party and didn't even know until they called. Told me to go straight to the hospital. There was nothing that could be done. I saw him one last time. He was only seven weeks old."

She blinked quickly. "So tiny. Can you imagine?" Now her eyes glowed with all the feeling she had been suppressing, her lashes moist. "I can still see his little face."

Natasha took a deep breath. "I really didn't remember that I had a brother."

"We don't talk about it. Even after all these years, it's still painful. I'm telling you now so you understand loss is a part of life for everyone. Not just you and not just our family." Her fingers brushed away the moisture on her cheek. "You can't stop living and loving because you might lose what you love."

It felt so strange to Natasha. There had been a boy in her family, not just girl children. She wondered what he would have been like if he had lived. Would he have been like her and Sonia, wanting his own way, standing up for himself, or more like Elena? Would he have had hair as dark as hers? Brown eyes?

"It's harder to lose a child than…well, than anything. In a way, Happy was your child. He depended on you. You looked after him." Mama bit her bottom lip and sighed. "So now you know."

A boy. Natasha tried to absorb this into the image in her mind of her household. The new knowledge made her feel as though she were part of the adult life of her family. She somehow felt, after this last eventful year, she was no longer a child. It was a strange feeling, yet a freeing one. She would need to think about everything a lot more.

Suddenly, she felt very tired, as though her body and soul had been pummeled from several directions. Finally she said, "But you had two more children. I mean, after—"

"That's right. We didn't have more children to replace Matvei. We can never replace him. But we have been blessed with two more wonderful girls. And in time you will have another dog. Not right now. It's not the right time. But the right time will come. And next time we'll know about the immunizations. Matvei's death was not anyone's fault and neither is Happy's. It's just the way life is."

Natasha reached out and embraced her mother. "I'm glad you told me." She could never replace Happy, but she could have another dog later. That was where Lorraine was wrong. She did not keep friends. She replaced them. Threw out the old for the new. Natasha would have new friends and would have a dog again someday. But she would keep, and treasure, the old.

Mama leaned her head against her daughter. "You are mature enough to know about your brother now."

"I feel older after all this."

Mama nodded. "Difficult things make you grow."

"I now understand why you were so sad after Grandpa died."

"Yes. Grandpa's death has taught me how to value the life around me. It was a hard lesson for me, and, unfortunately, for you, too."

With her chin digging into her mother's shoulder, Natasha asked, "What will we do, you know, with Happy's body?"

"The vet said he would take care of it. If you'd like you could have a memorial service here."

"I don't know yet." Maybe she could have her friends come and they could hold candles like they had for Grandpa; maybe have some incense. Mama could make sweet rice. He was a dog, but he wasn't *just* a dog. She could put a marker in the back yard for him. So she would remember him. Probably for her brother, for Matvei, it seemed strange to say the name, they probably had a real service and a real grave. "Is his grave in Shanghai? Matvei, I mean."

Mama stared at the floor for a minute, and then replied softly, "It was so hard to leave, knowing we would never go back."

Pulling at a loose thread on Ivan's stomach, Natasha said, "Papa has always wanted a son."

"Of course. And he wanted daughters, too. One is not better than the other, just different. He wants to have those experiences he can only have with a son. But he is learning that will not happen. We continue to learn lessons all through our lives."

"When we get old like Babushka, maybe we'll understand everything."

"I doubt it. The world changes. Can you imagine what it was like when Babushka was young? So very different. It will change as you grow older, too." Mama seemed herself again.

"So we can never understand everything?"

"Think how boring it would be if you could." A smile crept back into Mama's eyes.

"How about Sonia? Will we be able to afford everything she will need?"

"We'll work it out as we go. The doctor said she'd be fitted with strong hearing aids when she's bigger. And because she's never had hearing, she won't miss it like you would if you suddenly became deaf. She's strong, like you. She'll be fine, and so will you. It's hard, I know, but slowly other things besides Happy will come into your mind. That's how nature works."

"I'll never forget him."

"Of course you won't. He's been very important to you."

Papa knocked at the door. "Are you feeling better?"

"She's a bit better." As Mama rose from the bed, her hand touched the envelope in her pocket. "Oh, yes." She ripped it open.

"What's that?" Papa asked, but Mama kept reading.

Natasha shrugged. "It's from school."

"Look at this." Mama fluttered two pieces of paper that were attached in one corner. "The first sheet is from the New South Wales Department of Education. They want Natasha to go to their headquarters in the city to be tested for Opportunity School." She hugged Papa. "You know, the program for gifted children."

Looking back at the note, she said, "We have to sign this. And the second note is from Mrs. Wilkey. She says that Natasha should go. And even if she doesn't make it because her English is not perfect yet, she's sure she'll get into a selective high school. Do you remember what Vera said? Children who go to selective high schools can usually go on to university."

A broad grin erupted on Papa's face. He patted Natasha's shoulder. "Good girl. We are very proud of you."

For a moment, warmth seeped into the empty hole inside her. But, she wished the note had come on a different day, when she could have enjoyed it more. "I wish I could tell Happy."

Papa spoke out as though he were addressing an audience. "This is why we came to Australia. So you and your sisters could have these opportunities. This never would have happened in Shanghai, not the way it is now. Where do I sign?" With a dramatic flourish, he signed his name. "I'm glad I learned to sign my name in English even before we left Shanghai. I've signed it many times, but this is the happiest."

Taking the papers from Papa, Natasha was still thinking about Happy, when a new thought astonished her. Happy knew. She was quite sure he knew just how proud she felt and was even more thrilled for her than she was for herself. She realized she could talk to him in her mind, and no one needed to know.

Babushka's head poked around the door. "Can we come in?" She entered with her hand in Sonia's. When Sonia saw tears on her sister's cheeks, she ran to her and placed her chin on Natasha's knee, gazing up into her face. As Natasha stroked the fine hair across Sonia's forehead, her little hand reached out and grabbed at the papers.

"Stop."

Sonia's hand stopped in mid-air. Then she grinned, a big toothy grin.

"She understood." Natasha looked up at her parents. "I think she understood what I said.

"Was it the word, or the expression?" Papa asked.

Mama took in a deep breath. "Say it again and show her she was right." Mama reached for the papers and then stopped. "Stop." She shook her head.

Sonia laughed and imitated her.

"Try something else, quickly."

Natasha held up Ivan and shook her head. "Stop," she said. Sonia reached up, and then shook her head as she withdrew her hand.

Mama squealed, scooping up the baby and twirling her in the air. "She understands, she understands!"

Babushka clasped her hands to her heart. "God be praised." Tears shone in her eyes. "The dear child. I can say the word 'stop'. I'll learn English along with her. Do you think…perhaps they were wrong and she can hear after all?"

Papa pulled Mama into a silent embrace, Sonia giggling between them. "I don't think she can hear like we can. But maybe there's a little hearing. She's probably reacting to our actions even more than the word."

"And reading our lips, too," Natasha added. "The book says a deaf child learns through eyes instead of ears. I'll make up games to play with her. I'll teach her different short words."

"Good," Mama agreed. "Not too many words at once, but we need to expand what she learns. Lots of different games. We'll try everything."

Natasha lifted her sister from between her parents. "Yes," she whispered into her soft hair, "you've made me feel so much better." She breathed out a long sigh. Sonia would be all right. If she could understand one word, then she should be able to understand more. And in time, who knew, perhaps she would learn to say these words as well.

Sonia turned to her parents and made a funny face. As they laughed, a loud knock sounded on the back door.

"Is Natasha home?" Lizzie's voice called out.

"Would you like to see Lizzie?" Mama asked.

Placing Sonia onto the floor, Natasha nodded. She couldn't cry any more, not now, anyway. Her cheeks were stained and her hair stuck out at odd angles. She knew she would cry again in the night, but she needed her friends over the long two days of the weekend. Without Happy, the house felt too empty. "I'm glad Lizzie's come. Can Jan come over tomorrow and Gina, too?"

"Come in, Lizzie," Mama called, picking up the baby. "Of course, Jan can come. But you might want to brush your hair."

"Hair? I don't care about my hair. My friends like me just the way I am."

"My goodness, dinner will be late tonight," Babushka muttered as she hurried away. Papa walked out behind her and stopped to exchange a few words with Lizzie.

"You've got three good friends," Mama continued to Natasha. "When we first came to Australia, you didn't think you'd ever have a good friend."

"For a long while I didn't think I'd like it here. But it's okay. It's nice to have friends. It's funny. I don't remember making them. They sort of happened while I wasn't looking."

Lizzie rushed in and hugged her. "I know it's late, but I came right over when I heard about Happy. I'm so sorry. I always felt like he was my dog, too."

"I know. He loved you, too. He was such a great dog. I really miss him," Natasha was trying not to cry again.

Lizzie kneeled up on the bed. "Are you okay?"

"Better. I'm still sad, but better."

"Are you going to bury him?"

"The vet is taking care of him. But we could have a memorial service. I'll get Babushka to make some sweet rice. And, Mama, do we have skinny long white candles?"

"I'll get some first thing in the morning."

"When will it be? I want to come," Lizzie said.

"Tomorrow at two. I'll call Jan and Gina. And I'll call Vladimir, because he loved Happy, too."

"We'll all come," Mama said. "Papa, Babushka, your sisters. We all loved Happy."

"Some of my sisters and brothers will come, too. Do you want to come see Andrew's new hamster tomorrow? His name's Toby." Lizzie turned to Mama. "Mum's given in about a pet but says he can only have something that stays in a cage." She screwed up her face. "Not nearly as good as a cat or a dog."

"I'd love to see Toby. But a dog's best for me," Natasha said. "I'll get another one someday. When I'm ready. But tomorrow we'll have a Russian service for Happy, my wonderful Australian dog."

Acknowledgements

The creation of this book owes a debt to my Hong Kong writers' group, especially Michiko Okubo and Kathryn Lovatt. Also, I am indebted to Serena Lam and Lena Chan for help with Chinese words and phrases.

My Russian transliteration was greatly aided by Jill Foster and Alla Borodyansky. Thank you.

I wish to acknowledge, with gratitude, Jason Wordie for assistance with Hong Kong history and also the Hedbergs for their help.

Finally, thank you to my mother, my sister, my late father and both late Babushkas for keeping the 'Russianness' in our family life. And thanks also to my husband and three kids for being patient about all those burnt dinners.